Stepping back, Perdita trod hard upon the speaker's toe, and was gratified to hear a sudden curse. Smiling artlessly, she turned to face him.

'I beg your pardon, sir,' she said politely. 'How clumsy I must seem!'

The Earl of Rushmore caught his breath. This creature was quite the loveliest woman he had ever seen.

He didn't know what he had expected. Possibly blushes and maidenly confusion. Instead she looked at him direct. He was quick to make his apologies. 'Not in the least, ma'am. The fault was all mine. My foot was in your way...' He bowed and turned away.

'So it was!'

Something in her tone brought him round to face her again. There was no mistaking the light of battle in her eyes.

'Did I hurt you, sir?'

Rushmore was no fool. He understood her perfectly now. The chit had stamped upon his foot deliberately. His lip curled as he bowed again. 'You'll be delighted to hear that I am quite uninjured.'

Dear Reader

This book continues the story of the Wentworth family. The younger girls are now old enough to enter the world of high society in Regency London and Bath.

It was an exciting world of elegance and sophistication, when civilised living was based upon the highest standards of manners, fashions, architecture, furniture-making and a love of good food and wine. Certain essential accomplishments were demanded of both men and women, but in return the aristocracy enjoyed most delightful lives of luxury.

Yet there was a darker side to this world of pleasure. Intrigue and gossip were rife, and a woman was always in danger of losing her reputation by a single act of folly. Once lost it could never be recovered. Then there were those who prowled the fringes of society, searching out the vulnerable in an effort to make their own fortunes. They ran great risks, of course, as did their victims, for the law was harsh in dealing with fraud or offences against property.

This is the story of one such plot against an innocent girl. Fortunately she has good friends, like Perdita, the heroine of this novel. Amy, Perdita's sister, is the heroine of the next book in this series.

Enjoy your reading!

Meg Alexander

THE REBELLIOUS DÉBUTANTE

Meg Alexander

MILLS & BOON®

First published in Great Britain 2002
Large Print edition 2003
Harlequin Mills & Boon Limited,
Eton House, 18-24 Paradise Road, Richmond, Surrey TW9 1SR

© Meg Alexander 2002

ISBN 0 263 17987 7

Set in Times Roman 15 on 16 pt.
42-0103-80989

Printed and bound in Great Britain
by Antony Rowe Ltd, Chippenham, Wiltshire

After living in southern Spain for many years, **Meg Alexander** now lives in Kent, although, having been born in Lancashire, she feels that her roots are in the north of England. Meg's career has encompassed a wide variety of roles, from professional cook to assistant director of a conference centre. She has always been a voracious reader, and loves to write. Other loves include history, cats, gardening, cooking and travel. She has a son and two grandchildren.

Recent titles by the same author:

THE GENTLEMAN'S DEMAND

and in *The Steepwood Scandal* mini-series:

THE RELUCTANT BRIDE
MR RUSHFORD'S HONOUR

Chapter One

1816

Perdita Wentworth looked about her with a wondering expression. 'This Almack must be the cleverest man in London,' she announced. 'How on earth has he managed to persuade polite society that this is the place to be seen?'

Her mother hushed her at once. 'Do keep your voice down, darling. I know that you didn't want to come here, but at least look as if you are enjoying yourself. When Lady Castlereagh sent us the vouchers she believed that she was doing us a kindness. She had many other requests for them, you know.'

'I could wish that she had handed them out elsewhere.' Perdita was unrepentant. 'Stale sandwiches and weak lemonade? I'm surprised that there hasn't been a riot.'

'Now, love, you know that food is not the attraction here.'

'Well, it can't be the décor.' Perdita laughed. 'I've seen many a barn with a more inviting interior. The place is downright shabby.'

'You'll forget all that when the music starts, my dear. You know how you love to dance…'

'I do, but not as an exhibit, Mother. Just look at the old biddies seated by the walls. If they haven't priced each item of my clothing I shall be surprised.'

'Oh dear, and I was just about to join them.' Elizabeth Wentworth twinkled at her daughter. 'Sadly, I've forgotten my walking stick and my lorgnette.'

Perdita laid an affectionate hand upon her mother's arm. 'You had best not let Papa know that you fancy yourself an old biddy,' she teased. 'He would take it much amiss. In his eyes you will always be the girl he rescued all those years ago.'

'Your father does not change, thank goodness,' Elizabeth said fondly. 'Now, my dear, I see Emily Cowper by the door. I must go and speak to her. Your card is filled?'

'For every dance, Mama.' With an effort Perdita refrained from commenting upon her prospective partners, most of whom she regarded as barely out of leading strings.

The gentleman standing behind her was not so charitable. 'Dear God!' he said with feeling. 'What are we doing here? Almack's hasn't changed in all the years I've been away. Let us leave and go at once to White's or Watier's.'

'Adam, you can't!' his friend said bluntly. 'If you wish to launch your ward upon the world, you must make yourself agreeable to the lady patronesses.'

'And which of them do you suggest?' The Earl of Rushmore regarded the seated ranks of ladies with a jaundiced eye. 'Damned if they ain't a bunch of harpies, set on matching up these ninnies with a passel of schoolroom misses.'

The Earl had not troubled to lower his voice, and Perdita heard him clearly. It was unfortunate that at that moment her mother had chosen to seat herself with the other ladies. Her anger flared. To hear herself described as a schoolgirl was bad enough, but she would not tolerate the description of her mother as a harpy.

Stepping back, she trod hard upon the speaker's toes, and was gratified to hear a sudden curse. Smiling artlessly, she turned to face him.

'I beg your pardon, sir,' she said politely. 'How clumsy I must seem!'

The Earl of Rushmore caught his breath. This diminutive creature was quite the loveliest woman he had ever seen. Unfashionably dark, perhaps, with raven-black curls framing the perfect oval of her face, and emphasising a creamy complexion against which a pair of fine eyebrows stood out above huge lustrous eyes.

He didn't know what he had expected. Possibly blushes and maidenly confusion? Instead she looked directly at him. He was quick to make his apologies.

'Not in the least, ma'am. The fault was mine alone. My foot was in your way…' He bowed and turned away.

'So it was!' Something in her tone brought him round to face her again. There was no mistaking the light of battle in her eyes. 'Did I hurt you, sir?'

Rushmore was no fool. He understood her perfectly now. The chit had stamped upon his foot deliberately. His lip curled as he bowed again. 'You'll be delighted to hear that I am quite uninjured.'

His sneering tone brought the colour to Perdita's cheeks. She spun round and began to walk away, but was not out of hearing before she heard his comments.

'Who is the beauty?' The question was so casual as to appear almost uninterested.

'That is Perdita Wentworth. She is quite lovely, isn't she? You'll have heard of the family, of course. The Earl of Brandon is one of her connections. Her father is a younger son, and a naval man. This is the girl's first Season.'

'Has she caught herself a husband yet? With that face and those connections it shouldn't have proved too difficult.'

'I don't think so. Nothing has been announced. Why, Adam, are you thinking of trying your luck?'

'Good God, no! The lady is too obvious for me. I think she knows her worth and is aiming to become a countess at the very least. I've seen it all before—dropped handkerchiefs, twisted ankles, fainting fits, anything, in fact, to effect an introduction. I'll give her credit for one thing. She was, at least, original.'

Rigid with fury, Perdita stood riveted to the spot. Then, wheeling round, she turned to confront the speaker.

'Why, you insufferable popinjay!' she cried. 'You must think yourself the catch of the Season!'

The Earl was startled into silence, but he heard a snort of laughter from his companion. He ignored it. Always aware of his surroundings, he noticed at once that the young lady who stood before him, bristling with anger, had become the focus of all eyes.

With a winning smile, he took her hand as the music started, and led her into the dance. A young man barred their way.

'There must be some mistake!' he said stiffly. 'Miss Wentworth is promised to me for the waltz.'

'The lady has changed her mind.' The Earl's reply was uncompromising. 'She will dance with me...'

Disposed to argue, the young man caught the eye of Perdita's companion and changed his mind, retiring in some haste.

'How dare you?' Perdita struggled to release her hand. 'I won't dance with you!'

'You will, you know!' The grip on her hand and about her waist was too firm to allow of escape.

'Miss Wentworth, pray consider your situation. Every eye in the room is upon us at this moment. A public brawl will do nothing for your reputation.'

'Much I care for that!' she hissed.

'Then you are a fool, my dear.' The Earl swung her into the dance with expertise. 'You may dislike convention as much as I do myself, but we live in this world, and we must abide by its rules.'

As he spoke he was seized with a feeling of self-disgust. Even to his own ears he sounded like a prosy old bore. Clearly his partner shared that opinion.

'Don't glare at me!' he said sweetly. 'A smile would not come amiss. You dance very well, by the way.'

'But not with you!' Perdita slipped out of his grasp and turned, intent on leaving him alone on the dance floor.

It took but the barest hint of a hip throw and she stumbled. Then his arms were about her, lifting her off her feet.

'Make way!' he cried in clarion tones. 'The lady has turned her ankle.'

Perdita was unable to contradict him. A large hand cradled the back of her head, pressing her face into the fine fabric of his coat. Rushmore strode swiftly to an alcove and laid his fair burden upon a sofa. Then, conscious of the interested spectators, he knelt to examine her ankle.

'Don't touch me!' she cried hotly.

'You must try to be brave!' came the tender reply. Then, using his broad shoulders to shield her from the gaping crowd, he bent his face to hers. 'Use your head!' he muttered in a different tone. 'Do you wish to cause a scandal?'

A hand rested lightly upon his shoulder.

'Thank you so much, my lord,' a clear voice said. 'Pray don't feel obliged to trouble yourself further. I have asked that my carriage be brought round to the entrance so that I may take my daughter home without delay.'

The Earl rose to his feet and turned to face the speaker. There could be no doubt that this was Perdita's mother. They might have been sisters, but it was clear that the girl had inherited her beauty from the stunning creature who stood beside him.

The Earl bowed. 'I fear I am a clumsy dancer, ma'am. It appears that the young lady has turned her ankle. It is not broken, but it must be painful. If you will allow me, I will carry her to your coach. My name is Rushmore, by the way.'

'I know who you are, my lord, and I am sensible of your kindness to Perdita.' Elizabeth Wentworth looked about her. The interested crowd of spectators was pressing ever closer. 'If these people will make way for you…?'

'Mother…! There is no need!' Perdita's mouth set in a mutinous line as Rushmore bent towards her, but an icy glance from her mother silenced her. She was forced to submit to being carried from the

ballroom by this giant of a man, much though she
detested him. Then she noticed that his chest was
heaving.

'Put me down!' she hissed. 'I am too heavy for
you.'

'Light as a feather, ma'am!' He choked.

Then she realised to her chagrin that he was
laughing uncontrollably.

'You find this amusing?' she ground out.

'Vastly amusing, ma'am! Confess it now, you are
hoist with your own petard.'

'I don't even know what that means, but I make
no doubt that it is an insult…to add to your others.'

'Not so! I was merely pointing out that your
scheme to injure me has rebounded against yourself.
And when did I insult you, ma'am?'

'First of all you said that I was a schoolroom
miss, and then…and then…you said that I was planning to make myself a countess.'

Rushmore looked down at the vivid little face. It
was devoid of guile, but there was no mistaking the
dagger-look.

'Unforgivable!' he said gravely. 'I see now that
you are a lady of mature years…almost an ape-
leader, if the truth be known…and with not the
slightest prospect of becoming a countess.'

Perdita could have struck him, but she was helpless in his arms. He was grinning down at her with
every appearance of enjoyment. She was tempted to
put out her tongue at him, but that would have been

child-like. Her chin went up and she turned her head away, determined to preserve what shreds of dignity remained to her.

Her temper was not improved when Rushmore laid her in the coach with exaggerated care, solicitous for her comfort with the most tender of enquiries. Then he stood back to allow Elizabeth to take her place in the opposite seat. He bowed and then, expressing the hope that Perdita would be much recovered by the morning, he stood back to let the coach move away.

Elizabeth called him back.

'My lord, allow me to give you our direction. We are staying with the Earl of Brandon. My husband will be anxious to thank you for your kindness to our daughter, if you should care to call upon us.'

'I shall be honoured, ma'am!' Rushmore caught Perdita's eye and surprised a look of horror. He gave her a charming smile, stood back, and watched the carriage until it was out of sight.

'Oh, Mother, why did you ask him to call upon us? He's quite the most hateful man I've ever met.'

'I asked him for the best of reasons, Perdita. Tonight you made an exhibition of yourself. When, and if, the Earl calls, you will apologise to him for your behaviour.'

'Oh, no! I can't! You don't know what he said.'

'I don't care what he said, unless he made some coarse suggestion to you, which I think unlikely.'

'Of course he didn't. We are all beneath his touch, you know. He said that we were school-girls—'

'And you felt obliged to confirm that belief this evening?'

'It wasn't just that. He sneered at everything and he said that the older ladies were a bunch of har-pies.'

'So that was why you trod upon his foot? Must I remind you that you had been saying much the same yourself not five minutes earlier? You won't deny that your action was deliberate? I saw you do it.'

'I didn't hurt him,' Perdita mourned. 'My slippers were too soft.' She stole a sideways glance at her mother. 'Are you very angry?'

'Need you ask?' Elizabeth replied in an icy tone. 'That action was bad enough, but it might have passed unnoticed as an accident. Why did you go back to challenge him?'

'He was insulting, Mother. He told his friend that I was trying to attract his notice, in the hope of becoming a countess.'

'*You* knew that wasn't true, so why let it upset you?'

'He is detestable!' Perdita cried. 'Puffed up with pride, and convinced that he is the catch of the Season! Insufferable nincompoop!'

'You gave him your opinion, I make no doubt?'

'I did, but, Mother, I didn't mean to make a scene. I didn't want to dance with him, you know.'

'In another second or two that would have become obvious to everyone in the room. You may thank your stars that the Earl had more concern for your reputation than you have yourself. To leave him alone in the middle of the floor must have given rise to speculation, most of it unpleasant. You were already attracting attention before he led you out. No doubt that is why he did so. You have much to thank him for.'

'He's a stupid creature!' Perdita muttered.

'Indeed! Well, it may or may not interest you to know that the Earl was one of Wellington's most capable commanders. He will, no doubt, be glad to accept your opinion of him in preference to that of the Duke.'

Perdita was silenced.

Her mother did not speak again until they reached their destination. 'Pray do not allow the servants to help you. I know quite well that you have not turned your ankle.'

Once indoors, Elizabeth turned to her daughter. 'You had best go to your room,' she said. 'I shall speak to your father when he returns, but I can tell you now that he will not be best pleased to hear of this latest piece of folly. We shall see you in the morning.'

It was an utterance which promised little sleep for Perdita that night. Her fiery temper had got the better of her again, and she confessed as much to her sister.

'You are home early,' Amy said brightly. 'What was it like at Almack's? I want to hear all about it. I can't wait to make my own come-out...'

'It was the same as usual,' Perdita said heavily. 'Deadly dull, I must confess, unless one believes all the nonsense spoken by these hopeful younger sons.'

'*I* should not object to being told that my eyes were like stars,' Amy informed her wistfully.

'It's nonsense!' Perdita informed her. 'Stars are high in the heavens, millions of miles away. Are we supposed to believe such rubbish?'

'Oh, you ain't in the least bit romantical. No wonder all your beaux are afraid of you.'

'They are not *my* beaux,' Perdita said with dignity. 'And if they are afraid, I don't think much of their courage.'

Her sister gave her a quizzical look. 'You are crabby tonight. What has happened to upset you? Have you had more offers?'

Perdita shook her head. 'Nothing like that, but I'm in disgrace again. How was I to know that I should find myself beside the most obnoxious man in the kingdom?'

'Another one? You are mighty particular.'

'This one was different,' Perdita said slowly. 'Insulting, insufferable and far too sure of himself.'

'Well, that's a change!' Amy said brightly. 'You mean he didn't quake in his boots when you spoke to him?'

'Far from it! He...he actually laughed at me. I'll make him pay for that!'

'But who was he? You haven't spoken of him before.'

'He's one of Wellington's men, I believe, and just returned to this country.'

'A hero? Oh, love, how wonderful!'

'You would not think so if you met him. Doubtless he is in his element brandishing a sword, or charging over ramparts, or whatever soldiers do. He doesn't appear to much advantage in polite society.'

'But...neither do you. Mother is forever telling you to keep your opinions to yourself, and not to seem so independent.'

'She doesn't mean it, Amy. Mother was a force to be reckoned with, even as a sixteen-year-old.'

Amy nodded. 'Well, what happened tonight? What did you do that was so dreadful?'

Perdita explained. 'Was I wrong?' she asked at last.

'He sounds vile!' Amy spoke with conviction. 'You should have bitten him!'

'I would have, but he held my face against his coat!' Perdita caught her sister's eye and dissolved into peals of laughter. At last she wiped her eyes.

'Oh dear, it really isn't amusing,' she admitted. 'Mother is very angry with me. I suppose it isn't the kind of behaviour that one expects at Almack's.'

At that moment Elizabeth Wentworth was expressing the same sentiments to her husband. Perry had spent a convivial evening at a naval dinner, but his contentment vanished at his wife's expression.

'What is it, my darling?' he asked in some alarm. 'Are you not well? Sit down, my love! Let me get something for you—'

'Don't fuss, Perry! I am perfectly well, but we need to talk.' Swiftly, she related the events of the evening, and saw with dismay that her husband was trying to hide his amusement.

'Now, Perry, I beg that you will not laugh!' she reproached. 'Our daughter was in danger of losing what remains of her reputation. You shall not encourage her in her folly.'

'She's just a child,' Perry said cheerfully. 'Will you tell me that Rushmore is in the fidgets because of all this nonsense?'

'I'm glad you agree that she is still a child,' Elizabeth said gravely. 'We should not have allowed her to make her come-out, in spite of all her wheedling.'

'Well, we couldn't send her back to school,' Perry pointed out. 'Miss Bedlington would not have her.'

'Quite! Have you forgot her words? Let me remind you of them. ''Perdita is the most disruptive influence ever to enter my doors.'' Half London is aware of it.'

'Lizzie, let me ask you something! Did you blame her for what she did? We haven't raised either of our girls to be silent in the face of injustice.'

'Oh, my dear, I love her just as much as you do!' Elizabeth stretched out her hand to him. 'Perhaps she was right to throw a bowl of water over Miss Bedlington, but she's a young woman now, and must learn some self-control.'

'I'm glad she soaked the sour-faced old cat!' Perry was unrepentant. 'There was something sadistic about the way that woman took so much pleasure in humiliating the prettiest of her pupils. Perdita wanted to give her a taste of her own medicine, and I, for one, don't blame her!'

'You are incorrigible!' Elizabeth sighed. 'Miss Bedlington was wrong to force Charlotte Ingham's head beneath a tap just because the girl had curled her hair, but Perdita half-drowned her.'

Perry chuckled. 'Do you know, she reminds me strongly of a girl I used to know…I can't quite recall her name…'

His wife had the grace to blush. 'That was long ago,' she demurred. 'Times were different then. Now that we are at peace there won't be so much latitude allowed. Society will become more circumspect.'

'And you approve?' The question was accompanied by a quizzical look.

'I can't change attitudes,' his wife said softly. 'Oh, my dear, don't you see? If we are not careful, our girl will acquire the reputation of a hoyden. Neither of us has an eye to the main chance as far as marriage for her is concerned. She won't be co-erced in any way, but we must think of her happi-ness. It cannot serve to have the world regard her as a pert and wilful girl. She is deserving of much more than that. She has a heart of gold.'

Perry fell silent for a time. Then he gave his wife a rueful look. 'What are we to do?' he asked. 'Per-haps, in Gibraltar…?'

'I think not!' Elizabeth chose her words with care. 'I know that you promised her the trip, my dear, but it would be folly.'

'I don't care to go back on my word,' Perry said stiffly.

Elizabeth looked at him and sighed. When he set his mouth in that mutinous line he reminded her so forcibly of their elder daughter.

'Nor do I, Perry, but it is time that Perdita was taught a lesson. Aside from anything else, can you see her in Gibraltar, setting that bastion of respect-ability by the ears?'

'She might liven it up!' Perry twinkled, but he received no answering smile.

'I wish you will be serious, love. I think it best to send her to Aunt Beatrice in Bath for the time being. It will get her out of London, and she and

Amy can travel together when Amy goes back to school next week.'

'You can't mean it, Lizzie!' Perry looked his dismay. 'Perdita is like to die of boredom in the place. If you worry about her in Gibraltar, how do you suppose she'll go on in Bath?'

'I've thought about it carefully. Bath is not exactly in the depths of the countryside. It is a fashionable place.'

'It was used to be, my love, but that was in the middle of the last century.'

'Nevertheless, we are not condemning Perdita to a life of solitude. She may walk, and ride, and go to balls and picnics.'

'Behaving always with perfect rectitude?' Perry chuckled.

'I'm hoping that the loss of her trip to Gibraltar may cause her to think more carefully before she acts.'

'Are we not being too hard on her?'

'Oh, Perry, she has got to learn that she isn't a law unto herself. I know you hope, as I do, that she will make a happy marriage, but she frightens all the men away with her readiness to speak out.'

'More fools they!' her husband answered with conviction. 'Perdita need not trouble herself to find a husband yet. I'd rather she never wed at all than threw herself away upon some fool who did not value her. In any case, at seventeen she's much too young to think of marriage.'

His wife hid a smile. 'I was younger when we met,' she reminded him. 'You didn't allow that to stand in your way.'

Perry slipped an arm about her waist and hugged her to him. 'I saved you from a dreadful fate,' he teased.

Elizabeth rested her hands against the fabric of his coat and looked up at him. 'I wonder,' she said solemnly. 'Most certainly I did not bargain to be saddled with a fond papa who will not discipline his daughter. Oh, my darling, let me have my way in this. It will be hard for all of us, but it seems to me to be the only thing to do.'

Perry kissed her then. 'She'll be very disappointed, Lizzie, and so will I. I was looking forward to having both of you aboard my ship for this trip to the Mediterranean.'

'There will be another time,' his wife assured him. 'Won't you make do with me alone?'

'That won't be a hardship, love.' Perry kissed her again. 'You won't change your mind about Perdita?'

'I think not, Perry. Nothing we have said or done to date has changed her behaviour in the least. Trust me, my dear. We *can't* allow her to run wild.'

Perry was silent for a time. He wasn't convinced that Perdita's behaviour needed changing. Her disregard for convention always amused him, but he would not see his wife distressed.

'Very well,' he said at last. 'I'll agree if you think it best.' Then a thought struck him. 'Aunt Trixie may not wish to have her, though. Don't she spend her time drinking that filthy water in the Pump Room, playing cards, and gossiping with her cronies?'

Elizabeth saw the hopeful gleam in his eye. 'Perdita need not take the waters, nor need she play cards or gossip. Aunt Trixie loves our girls, you know. She has been begging for this age to have them stay with her. You must recall how good she was when they were at school, taking them out on holidays? She tells me that they brightened up her life.'

Perry repressed a smile. Miss Beatrice Langrishe clearly had no idea just how much brighter her life could become with a lively seventeen-year-old in her care.

Elizabeth read his mind. 'I think you need not fear that Perdita will upset her. She is too kind for that. Perdita thrives on opposition, but I doubt if she will set her will against that of a gentle, elderly lady who sees the best in everyone.'

'Perdita's arrival will mean extra work for her staff,' Perry insisted.

'No, it won't. I shall send Ellen with her.'

Perry whistled. 'By Gad, you mean it this time, don't you? Perdita won't like that. She'll think you're sending her old nurse to keep an eye on her.'

'She will be right. Perdita may dislike the idea, but I shall explain that she mustn't be a trouble to

Aunt Trixie. Officially, Ellen will be there to augment the staff.'

Perry raised a quizzical eyebrow. 'She won't believe you, love. Will you not sleep on this decision?'

'I will, but I shall not change my mind. Now, Perry, you must back me up. I sent Perdita to her room. She is not to leave it until we summon her tomorrow.'

Perry took a turn about the room. Then he gave his wife a guilty look. 'I won't be here,' he told her hastily. 'Tomorrow I must make an early start. I have an appointment with my Lords of the Admiralty.'

'How convenient!' Elizabeth's tone was dry. She was disposed to argue and then thought better of it. Perdita could always twist her father around her little finger. Knowing him, Elizabeth realised that his resolve would melt in the face of his daughter's disappointment. It would be best if she spoke to Perdita alone.

'Very well,' she continued. 'You are leaving it to me, my dear. Now tell me about your naval dinner. Did you see any of your old acquaintance?'

It was a clear invitation to change the subject, and Perry bowed to the inevitable.

Perdita was up betimes next day. In spite of her forebodings, she had enjoyed a good night's sleep, and was ready to defend her actions. Her father would take her side. She felt sure of it. Mother would be more difficult, but if she was suitably contrite, all might still be well.

As for the obnoxious Earl of Rushmore—she thought it unlikely that he would trouble to call. Doubtless, at that very moment, he was congratulating himself upon his lofty position, and denigrating lesser mortals.

She sipped her morning chocolate and nibbled at a roll. A glance at the clock surprised her. She had slept late, it was almost noon. Reaching out, she rang the bell for Abby, her little maid. Abby would dress her quickly. She must be ready when her mother sent for her.

It was Ellen who entered the room.

Perdita greeted her politely, but an enquiry as to Abby's whereabouts was greeted with a grim smile.

'Your ma asked me to look to you this morning, Miss Perdita. No need to rush. She ain't ready for you yet.' The old woman walked over to the clothes press and lifted out a gown.

'Ellen, I haven't decided what I'll wear today,' Perdita said with some hauteur.

'Then you won't have to trouble your head. You ain't going out, I think. This blue will do well enough.'

Perdita's temper flared. She would not be treated as if she was still in the nursery. 'How do you know what I will do today?' she asked. 'I may decide to ride, or to do some shopping, or visit the beasts in the Tower of London.'

'You won't be doing any of that,' Ellen forecast darkly. 'Though it's a toss-up which has the worst temper—you or them beasts. Been up to your old tricks again, have you?'

'I don't know what you mean,' Perdita said with dignity. She slipped out of bed, cast aside her night-robe, and walked over to the ewer and basin on her wash-stand.

Ellen watched her with a critical eye. 'You could do with some flesh on them bones,' she announced. 'Been following that Lord Byron, have you? I hear he lives on vinegar and potatoes.'

'I have not. If you must know, Ellen, I have an excellent appetite.'

Ellen chortled. 'Then it's that nasty temper of yours as keeps you thin. Them hip-bones would cut a man to ribbons, if your tongue hadn't done it first.'

'Don't be vulgar!' Perdita said coldly. She sat down at her dressing-table and picked up her hair-brush.

'I'll do that!' Ellen snatched it from her. 'It comes to somethin' if I don't know how to brush your hair.' She set about her task with enthusiasm

'There's no need to knock my head off!' Perdita's eyes were watering.

'Might do you some good—knocking sense in, as you might say.' She paused as Amy burst into the room. 'Well, miss, where's the fire?' she demanded in caustic tones. 'Don't they teach you anything at that fine school of yours? Wasting their time, they are, in my opinion. No lady rushes about as if the fiends of hell were after her.'

'Sorry, Ellen!' Amy was too full of her news to spare more than a winning smile for her old nurse. 'Perdita, you'll never guess. Mother has a morning caller!'

Perdita smiled at her. 'The Prince Regent, at the very least, to judge by your expression?'

'No, not him!' her sister cried impatiently. 'Can't you guess?'

'The Duke of Wellington, Marshal Blücher, the Tsar of Russia?'

'Of course not, silly! It is your enemy...the Earl of Rushmore!'

Perdita stared in disbelief. 'It can't be! Are you sure?'

'Of course I'm sure,' Amy cried indignantly. 'I heard the commotion at the door and went to see who it was. I heard Knox announce him.'

'Who...who did he ask for?' Perdita said in hollow tones.

'He asked for Father first, but Father is gone out. Then he asked for Mother.'

Perdita's heart sank. Her father was her staunchest ally. He, at least, might have taken her part in what she guessed would be a humiliating confrontation.

'The man's a monster!' she ground out. 'He hasn't wasted much time in coming to claim his pound of flesh...'

Ellen cackled aloud. 'He won't get much flesh from you, but you've done it now! I shouldn't be surprised if your ma and pa don't send you back to school with Miss Amy. I never heard of such a thing—setting yourself up against his lordship in the way you did.'

Perdita's eyes flashed. 'You know nothing about it, Ellen!'

'I've heard some—and I can guess the rest. We'd best get out our boxes. You'll be on your way to Bath next week.'

'No, I won't!' Perdita stamped her foot. 'I'll run away before I go back to that awful place.'

Ellen's smile broadened. 'And how will you earn your living, Miss Perdita? You won't do as a lady's maid, seeing that you've never yet set a straight stitch in your sewing, and young gels ain't popular as governesses. They ain't yet taking women in the army or the navy, though I make no doubt you'd fire a gun with the best of them. It's a pity that the war is over. You might have won it on your own.'

'Ellen, you may go,' Perdita snapped. 'You may keep your spiteful remarks to yourself.'

'I don't doubt that you'll hear worse this day,' the old woman forecast with some satisfaction. Nodding to herself, she left her charges to their lamentations.

'Did you see Rushmore?' Perdita asked.

'Yes, I peeped at him through the banisters. He..he's very grand, isn't he?'

'Grand, and proud, and arrogant, and hateful! Did...did he seem very angry?'

'I couldn't tell,' Amy said honestly. 'He seemed to cross the hall in a couple of strides. I didn't see his face. Knox showed him through to Mother in the study.'

Both girls were silent. Then Amy sighed. 'I wish we could be a couple of flies upon the wall,' she said. 'I'd like to know what he is saying.'

'Well, I can guess,' Perdita announced. 'His precious feathers have been ruffled. Most probably he's insisting that I grovel on my knees before him. Well, I won't do it. Mother can lock me in my room and make me live upon bread and water, but I won't give in.'

Amy laughed. 'Mother won't do that, and well you know it.'

'I know.' Perdita hung her head. 'But I'd rather she did that than look so disappointed in me. I wish I were more like you. You don't fly out as I do. You've even managed to charm Miss Bedlington, which must be the wonder of the age. Don't you mind that awful school?'

'I can stand it for another year,' Amy reassured her. 'Miss Bedlington doesn't bother with me. I'll never be a beauty, which is all that seems to worry her. Besides, I have my friends. They miss you, love.'

'I miss them too. It will be fun when you make your come-out with the others.' Perdita stirred uneasily. Her expression belied her words. It was clear that fun was the last thing on her mind.

'I wish that Mother would send for me,' she said at last. 'I'd rather get my scolding over with, whatever the result.'

'It may not be so bad,' her sister comforted.

'I don't know.' Perdita shook her head. 'What can be taking the Earl so long? I thought that morning calls were to last no longer than a half-hour.'

'They may be speaking of Wellington's campaign,' Amy suggested.

'Some hopes!' her sister cried. 'Mother is being given a blow-by-blow account of what took place at Almack's. It's sackcloth and ashes for me, I fear.'

Chapter Two

Perdita was mistaken. She would have been astonished to find that her mother was, at that moment, engaged in a battle of wills with the redoubtable Earl of Rushmore.

In the absence of the head of the Wentworth family from his home, Elizabeth had taken over the running of the household from the Countess. It had been a busy morning. She had managed to negotiate menus for the following week without offending the susceptibilities of the Earl of Brandon's treasured chef. She had also studied the household accounts. Now she turned to a pile of correspondence. There were invitations to so many functions, some to accept and some to refuse. Always at the back of her mind was the problem of Perdita.

Even so, she was startled when her visitor was announced. When she'd issued the invitation she had not expected him to call. Now, it seemed the Earl was intent upon an apology. Petty-minded, she thought scornfully. Perdita had been wrong, of course, but no man worth his salt would think it incumbent on him to pursue the matter. It was in no charitable frame of mind that she greeted her morning caller, but she offered at once to summon Perdita.

The Earl regarded her with a quizzical expression. ''I beg that you will not do so,'' he remarked.

'But, my lord, she must apologise to you. You are generous to waive the need, but it is necessary.'

'Do you think so, ma'am? You must do as you think best, of course. Certainly it will give me the opportunity to explain to the young lady that the fault was mine alone.'

Elizabeth stared at him. 'Sir, this will not do. Perdita is at fault and cannot be excused.'

'But nor can I, ma'am, nor can I. My remarks were not such as might be tolerated by any woman of spirit.'

'Perdita is overly endowed with that particular characteristic,' her mother observed drily. 'I fear it will not serve her well in present-day society.'

'You think not?' The hooded eyes rested with interest upon his companion's lovely face. Elizabeth was a famous beauty, but there was character in the set of that delicious mouth and her steady gaze. The girl had inherited more than her mother's looks. The Earl began to smile and that smile transformed his somewhat saturnine countenance.

Elizabeth was surprised. For the first time she was aware of Rushmore's famous charm as his blue eyes twinkled at her. He was deeply tanned and as he threw back his head to laugh, she caught a glimpse of strong white teeth.

She shook her head at him, and was about to speak when he lifted a hand to stay her.

'I don't mean to interfere in family matters,' he assured her. 'Perhaps you will allow me to explain. I am ashamed of my behaviour. I was bored and somewhat at odds with the world last evening. Life seems somewhat tame at present in the time of peace. For these past few years we have lived so close to the edge of existence. God knows, I had no wish for the war with France to continue, but we were not concerned with petty undertakings. Can you understand?'

'I do indeed, my lord. I had the same experience many years ago. It takes some time to settle into a more staid way of life.'

Rushmore smiled again. There would never be anything staid about this woman or her family. 'Then, ma'am, may I beg that your daughter be excused from making a totally unnecessary apology? She is very young, and I would not humiliate her. Summon her if you must. I will assure her of my regrets and ask her pardon.'

Elizabeth threw up her hands. She knew when she was beaten, but she frowned in mock annoyance. Then she caught Rushmore's laughing eyes, and her own lips curved in a smile. The more she knew of this man the better she liked him for his refusal to attempt to crush Perdita's spirit.

'That would be going too far, my lord. You are most generous, but Perdita may not be so lucky on the next occasion. Let us leave matters as they are. It will do my daughter no harm to reflect upon the wisdom of keeping a still tongue in her head, for a time, at least.'

'And will it last, ma'am?' Rushmore grinned at her.

'I think it highly unlikely, sir.' Elizabeth regarded her visitor for a long moment. 'Will you tell me something?' she asked at last.

Rushmore bowed. 'Most certainly, if I can.'

'Why are you here, my lord? It cannot be to en-quire about Perdita's health. You know quite well that she did not turn her ankle. Nor have you come for an apology. Is there something else?'

Rushmore was silent for a time, and Elizabeth did not speak. She guessed that he was attempting to come to some decision. Then he looked up at her.

'I'd like your advice,' he told her bluntly. 'I find myself in something of a quandary.'

Elizabeth's face did not betray her astonishment, though she could think of no possible subject upon which she could advise this powerful man.

'Go on!' she encouraged.

'Well, ma'am, I seem to have acquired a ward— a girl of the same age as your daughter, and I don't know what to do with her.'

Elizabeth hid a smile. 'A serious problem, I agree. How do you find yourself in this position, sir?'

'Her father was my closest friend. He was killed at Waterloo. The girl has no other relatives, I believe, so I promised to look out for her.' Rushmore's face grew sombre. 'I could not refuse a dying man.'

'Of course not, but must this be a problem for you? Perhaps your own female relatives might take an interest in her?'

'They won't be given the chance,' Rushmore told her grimly. 'The girl is a considerable heiress. I won't leave her to their tender mercies. They'd have her wed to some impecunious younger son before she could draw breath.'

Elizabeth felt it wiser not to comment upon this remark.

'Have you met the young lady?' she asked.

'Not yet, ma'am. I've written, of course, and had some duty letters in return, but it is most important that I see her without delay. The child must have suffered in her loss. She and her father were very close. I understand that her mother died in child-bed.'

'That is a tragic story,' Elizabeth said quietly. 'Where is your ward now?'

'She is at school in Bath, but I can't leave her there.' Rushmore ran his fingers through his hair. 'What am I to do with her?'

Elizabeth smiled at him. He was clearly at a loss and there was something endearing about his air of distraction. This was a problem well outside his previous experience.

'Then you have no plans for her?'

'I'll have to bring her out, of course—give her a Season, I suppose. I'd like her to marry well. That is why I went to Almack's. It wasn't very encouraging.'

'May I ask why you have come to me? Perdita can have given you no good impression as to how I raise my daughters.'

'Miss Wentworth is no milk-and-water creature, simpering and swooning, and making sheep's eyes at the men.'

It was Elizabeth's turn to laugh. 'And that is a recommendation in your eyes? Such girlish nonsense is thought to be attractive?'

'Not to any man of sense. Your daughter, ma'am, is the first intelligent girl I've met since my return from the Low Countries.'

'For heaven's sake, don't tell her so,' Elizabeth exclaimed with feeling. 'Between you and her father there will be no controlling her. Now, sir, what are we to do about your ward? I'll help you in any way I can.'

Rushmore rose, walked over to Elizabeth and kissed her hand with courtly grace. 'I felt that you would not fail me,' he said more cheerfully. 'I'll go to Bath and make myself known to her. If she'll agree to stay at school until next year, it will give me time to look about me. You have the entrée to Almack's, ma'am, so if I could persuade you to use your influence with the patronesses?'

'I'll do so gladly, but the girl must have a sponsor. My younger girl comes out next year. I wonder…? Would you care to have me present the girls together?'

Rushmore's harsh face lit up. 'Ma'am, I can think of nothing more suitable. You are too good. I should be at a loss myself. I suppose there must be gowns to consider and bonnets? Faced with such decisions I'd consider the provisioning of an army much less onerous. You will not find it tedious? I'm aware that I'm placing an extra burden on your shoulders…'

'It will be a pleasure,' Elizabeth told him truthfully. 'There is little enough we can do to serve the dependents of those men who gave their lives for us. It will be a privilege to be allowed to help in some small way.'

'Then we are agreed?' Rushmore's smile transformed his face. 'I am much in your debt, my dear ma'am. Naturally, expense will not be a consideration… You will not hesitate to let me know how I can help? There must be something I can do.'

Elizabeth returned his smile. 'Not for the moment, my lord. We have many months ahead of us before your ward leaves school. You say she is in Bath?'

'Yes! At Miss Bedlington's Academy. I do not know of it, do you?' He was surprised by Elizabeth's startled look. 'What is it, ma'am? Is something wrong? If the place is unsuitable she must leave at once.'

'It is a respectable establishment,' Elizabeth said with some reluctance. 'I know it well. My younger girl is there.'

'Miss Wentworth also attended the school? That gives me an excellent opinion of the place. Clearly there was no attempt to crush her spirit.'

'Er…no! At least, the attempt did not succeed.' Elizabeth's tone was hollow. She had no wish to supply the Earl with details of Perdita's stay at the Academy, nor to inform him that her daughter had been expelled.

Then she heard a laugh of pure delight. Rushmore had understood her perfectly. Now he rose to take his leave of her.

'I'll go to Bath at once,' he promised. 'I must get to know my ward and tell her of your kindness. There will be many details to discuss. When may I call on you again?'

'Not for some months, I fear. My husband is ordered to his Mediterranean station. We sail for Gibraltar in ten days' time.'

Rushmore nodded. 'You will be glad to escape the English winter, I make no doubt. Then, ma'am, I shall look for your return.' He handed her his card.

'Letters to this address will find me if you have need of my assistance, or if you change your mind.'

'I won't do that,' she told him simply. 'We have one great advantage, sir.'

'And what is that, may I ask?'

'I imagine that the girls already know each other. My Amy is a friendly little creature. She will be glad to have her schoolfriend stay with us throughout the Season. Then neither girl will find it quite so daunting.'

Rushmore kissed her hand again. 'You have lifted a great weight from my mind. I am deeply in your debt, ma'am. I hope you will not hesitate to command me in any way you wish.'

He did not wait for her to summon a servant to show him out. 'I have taken up far too much of your time,' he said. He bowed again and strode into the hall.

Knox stepped forward at once with his hat and cane. It was unfortunate that the Earl should have chosen that particular moment to glance at the ceiling, at the exquisite work of Robert Adam. On this occasion his eye was drawn to a movement on the first floor. Two faces were gazing down at him.

Perdita drew back at once, but not before she had become the recipient of a ravishing smile and an extravagant salute. Then the Earl was gone.

'Insolent creature!' she muttered. 'I suppose that he is well pleased with himself after treating Mother to a diatribe about my behaviour.'

'Well, at least he's gone,' Amy pointed out. 'And you weren't asked to apologise... That's something!'

'I don't trust him,' Perdita remarked in a gloomy tone. 'He'll have thought of something much much worse.'

'Oh, don't be such a goose! What could be worse?'

Perdita soon found out. Summoned to the study without delay, she could not believe her ears.

'You mean I am not to sail with you and Papa?' she cried. 'Oh, Mother, you promised...'

'That was before I realised that you have learned nothing in these past few months, Perdita. It was much against my judgment that we agreed to give you a Season after your expulsion from the Academy. It was a mistake. You are not yet ready to take your place in society.'

'But, Mother, I would have apologised to the Earl. Indeed I would! Anything but this.'

'His Lordship did not wish for an apology—'

'No, I expect he wouldn't,' Perdita cried bitterly. 'He'd prefer to ruin my life with his demands.'

'Nonsense! You are quite mistaken. For reasons which I find it difficult to fathom, his lordship did not take offence at your behaviour. You don't deserve such charity—'

'And I don't want it from him!'

'Perhaps not. You will not find *me* so charitable. For reasons which are known to you, I can't send you back to school, so you will go to Aunt Beatrice for the winter.'

'To Bath? Oh, Mother, please! It is a dreary place. I'd rather die!'

'That option is not open to you,' Elizabeth said austerely. 'Now let us have an end to these dramatics. We are not condemning you to a life of solitary confinement.'

'It will be almost as bad!'

'Don't put me more out of patience with you than I am already, Perdita. Aunt Beatrice is the kindest of women. She may not care to attend the Assembles, but there is still the Pump Room...'

Perdita threw her eyes to heaven, and Elizabeth was hard put to disguise a smile.

'No one insists that you drink the waters, my dear.'

'But, Mother, they are all decrepit. One cannot walk about the place for fear of falling over bath-chairs...'

'The Pump Room is not the only place to visit. You may go to the Sydney Gardens—'

'Almost as bad!' Perdita announced in dismal tones. 'Papa had promised to show me the Barbary apes, and to take me into Spain. Besides, you can see Africa across the Straits.' Her look at her mother was beseeching. 'Don't punish me like this!' she begged. 'I will be good! I will!'

Elizabeth was torn, but she had resolved that she would not weaken. 'Then show us that you mean it, my dear. Go to your aunt and spend the winter with her. You will be close to Amy and your friends, and the libraries and shops in Milsom Street will save you from a living death. Perdita, your Aunt Beatrice loves you dearly. She has been hoping for this age to have you stay with her. Can you not be generous with your time?'

Perdita was too distraught to speak, but she managed a brief nod. Open attack would have brought a sharp response from her, but an appeal to her better nature was something else.

'Very well, then,' her mother continued. 'You will travel with Amy when she returns to school, and Ellen shall go with you.' Her raised hand quelled the expected objection from Perdita. 'I am sending Ellen to help out. Your aunt's staff must not feel that you are an added burden.'

Perdita was reduced to silence.

'There is one other thing I have to say to you.' Her mother's tone was inexorable. 'You will not, I hope, attempt to persuade your father into altering this decision. Have I your word on that?'

Perdita nodded again. She was close to tears, but her own pride made her blink them back.

'I won't ask him,' she choked out. Then she fled to her room.

Amy found her huddled in the window-seat, weeping as if her heart would break.

Amy was dismayed. Her strong-willed sister seldom gave way to tears. 'What is it, love?' she cried. 'Mother can't be thinking of sending you back to school?'

'I'm sure she would, if Miss Bedlington would have me, but you know she won't. Still, I am to be sent to Bath, to stay with Aunt Trixie.'

'That isn't so very dreadful,' Amy comforted. 'Our aunt is such a dear.'

'But I wanted to sail with Father. Both he and Mother promised. It was to be my treat, and I've thought of nothing else for these past weeks.'

'You could speak to him,' Amy suggested.

'No, I can't. Mother made me promise…'

'Well, *I* could speak to him.'

'No, that would be almost the same thing. Oh, Amy, this is all the doing of that hateful creature, Rushmore. I can't think what he told Mama, but it was probably some heavily embroidered tale about our conversation.'

'He is a swine!' Amy agreed. 'Imagine a man like that attempting to damage your reputation! What a cur!'

'He is all of those things. I would have apologised, you know, in spite of what I said, but it wasn't enough for him. He wants to ruin my life!'

'He can't do that, for we shan't allow it.' Amy slipped an arm about her sister's waist. 'Cheer up, love! I know that you are disappointed, but selfishly,

I am not. We shall be together in Bath, which will make all the difference to me at least.'

'I shan't be able to call on you. Miss Bedlington will not allow it. I am forbidden to cross the threshold.'

'She won't refuse Aunt Trixie.'

'You think not? Our aunt is such a gentle soul.'

'You haven't seen her in action, dearest. That sweet manner hides a will of iron. Aunt has an astonishing ability to get her way when it suits her to do so. You don't know her as well as I. We were thrown much together after you left Bath.'

'Oh, pray don't think that I shall find her company a trial. She is the kindest of women. It is just that…well…I think my punishment is unjust. At least I can be in no doubt as to who is to blame.'

'Don't worry about Rushmore,' Amy advised. 'He isn't worth a second thought. Let us save our pity for his wife. What must it be like to be married to that monster?'

'I can't imagine!' This wasn't strictly true. Young as she was, Perdita had been well aware of the latent strength in the powerful arms which had swept her off her feet and carried her from the ballroom floor. Crushed against that brawny chest, she had felt a curious frisson of excitement behind her outward rage. If nothing else, it had given her a taste for battle. It was a pity that she was unlikely ever to meet the Earl again. A longing for revenge swept over her. It was so strong that she could almost taste it. God help him if he crossed her path again.

She wiped away the traces of her tears. 'I'm sorry, Amy,' she whispered. 'I've been thinking only of myself. You didn't complain when Mother and Father promised to take me to Gibraltar, though you couldn't go yourself.'

'I thought there would be another time,' Amy said cheerfully. 'Besides, I'm always seasick. Apart from that, the life on a naval station is too stiff for me—all those disapproving matrons, and more etiquette than one is likely to find in London.'

Perdita smiled at last. 'Amy, you are a jewel!' she announced. 'You have reconciled me to my fate!'

'Oh, it won't be so bad!' Ever practical, Amy was ready with words of reassurance. 'Think of the shops in Milsom Street! Papa is sure to make you a handsome allowance... And then there are the libraries. Confess it, Perdita, you haven't enjoyed your first Season here in London...it can only be better in Bath.'

'It will be quieter.' Perdita grimaced. 'I doubt if there will be a gentleman under the age of sixty-five...'

'And shall you mind that?' Amy gave her sister a sly look. 'You've given me a scathing report on the younger men you've met.'

Perdita frowned. 'There must be something wrong with me. I can't find a single man I care to talk to. With one eye on my dowry, they mutter platitudes, and if I try to speak of things which interest me they look quite shocked. I won't be patted on the head and consigned to the nursery to rear a passel of children.'

'You make them uncomfortable!' Amy told her. 'Your sympathy for the Luddites hasn't gone down too well, nor have your views on the slave trade.'

'I won't change them!' her sister retorted fiercely. 'No civilised person can condone the trafficking in human lives.'

'Love, you are preaching to the converted, as you well know.'

'You keep your opinions to yourself far better than I do,' Perdita said ruefully.

'It doesn't stop me making up my mind to do something about it, as soon as I have the chance.'

'A blue-stocking, Amy?'

'Something like that!' her sister agreed cheerfully. 'I'm saving my ammunition until I can hit the target.'

Perdita was intrigued. 'And does Miss Bedlington know of your views?'

'She has not the slightest notion.' Amy's eyes were sparkling with amusement. 'As far as she is concerned, I am the unfortunate ugly duckling of the Wentworth family, and much to be pitied. My ravishing elder sister gets all the limelight, in spite of her scandalous behaviour. It is much to be deplored.'

Perdita smiled in spite of herself. 'You are like to give her a dreadful shock. My own exploits will pale into insignificance.'

'But not just yet, Perdita. You must give me time.' Amy leaned back in her chair. Her coltish figure gave little promise of the woman she would become. 'Is that the door?' she asked. 'Papa must be home. Shall we go down to nuncheon?'

Perdita straightened her shoulders. 'Do I look a wreck?' she asked anxiously. 'I don't wish to upset Papa, or Mother either.'

'I'd be glad to look as much of a wreck as you do at this moment,' Amy reassured her with a laugh. 'Come on! Just think of the hateful Earl of Rushmore. That will stiffen your resolve not to give way to a fit of the dismals.'

Perdita determined to heed this excellent advice. She managed a smile for her Mama, and was greeted with a loving bear-hug by her father. No comment was made about her reddened eyes, but Perry was stricken to the heart.

'What do you say to a drive in the park this afternoon?' he suggested. 'I'm promised that it will not rain, and I haven't yet seen your latest toilettes. From the size of the account, they must be something special indeed!'

'They are, Papa.' Amy grinned at him. 'Mother didn't insist upon my choosing white this time, so mine is a heavenly shade of blue and my bonnet has delicious feathers.'

'Perdita?'

His elder daughter looked up at his troubled face and forced an enthusiastic response. 'Mine is a primrose colour, Father. I like it above anything, and my bonnet too. Shall we need to bring a calash, do you suppose?'

'Great heavens, no!' Perry said with feeling. 'I draw the line at that. I won't be taken for a bee-keeper by my friends. Those frightful bonnet-protectors resemble nothing so much as hives.'

Even Perdita giggled at that, and the slight air of tension eased. Elizabeth gave her daughter an approving look. At least the child wasn't sulking in disappointment. Had she been too harsh? She thought not. What Perdita needed for the next few months was time to come to terms with the adult world.

Elizabeth was under no illusions as to the nature of the society in which she and her family lived. Allow the least breath of scandal to attach itself to either of her daughters and they would be ostracised.

Perry might claim that he didn't care if neither of the girls were to wed. She doubted if he had given serious thought to the alternatives. She and her beloved husband would not always be there to care for Amy and Perdita. What would happen to them then? Did Perry consider what a lonely spinsterhood might mean to them?

Women had no rights. In the eyes of the law they did not exist. She'd had some little experience of these matters herself. Even a visit to her bank to enquire about a point concerning her inheritance had brought a pained smile of sympathy and the suggestion that perhaps her husband, her brother, or some male relative would be better fitted to understand the legalities.

With Perry's blessing, Elizabeth had moved her account at once. Dear Perry, he understood her fiery nature perfectly. She looked across the dining-table and gave him a loving smile. If only her girls could meet men who were happy in their own skins, who didn't feel threatened by allowing the female sex some modicum of freedom. Perry understood the need for women's suffrage, but she doubted if it would come in his lifetime, or even that of her daughters.

The light nuncheon of cold meats, sallets and fruit was soon disposed of. Then Perry consulted his watch.

'Well, girls,' he teased. 'How long will it take for you to beautify yourselves? Shall I have time to answer all my letters? You must give me fair warning before I summon the carriage. We cannot have the horses standing.'

'You are making game of us, Papa!' Perdita dropped a kiss upon his brow. 'When have we ever kept you waiting?'

'Not often.' Perry twinkled. 'The thought of an outing speeds you up amazingly.' He waited until the door had closed upon them. Then he turned to his wife.

'Perdita is behaving well,' he said. 'You must be proud of her.'

'I am. Perry, I need not tell you of her disappointment, but believe me, it is for the best…'

Perry let that pass. 'I hear that Rushmore called this morning,' he observed grimly.

'Now don't fly into the boughs, my dear. As far as Perdita is concerned he is as foolish as you are yourself. He would not hear of an apology—'

'I thought you were determined on it.'

A faint tinge of pink coloured Elizabeth's cheeks. 'The Earl announced that he alone was at fault. If I had summoned Perdita, he was determined upon assuring her of that fact. I could not allow it. She was at fault herself.'

Perry regarded his wife with interest. 'You crossed swords with him?'

'Well, not exactly! Rushmore did not call upon us for an apology. He came to make a request of us.'

'The plot thickens!' Perry teased. 'From your guilty expression, my love, I take it that you have agreed to the request?'

'Only if you have no objection, Perry. It seems he has a ward, through no fault of his own. He doesn't know what to do with her. I thought perhaps that we might help?'

'Indeed! And what made you agree?'

'Oh, I don't know. I liked him very much. I found him generous-minded. He would not hear that Perdita was at fault.'

Perry was not yet ready to forgive the author of Perdita's fall from grace. 'Overlooked, perhaps, because he needed a favour?'

'No, I don't think that of him. When you meet him, Perry, you will like him as I do.'

'And this girl?'

'The daughter of his friend who was killed at Waterloo. The girl has no other relations, or so I understand. Rushmore has promised to take care of her. She is at school in Bath.'

'Miss Bedlington's?'

Elizabeth nodded. 'Our girls must know of her. Sadly, I forgot to ask her name. Shall you object if I bring her out next year with Amy?'

'Of course not, my love! When did anything you decided ever come amiss with me?'

'Not recently!' Elizabeth teased. 'Though when we first met you found me something of a trial.'

'I never heard a truer word,' Perry said solemnly. 'When compared with you as a girl, Perdita is an angel!'

'You are biased in her favour.' Elizabeth gave him a mock frown. 'I'm glad you thought of driving in the Park, my dear. Perdita must not hide herself away today. That would give rise to gossip about the scene at Almack's.'

'She could always contrive to limp a little.' Perry was unrepentant about his daughter's behaviour. 'But even that will not be necessary if she is seated in the barouche. I must remind her to groan a little every now and then...'

'You are as bad as she is,' his wife told him severely.

'But you love me still?' Perry took his wife into his arms and kissed her soundly.

As Perry had predicted, the fine weather held for the rest of the day, so the collapsible roof of the family barouche stayed down, allowing the ladies both to see and be seen by the crowds in Rotten Row.

They were soon surrounded as friends pushed towards them through the press of gigs, tilburies and curricles. Perry cast a longing glance at several dashing phaetons, but his attention was soon diverted as three of his nephews rode towards him. There was no mistaking the family resemblance. Sebastian's boys bore a striking likeness to both his brother and himself, tall, dark, and blessed with a massive breadth of shoulder.

'Out to make your fortunes, lads?' he joked. 'Have you thrown your handkerchiefs to any of the heiresses?'

This sally was greeted by chuckles of amusement. 'We ain't ready to be handfasted yet, sir. Besides,

which of them can compare with our own family?'
Thomas beamed upon his cousins and his aunt.

Elizabeth shook her head at him. 'Are you just
come from Ireland, then? You must have kissed the
Blarney Stone, my dear. Your mother must be in
despair. Is she never to be rid of you?'

'She hasn't said...' Thomas paused and cocked
his head. 'What on earth is that noise? Surely it
can't be rioting?'

'Sounds more like cheering to me,' his brother
observed. 'Some bigwig must have decided to take
the air today.'

As the noise increased a rumour rippled through
the crowd. 'Wellington! It's Wellington! The Duke
himself...!'

At Perry's order their coachman drew the barouche to the side of the main concourse in the Row.
In the distance he could see a party of horsemen
making their way towards him. They were well
mounted and splendidly attired, but for the figure in
the centre of the group.

Perdita craned her neck to study this man who
was dressed in the plainest of riding garb without a
star, a riband, or a decoration of any kind. Even had
she not glimpsed the famous profile she would have
known at once that this was the saviour of her country. There was no mistaking that air of authority and
assurance.

Then her eye fell upon the man beside him and
her pleasure vanished in an instant. Praying that

Rushmore would not see them, she turned her head away.

Amy had noticed nothing amiss. 'Do look, Perdita,' she begged. 'The Duke is riding Copenhagen—the most famous horse in the world.'

Perdita stole another look at the group of riders. By now they were abreast of the barouche, and as she raised her head her eyes met those of Rushmore. With a word to his superior officer he left his companions and cantered over towards her.

His greeting was, however, for her mother. 'Ma'am, I am glad to see you here today and to have the opportunity of making the acquaintance of your husband.'

Elizabeth made the necessary introductions and the two men shook hands.

'I understand that you are about to leave for Gibraltar, sir. Do you know Spain at all?'

'No, my lord, at least, not nearly as well as you do yourself. You were at Salamanca, I believe?'

Before the Earl could reply, a hand descended upon his shoulder. 'Rushmore, you are the slyest of dogs,' a jovial voice remarked. 'Now I understand why you were so anxious to return to England...' A pair of bright blue eyes smiled down on the ladies.

'Your Grace, allow me to make the Wentworth family known to you.' Clearly, Rushmore was unfazed by the presence of the Great Man, though his voice and manner told of his respect.

'Ha! A naval man!' The Duke seized Perry's hand and pumped it with enthusiasm. 'Between our navy and our army we made short work of England's enemies, did we not?'

It was impossible to resist this easy camaraderie and soon Perry was deep in conversation with the Duke.

Both Perdita and Amy stared at Wellington as if they couldn't believe their eyes. For the moment Perdita had forgotten Rushmore. Then he addressed her directly.

'I trust I find you in good health today, Miss Wentworth? The foot is not giving you much pain, I hope?'

Perdita affected not to have heard him, but Elizabeth intervened.

'My love, the Earl is speaking to you,' she said sternly.

'Oh, I beg your pardon, sir, I was looking at the Duke.' Perdita avoided her mother's eye. Part of that statement was true, but she had heard the Earl quite clearly, and she had determined to ignore him.

'Deafness is a terrible affliction,' he whispered in a low voice. 'A tragedy in one so young. I'm told that an ear-trumpet helps to remedy the condition.'

Perdita would not be drawn. She kept her eyes fixed firmly upon the Duke, so Rushmore turned to Amy. 'And how do you go on, Miss Amy?' he asked. 'I hear that you are at school in Bath.'

'Yes, sir!' Amy's tone was uncompromising. 'I am to return next week.'

'And Miss Wentworth? Are you to travel to Gibraltar with your family?'

It was the most unfortunate of questions, and Rushmore was surprised to see Perdita's knuckles whiten as she clenched her hands. The enquiry had seemed to him to be innocuous, just part of the trivia which passed for conversation in polite society.

She looked at him then, and he was startled to see the enmity in her eyes. It was unmistakable.

'No!' she hissed. 'I am to stay with my great-aunt.'

Amy moved closer to her sister as if for comfort and both girls looked away. Rushmore was no fool. It was clear to him that the younger members of the Wentworth family had decided to close their ranks against him.

He shrugged. He'd been mistaken in Perdita. She was a silly, mannerless child, no better than the brainless females he had scorned at Almack's. He turned away and engaged Elizabeth in conversation.

Chapter Three

Always an admirer of feminine charms, Wellington was quick to join in their conversation. He eyed Elizabeth with fresh admiration.

'Ma'am, I trust you will be able to persuade your husband to bring you to my next reception?'

'You honour us, your Grace. Alas, we leave for the Mediterranean in ten days' time. I am so sorry…'

'The loss is mine, I assure you. Perhaps when you return?' He turned to Perry. 'My dear sir, you are a fortunate man. I envy you this bevy of beauties.' Doffing his hat to them, he turned to canter back to his waiting entourage. Then he noticed Thomas and nodded an acknowledgment.

'Good day to you, my boy! I hope I see you well?'

Thomas flushed with pleasure at this sign of recognition for one of his most junior officers from a man he regarded as almost a god. He bowed and muttered a reply.

The Duke laughed as he addressed Elizabeth again. 'This young man is also a credit to your family...a warrior who is an excellent dancer.' Still laughing, he rode away with Rushmore at his side.

Elizabeth was aware that her family party was the cynosure of all eyes. There could be no question now of Perdita's behaviour giving cause for censure. The Duke of Wellington himself had honoured them with his notice. She hid her pleasure in this fact as the carriage was besieged by curious members of the *ton*.

Perdita beckoned to Thomas to come close.

'The Duke is not in the least as I expected,' she whispered. 'He is quite charming... I had thought he would be hard and cold.'

'He's a dear!' Amy informed her cousin. 'He even said that I was a beauty. Do you think he meant it?'

Thomas grinned at her. 'Not for a minute!' he teased. 'Such ugly creatures as you are. How could he possibly mean it?'

'Now you are making game of us,' Amy announced with dignity. 'I can't think why he should imagine that you are a good dancer. You always tread upon my feet!'

'That's because they are always in the way.' Thomas was unrepentant.

As the usual banter between the two of them threatened to become heated, Perdita intervened.

'The Duke still puzzles me,' she said thoughtfully. 'One cannot doubt his habit of command, of course, but I can't believe some of the stories I have heard about him.'

'Which stories are those?'

'It is said…that he hanged some of his own men and flogged some others.'

'That's true, Perdita, but you do not know the circumstances. The men were hanged for ra—'' Thomas caught his aunt's eye and hastily amended his words. 'I mean that they showed no respect for the women in the Spanish towns we took. Others ignored his orders not to loot those towns. They were flogged for disobedience.'

'It seems harsh. Did he really refer to his army as ''the scum of the earth''?'

'He did, but that same army is always fed and housed with the best that he can find for them. I've only seen him lose his temper once. That was when he arrived in a village to find that certain of his officers were comfortably installed in the best billets in the place, leaving their men without shelter or provisions. He turned them into the street. They weren't flogged, but his tongue was flaying enough.'

'I suppose that Rushmore was among them?'

'Good Lord, no!' Thomas stared at his cousin. 'What on earth gave you that idea? Do you suppose that his Grace would make such a close friend of the Earl if they were not of the same mind?

Rushmore is as much a stickler for the comfort of his men as the Duke himself.'

'You sound as if you like him,' Amy ventured.

'I do. He is a great gun. Some find his wit a little trying, but he makes me laugh.'

A silence greeted these words, and Thomas grinned again. 'Has he been teasing you, my dears? You must give him as good as you get. That is what appeals to him.'

'Perdita has already done so,' Amy replied.

'Yes, and I don't care if it appealed to him or not. I find him hateful, Thomas. You are welcome to your own opinion. No doubt he is a marvel upon the battlefield. I could wish that he would go back there.'

'Difficult, Perdita! There are not more battles to be fought, unless you care to provide him with one of your own?'

'I hope never to be in his company again.' Perdita turned to the gentleman by her side. It was the young man who had been cut out by the Earl. Now Perdita gave him a brilliant smile, raising hopes within his breast which were destined to remain unfulfilled.

Thomas was puzzled. It was unlike the normally sunny-natured Perdita to be so dismissive of one of her country's heroes. He raised an eyebrow in enquiry as he looked at Amy.

A quick glance at her mother told Amy that her mother was deep in conversation with Lady Castlereagh.

'I'll tell you about it later,' she whispered. 'Do you dine with us tonight?'

'I believe so. My aunt has asked the three of us. Do you go to the play with Perdita and your parents?'

Amy grimaced. 'No, alas! I'm not yet out, you know.'

'Never mind! We don't go either. We'll keep you company.'

Amy eyed him with interest. 'Will you teach me some card games? I'll need to understand about loo and faro if I'm not to become a flat next year.'

'I doubt that, you monstrous child. I trust you ain't planning to become a gambler? And where do you pick up these expressions? You ain't supposed to know them.'

'Don't preach, Tom!' Amy was unrepentant. 'Shall you go on later to a den of vice?'

A fit of coughing brought Thomas to the notice of his aunt. 'You must not stand about, my dears,' she said kindly. A glance at Perry caused him to give his coachman the office, and they continued their slow progress through the Park.

'The boys looked well, I thought,' Elizabeth observed to her husband. 'Though Thomas has a nasty cough…'

'I think he had a frog in his throat, Mama.' Amy was hard put to keep her countenance. She knew well enough that Thomas had almost choked upon her own outrageous question.

His scarlet face had aroused her curiosity. To-night she would ask him to explain exactly what went on in a den of vice.

But Thomas was unforthcoming on the subject. 'Blest if you and your sister ain't the world's worst for asking questions,' he complained when his host and hostess had left with Perdita for the play. 'And you are worse than she is. What ails her, Amy? She wasn't her usual self tonight.'

'She's in disgrace…at least, she was… Did you not know what happened at Almack's?'

'Never go near the place,' Thomas said with feeling. 'I ain't ready to be handfasted yet. Those old biddies frighten me to death. Dance more than once with any of the girls and the announcement will be in the *Gazette* next morning.'

Amy laughed. 'You are allowed two dances, so I hear. Besides, who'd have you, Tom?'

This cheerful insult left her cousin unmoved. 'What happened?' he asked. 'I don't care to see Perdita looking so…well…subdued.'

'She's disappointed,' Amy told him. 'Now she is to go to Bath, instead of to Gibraltar.'

'As bad as that?' Thomas whistled. 'What has she done? It must be murder, at the very least.'

'Don't be stupid!' Amy snapped. She felt Perdita's disappointment almost as keenly as if it had been her own. 'If you must know, it is all the fault of that creature you admire so much…'

'Wellington? That cannot be! She hadn't met him before today.'

'Of course it isn't the Duke of Wellington. It's that…that Rushmore!'

'Good Lord! Has he offered for her? Don't tell me she has refused him?'

Amy was aware that all three of her cousins were staring at her open-mouthed. 'Are you mad?' she asked. 'That puffed-up creature would not dream of offering for Perdita. He made that all too clear.'

'Has he insulted her?' The young men caught each other's eyes. Much as they admired Rushmore, they were ready to defend their cousin's honour.

'Not exactly!' Amy said hastily. 'It sounded as if…well…as if mutual insults were exchanged. Rushmore doesn't care for Almack's, and Perdita overheard his comments.'

'But she don't like the place herself,' Henry objected. 'She can't complain if others feel the same.'

'It wasn't just that. It was unfortunate that Mother had just sat down when Rushmore made a reference to harpies. It was the outside of enough. He had just been holding forth about the ninnies and schoolroom misses.'

Crispin chuckled. 'Perdita wouldn't like that!'

'She didn't. She stepped back and stamped upon his foot.'

Amy heard a ripple of amusement. 'That ain't so bad, Amy. Most probably he thought it was an accident.'

'No, he didn't. He thought that Perdita was attempting to attract his attention. His comments to his friend were...well...unkind. He said that she was hoping to make herself a countess.'

'And she heard him?' Crispin closed his eyes. He was the youngest and the gentlest of the brothers. He could well imagine the furore which ensued.

Thomas gave a shout of laughter. He had a lively appreciation of Perdita's fiery nature. 'Go on,' he begged. 'This is better than the play. What did she do?'

'She...er...told him that he was a popinjay who fancied himself the catch of the Season.'

For some strange reason this reduced her three companions to fits of helpless laughter.

'It isn't funny!' she told him with dignity. 'Everyone was staring! You know what gossips people are. Then Rushmore led Perdita into the dance. Mama says that it was to stave off comment.'

With eyes streaming, her cousins begged for more.

'Well...naturally, Perdita didn't care to dance with him. She tried to walk away, but he pushed her into a stumble. Then, if you please, he pretended that she had turned her ankle and carried her off the floor.'

'And to think we missed it!' Thomas mourned. 'I'd have given a month's pay to see Perdita's face.'

'And the Earl's, too.' Henry went off into fresh paroxysms of laughter. 'Rushmore must have been startled, to say the least, to be tackled by a bantam-weight.'

Amy looked at the circle of grinning faces. 'I thought you all admired the Earl,' she told them stiffly. 'He is not the gentleman you think him to be. He came to see Mama, and now Perdita is to be punished for behaving so badly. He is a petty creature. I have no time for him.'

Thomas frowned at her. 'You are mistaken, coz. There is nothing petty about Rushmore...rather the opposite.'

Henry was quick to agree with his brother. 'You can't know that he came to complain about Perdita,' he pointed out reasonably. 'That is, unless you were party to the conversation?'

'I wasn't.' Amy would not be convinced. 'But why else should he call upon us? It was only after his visit that Mama told Perdita that she was to go to Bath, rather than Gibraltar.'

'It could have been coincidence.' Crispin, always the peacemaker, decided to intervene. 'Aunt Elizabeth reaches her own decisions. I doubt if even Rushmore could influence her. Is it not possible that she'd made up her mind to punish Perdita before he came to call? I imagine she was none too pleased to see her daughter in a public quarrel with one of the most powerful men in the kingdom.'

Amy looked at her cousin in disgust. 'Defend Rushmore if you must! You sound like a bunch of prosy old women. Since when are you on the side of caution and decorum?' She tossed her head. 'Perdita was right, in my opinion. I should have done exactly the same.'

'That don't make it right, Amy. The pair of you have never learned to fight your weight.' Thomas ruffled his cousin's hair. 'Bless me if you won't insist on taking on the heavyweights.'

Amy glared at him. 'You won't convince me,' she insisted. 'It is my fondest hope never to set eyes again upon the Earl of Rushmore, and Perdita feels the same.'

'Then you are in luck!' Henry announced. 'I understand that the Earl is to leave London as soon as Wellington can spare him. I doubt if he'll go to Bath. He don't look much in need of doctoring as far as I can see.'

This brought a smile, even from the irate Amy. 'Then let's forget him,' she begged. 'The cards are in the bureau, Crispin. Will you get them?'

Thomas threw up his eyes to heaven. Clearly, Amy had not forgotten her wish to be initiated into the mysteries of loo and faro. Shuddering at the likely reaction from his aunt, he was moved to suggest a game of spillikins, but Amy threatened to box his ears.

'Try it.' He grinned. 'I'll put you over my knee.'

Amy thought better of her threat. Perhaps it might be as well to use a little diplomacy. She laid a hand upon his arm and gave him a winning smile.

'You did promise,' she cooed.

'No, I didn't. How about a game of backgammon?'

'Backgammon is a game for two. Oh, don't be such a bore! We shan't be playing for money, because I haven't any. We can only play for counters. Of course, we could pretend that they have a certain value.'

'Well, be it upon your own head! We'll give you the thrashing of your life.' Thomas looked at his brothers and between them they settled down to trounce her.

This was not so easily accomplished. Amy had a head for cards and retentive memory, as they soon discovered. The counters mounted up before her and in less than a couple of hours her cousins found that their pockets were to let.

It was only when Ellen came in to claim her charge that Thomas admitted defeat.

'Remind me to warn Society at large,' he said darkly. 'Lord help all of our acquaintances when you are let loose upon the London scene.'

Amy was delighted. 'You owe me thousands,' she announced. 'But I'll cancel the debt if you'll call for me tomorrow. I want to see the wild beasts in the Tower.'

'I doubt if they are ready for you. When they see you coming they'll hide in the furthest corners of their cages.'

Amy giggled. 'Promise?'

'Very well, we promise. Tell Perdita, won't you? An outing will cheer her up.'

Amy beamed at him. It had been a pleasant evening, and best of all was the news that Rushmore would no longer trouble them. Perdita would be delighted. With any luck she would never see her enemy again.

Amy's hopes were premature. The Wentworth family had not been settled in their box at the theatre for above a minute or two when they heard the sound of cheering.

Perdita's heart sank. The new arrival could not be the Prince Regent. The London crowds were more likely to boo and hiss him rather than to cheer. One man alone could be the recipient of such an enthusiastic reception. She was not mistaken. The audience rose as the Duke of Wellington made his appearance.

As always, his dress was plainer than that of any man in his entourage, except for Rushmore. Though that gentleman was faultlessly attired in evening wear which was the pride of his tailor, it was Wellington who was the focus of all eyes. He wore no stars or decorations, and Perdita smiled to herself, realising that he had no need of them. The eagle profile was unmistakable, as was his erect carriage, and the clear air of authority.

Perdita sank down in her chair and grasped at the curtained drapes, intending to draw them slightly, so that she might hide herself from Rushmore's view. It was her mother who objected.

'Leave them, my love,' her mother asked. 'You won't be able to see the stage.'

To gain a clear view of the stage was not the object uppermost in Perdita's mind at that particular moment, but she did as she was bidden. Perhaps if she could move her chair back into the shadow she might escape Rushmore's notice? After all, he was in the middle of an excited throng, all milling about the Duke.

For a time she thought that she had succeeded, but in the end it was Wellington himself who spied the Wentworth party. Just as the curtain rose upon the play he bowed to her mother and father.

Perdita murmured a most unladylike expletive beneath her breath. She had no objection to the Duke; in fact, she admired him as did all his fellow-countrymen. But if he should take it into his head to pay her mother and father a visit during the interval, Rushmore would be certain to accompany him.

It was too much to bear. Wildly, she cast about for some excuse which would remove her from his presence. The headache, perhaps? No, that would not fool her mother for an instant. Perdita did not suffer from headaches. And neither could she lay claim to another twisted ankle. There was nothing for it but to sit demurely in the box and pray that the Duke had other claims upon his interest during the intervals.

It was a forlorn hope. The Duke had taken a fancy to both Perry and Elizabeth Wentworth, and their beautiful daughter was a pleasure to behold. He was quick to tell her so, when, as Perdita dreaded, he came to greet them. Rushmore merely smiled and bowed, but there was an ironic look upon his face.

Conscious that her mother's eyes were upon her, Perdita made her curtsy to both gentlemen, with a shy word of thanks to Wellington for his graceful compliments.

How fortunate that upon this particular evening she had chosen to wear her newest and most expensive gown. It was a creation of pure silk chiffon in a dark rose colour, worn over a white satin slip and trimmed at the hem with a band of appliqued flowers in toning shades of pink and cerise. A narrow trimming of the same fabric edged both neck and sleeves.

'You are in famous looks tonight, Miss Wentworth,' a low voice whispered in her ear. 'How well that toilette becomes you!'

Perdita was tempted to give the Earl a dagger-look. A dozen sharp retorts rose to her lips, but she uttered none of them. She had not worn the gown to impress him, nor was her appearance any concern of his. She managed a distant smile and turned away to listen to Wellington's comments upon the play.

Rushmore's lips twitched. Evidently he was not to be forgiven so easily, but the chit could not be allowed to continue to regard him as her enemy. If his ward was to join the Wentworth family for the coming Season, he was determined that the girl would be welcomed and made to feel comfortable. The loss of her father had been tragedy enough for her. It was his hope that a change of scene and the friendship of the Wentworth girls would go some way towards lessening her grief.

He studied Perdita's face in silence, marvelling at the wonderful bone structure and the fine carriage of her head. This was no simpering miss. She had accepted Wellington's compliments gracefully, but in a curiously detached way, as if her beauty was of no concern to her. He was intrigued.

'Are you aware that you are quite the loveliest creature here tonight?' he whispered.

Perdita turned to look at him. She could do no other, as he had addressed her directly.

'That is a matter of opinion,' she told him coolly. 'I can claim no credit, my lord. I did not design my face.'

Rushmore smiled at her. 'Well said, Miss Wentworth! I agree that it is a gift from God.'

Perdita was not listening. She had turned away to look at Wellington once more. The Earl saw her intent expression and was inspired. The girl had no time for compliments, but he had another ace to play.

'How do you find the Duke?' he asked. 'Is he all that you imagined?'

He had her attention then. Perdita forgot her private vow not to speak to him more than was absolutely necessary.

'He is all that I imagined and more,' she said. 'When I look at him I realise that he has hidden depths. Meeting him socially as we have done, it is hard to imagine that this one man held the fate of Europe in his hands. Yet always there is the sense that behind that affable exterior lies a will of iron.'

Rushmore smiled. 'He is already known as the Iron Duke,' he agreed. 'Yet I have seen him in tears, Miss Wentworth. The loss of life at Waterloo was a grievous trial to him. So many of his friends were gone, but he mourned the common soldier just as much.'

'The slaughter must have been appalling,' Perdita said simply. 'It is such a hideous waste of good men's lives.'

'In one way, perhaps, but they did not die in vain. Had Napoleon not been defeated we should have been living beneath a tyrant's heel… Would you have wanted that?'

'No, of course not.' Perdita grew thoughtful. 'What will the Duke do now, do you suppose? With his concern for the common people, perhaps he will enter politics.'

Rushmore stared at her. Clearly, there was more to Perdita than a lovely face. He had not expected to find her ready to discuss the political scene. Well, he would not talk down to her. Instead, he paid her the compliment of taking her question seriously.

'The Duke is no democrat,' he told her with a wry smile. 'I suspect that you have liberal views, Miss Wentworth. Wellington does not share them. He is against any extension of the franchise, believing as he does in the status quo. In his eyes this country is well governed by the aristocracy. He would not have the system changed.'

'But surely change must come? There are other worthy men who must have much to offer. They pay their taxes. Are they not entitled to have some say in how the country is run?'

Rushmore rose to his feet as the bell sounded to warn that the second act of the play was about to begin.

'An interesting topic, is it not? We must discuss it further.' Bending to kiss her hand he followed his superior officer from the box.

He left Perdita wondering. It went much against the grain to admit that she had enjoyed their conversation, but it was true. Rushmore had not been patronising. Other men had patted her upon the head, figuratively speaking, and had indicated that subjects beyond fashion, gossip and thoughts of marriage were far beyond the grasp of the female mind.

Next time she saw him she would quiz him upon the rights of women in this male-dominated society. If he didn't agree that they were treated as non-citizens, at least he might discuss it with her.

Then she caught her mother's eye. 'Well done, my dear!' Elizabeth said. 'I am glad to see that you do not bear a grudge. The Earl is interesting, is he not?'

'I suppose so.' Perdita was not yet ready to forgive her enemy so easily. 'He was telling me about the Duke of Wellington.'

Elizabeth smiled to herself. It had not taken Rushmore long to find a way of undermining her daughter's resistance to him. 'You must tell me about it later, Perdita. We cannot hear enough about the Great Man, and I must suppose that Rushmore knows him as well as anyone.'

The Earl himself heard little of the rest of the play. Perdita had astonished him. How old could she be? Possibly eighteen? It had come as a shock to find that the girl had a head upon her shoulders and was capable of thinking for herself. He'd found her fiery and quick-tempered, but now he realised that there was far more to her than he had suspected.

Thoughtfully, he saluted her parents. It was clear that Perdita had been encouraged to read and to take part in discussions upon the topics of the day. Now he looked forward to their next encounter.

She hadn't mentioned Bath again. He'd surprise her there, guessing that Elizabeth had not yet mentioned her offer to sponsor his ward for the coming Season.

His thoughts turned again to Louise. Too much to hope, perhaps, that she would have Perdita's sparkle and quick intelligence, but he'd do his best by her, whatever her character. Again he blessed Elizabeth Wentworth for her understanding. Without her help he would have been hard put to launch the girl upon Society.

Now it was important that he visit Bath without delay. The Duke, he knew, was anxious to visit the property bestowed upon him by a grateful nation. With any luck he would release some members of his entourage to go about their own affairs.

Rushmore frowned. He need not stay too long in Bath. He'd been out of England for many years. His vast estates had claims upon his own attention, though they were well administered by his men of business.

Suddenly he longed to get away from London. Fastidious to a degree, the smell of death was still in his nostrils, and the stench in the capital was little better, compounded as it was of horse droppings, inadequate drainage, and streets which resembled open sewers.

And then there was the noise. The sounds of battle were bad enough, but they were over quickly. Here in London there was a constant cacophony of sound.

Rushmore grimaced. For a battle-hardened warrior who had fought his way across half of Europe, he was becoming much too nice in his requirements. What did the constant assault upon his eardrums matter? The cries of the muffin-men, the flower-sellers, the rattle of carriage wheels and the non-stop bustle were of small matter, surely?

Yet he longed for the peace of the countryside, and knew his longing for what it was...a simple case of battle fatigue. In time he would come about, and take up the threads of his life again. But to what end? He was unwed, and but sparsely provided with relatives, most of whom he hadn't seen for years. If he died tomorrow, who would mourn him? It was a sobering thought.

Perhaps he needed a family of his own. Unless he provided an heir his line would wither and die. To date he had had no opportunity to look about him...to drop his handkerchief in any direction. Such females as he had encountered had not moved him, unless it was to a sense that breeding was the only way in which they could deal together. The thought repelled him.

Then, unbidden, a vision of Perdita floated across his mind. Ridiculous, he told himself sternly. The child was half his age. She disliked him intensely. That much, at least, was clear. Aside from that, she'd had no chance to look about her. Her parents, he surmised correctly, would examine her choice of husband with great care, vetoing anyone to whom her heart was not given fully.

Rushmore shrugged. What was he thinking of? A lovely face, a spirited temperament, and the exchange of a few words. It was no basis for marriage, and he knew it. Aside from anything else, the lady would not have him. It was a sombre thought.

Even so, he was forced to admit that both of his encounters with Perdita had raised his spirits, lifting for a time that cloud of boredom and lassitude which seemed to have enveloped him since his return to England.

Half his age she might be, but already there were signs of the woman she would become—an independent soul who was fully capable of thinking for herself. Had he found a kindred spirit? He dismissed the idea before it was half-formed. The notion was ridiculous. His lips curved in a grimace of self-mockery.

The trouble was that he had been celibate for too long. Now he was indulging in fantasy, seduced by his own imagination. The ideal creature of his dreams had no existence in reality.

The long years spent in Spain and Portugal during the Peninsular War had offered little chance of feminine company. The menfolk of those countries guarded their women closely, even from Wellington's senior officers. Some beauty might be glimpsed from behind an iron grille, or peeping from a closed carriage, but they made no public appearances.

He could not blame their protectors. The sight of an army on the march, followed by a motley rabble of camp-followers, would be quite enough to persuade fathers, husbands and brothers to keep their female relatives well hidden.

Some soldiers' wives had followed the drum, but for the most part the women were blowsy creatures, drawn from the poorest of the poor, and ready to sell themselves for what pickings they could glean from the men they tramped behind.

Rushmore didn't despise them. No one who had seen them in the aftermath of battle could possible do that. He'd watched them bind up sickening wounds, and carry water to the dying without regard for their own safety, but they were no more of a temptation to him than the cloistered Spanish beauties.

Later, as Wellington's army waited for Napoleon in the Low Countries, there had been opportunity enough for dalliance. In the hectic atmosphere of Brussels before Waterloo even the normally respectable had snatched at the chance of one last fling at life before it was snuffed out for ever. No one had expected Wellington to win. Napoleon's armies were considered invincible.

Rushmore had resisted the lures thrown out to him, uninfluenced by the general hysteria. He knew his commander well, and was quietly confident of victory. His lip curled in disgust. During those final days he had learned much about the female sex, confirming his belief in the fragility of feminine virtue.

He would not cuckold a friend, though on more than one occasion he had been offered the opportunity to do so. The camp-followers were more honest, he'd decided, though the high-born ladies who smiled their invitations at him would have been shocked to hear him say so.

Well, there were other remedies now that he was back in England. He had means enough to offer *carte blanche* even to the most expensive of the fair Cyprians who frequented the London scene. Years ago he'd set up one or two of them in charming little houses, placing no limits upon their expenses and making sure that their carriages and bloodstock were of the finest money could buy.

It was strange that the idea should hold so little attraction for him now. He gave an involuntary sigh, and Wellington turned to him at once.

'I can only agree!' his superior officer told him with a smile. 'The play is poor. Thank heavens it is almost time for the second interval.'

This time they were summoned to the box of the Princess Esterhazy. Rushmore knew her to be one of the Lady Patronesses who ruled the roost at Almack's, but he was surprised to hear her scolding Wellington for his late arrival there in the previous week.

'We make no exceptions, your Grace. No one is admitted after eleven in the evening.' Her smile robbed the words of all offence.

'Quite right, ma'am!' the Duke agreed. 'Rules are rules and must be obeyed. Turn one away, and you must treat everyone alike.'

Rushmore warmed to the Great Man as he had done so often in the past. Wellington never stood upon his consequence. Clearly he had not taken offence at the refusal to admit him through Almack's hallowed portals, though a lesser man might have done so.

The Earl's eyes strayed to the opposite box to find it filled with friends and acquaintances of Perry and Elizabeth Wentworth. Perdita was invisible, surrounded by a crowd of hopeful suitors. The child would be certain to find a husband soon. That was only too clear. He didn't care to examine too closely the reason why he found the thought depressing.

He didn't see her again that evening. At the end of the play the Duke and his party were surrounded by well-wishers and the Wentworth box was empty by the time they were able to take their leave.

Refusing the suggestion of a visit to Watier's, Rushmore made his way back to his huge establishment in Grosvenor Square. Tonight, for some obscure reason, he found it little more cheerful than a mausoleum. He picked up a book and settled himself by the fire in the library, with a glass of brandy in his hand, to while away the hours before he went to bed. As he read, his black mood lifted, and he retired in a more contented frame of mind.

Perdita too had thrown off her depression. She'd enjoyed the evening, although the play had been dull and the acting indifferent. As always, Amy was still awake and anxious to hear the latest gossip about the world she was so soon to enter.

'Who was at the theatre?' she demanded eagerly. 'Did Wellington attend?'

'He did! Don't you ever tire of asking about your hero?' Perdita teased. 'He came to speak to us in the interval.'

'Really?' Amy's eyes were sparkling. 'I wish I had been there. Did you learn any more about his triumphs?'

'Yes.' Perdita grew thoughtful. 'The Earl of Rushmore told me something of them.'

'Rushmore? You mean you had a conversation with him?' Amy's astonishment knew no bounds.

'I couldn't ignore him, Amy, without disgracing myself further. And what he had to say was interesting.'

'Good Lord! Tell me all!'

For the next few minutes Amy hung on every word. Then she laughed. 'Rushmore has his uses, after all,' she announced. 'Have you quite forgiven him?'

'The man does not enter my thoughts,' Perdita said with dignity. 'Now I have no feelings about him one way or the other.'

'Fibber! I think you dislike him as much as ever.' Amy was undeceived. 'Don't worry, love. He will not stay in London. Thomas tells me that he is to leave as soon as the Duke releases him. I doubt if we shall see him again. Surely that is welcome news?'

Oddly, Perdita did not find it so. She could think of no suitable reply, so she summoned her maid and retired to her own room.

Chapter Four

Amy was disposed to tease her cousins on the following day.

'Up before noon?' she cried. 'What happened? Were you turned away from the gambling halls?'

Thomas appealed to Perdita. 'Where does your sister get these notions?' he asked. 'It ain't ladylike even to be aware of such places.'

Both the girls laughed at him. 'Are we supposed to be blind and deaf?' Perdita said. 'Thomas, it is time that you grew up.'

'I ain't the only one. Are you ready for our outing, or must we wait for you to primp and preen before we set out?' He looked at his brothers and raised his eyes to heaven.

'We are quite ready.' Perdita picked up her reticule. 'Amy, where do we go first?'

'The Tower, I think. Then on to the Exeter Exchange to see the lions and tigers and the water spectacle. After that we might visit the waxwork effigies at Madame Tussaud's.'

Thomas groaned as he saw the list in Amy's hand. 'Anything else? Have you forgot the Peerless Pool and Astley's Amphitheatre? It shouldn't take more than a month to see them all.'

'Don't be such a misery! We haven't asked you to take us to see the Elgin Marbles, Thomas, or the rest of the sights at the British Museum.'

'Thank the Lord for that. You'd be wasting your time, my girl. Headless statues ain't the thing for me. Well, come on! Let's get on with it. Then we can take you for an ice at Gunter's.'

Though Thomas affected to despise his cousin's choice of entertainment he enjoyed it. The beasts in both the Tower and the Exeter Exchange were savage enough to still his criticism and the water spectacle was well staged.

At Madame Tussaud's he made an effort to dissuade Amy and Perdita from entering the Special Room, but they would have none of it.

'Well, inspect the horrors if you must,' he said. 'But don't expect me to catch you if you faint. It's all executions and the like.'

'I've never fainted in my life,' Perdita told him. 'Don't be such a milksop!'

Even so, both girls were looking rather pale when they emerged from the chamber.

'I told you so,' Thomas said triumphantly. 'You both look sick as parrots.'

'I'm glad we've seen it,' Perdita told him coolly. 'We don't wish to be sheltered from the uglier side of life.'

Thomas whistled. 'Perdita, you ain't turning into a blue-stocking, I hope? That will scupper your chances of making a good match.'

Perdita fixed him with a basilisk look. 'What makes you think that I am seeking a ''good match'' as you are pleased to call it. Let me tell you, cousin, from what I've seen of men, I shall be happier on my own.'

This remark brought shouts of glee from all three cousins. 'So will they!' cried Henry. 'That is, unless you choose a bare-knuckle fighter.'

Perdita treated this remark with the disdain which it deserved. It was only when they reached Gunter's that she looked upon her irrepressible cousins with any degree of favour.

She sank into a chair with a sigh of relief. Three hours of sight-seeing had caused her new half-boots to nip her toes cruelly. It was Amy who noticed that the pale blue fabric uppers were becoming discoloured by a spreading stain.

'Dita, have you cut your foot?' she asked. 'That looks like blood to me.'

'It's nothing,' Perdita told her hastily. 'Though my boots do hurt after all this walking. Will you wait here for me whilst I go and change them?'

'I'll go with you,' Amy said at once.

'No, Jenkins shall take me in the coach and bring me back again. It won't take half an hour…'

'But shall you wish to go on walking, love?'

'Oh, Amy, we haven't done one half of what we planned for today, and we haven't much time before we leave for Bath.' With that Perdita rose to her feet, and hobbled out to the entrance, feeling as if she trod on knives.

By the time the coach reached Grosvenor Square she was in agony. Jenkins helped her down with a look of concern, but it was as much as she could do to mount the steps to the front door without crying out in pain.

'More trouble with your ankle, Miss Wentworth?' a deep voice enquired. 'Who is the unfortunate gentleman this time?'

Perdita turned her head and looked into the grinning face of the Earl of Rushmore.

'What are you doing here?' she demanded abruptly.

'Well now, I had supposed that I might make morning calls as well as any other man in London. If you will have the truth of it, I came to see your Mama.'

'Again?' Perdita tried to review her behaviour at her last meeting with the Earl, but she could think of nothing but the excruciating pain as she took another step towards the door. A muffled shriek escaped her lips.

'What's wrong?' Rushmore swung her round to face him. 'Are you ill?'

'No…it's just that…well…I think I've hurt my foot.'

His glance travelled to the little half-boots.

'I think we might say that,' he told her grimly. 'Your boots are soaked in blood.' Without more ado he picked her up and strode past the butler into the hall.

'Fetch Miss Wentworth's maid,' he ordered as he passed the startled man to walk into the salon. He laid Perdita down upon a sofa and dropped to his knees beside her, unlacing her boots with deft fingers.

'Good God!' he said with feeling. 'You've taken the skin off most of your toes and damaged your heels as well. What have you been doing?'

'We were sight-seeing,' she told him faintly.

'Well, you won't see an uglier sight than this. Had you no comfortable shoes?'

'They didn't match my toilette,' she said lamely. 'My boots are new…'

'Women!' Rushmore threw his eyes to heaven. Then he tossed the offending boots aside. 'You won't be wearing these again.' He looked up as Ellen entered the room, startled to see her charge with bare and bleeding feet, and being tended by a gentleman unknown to her.

'Good morning.' Rushmore said briefly. 'Miss Wentworth needs your help. Her feet are in sad case, I fear. Will you send for bandages and hot water? Then you may direct me to her room.'

A protest died on Ellen's lips. She knew quality when she saw it and this, she recognised at once, was a gentleman accustomed to being obeyed without question. She picked up Perdita's blood-stained stockings and rang the bell in reply to his request.

Ignoring Perdita's angry refusal to be helped, he took her into his arms once more and carried her up the staircase in Ellen's wake.

'I'll see to her now, my lord.' Ellen had been apprised of the gentleman's identity by the footman who came to do her bidding.

'Well, do please hurry, Ellen,' Perdita said. 'The others are waiting for me at Gunter's. I said that I should not be above half an hour.'

She heard a snort of disbelief from Rushmore. 'Are you quite mad?' he asked. 'You won't be walking on those feet again today.'

'Oh, yes, I shall.' Perdita winced as she dipped them into the bowl of water. 'They look worse than they are. I shall go on quite well if they are bandaged.'

'You can try, of course. Perhaps you hope to emulate the Indian fakirs who walk upon beds of nails or burning coals?'

'I shall manage!' Perdita glared at him as she waved away Ellen's attempt to coax her into lying upon her day-bed. 'I can't wear those,' she protested as Ellen produced a pair of her oldest and most comfortable slippers. 'Bring me my walking shoes.'

'Now, Miss Perdita, you'll never get them on over they bandages. You should listen to his lordship.'

'Why? This has nothing to do with him!' Perdita ignored the scandalised gasp and thrust the slippers aside.

'Miss Perdita, please…'

'Oh, let her try!' Rushmore was growing impatient. 'Some stupid human beings insist on learning the hard way.'

He was right, of course. Struggle as she might, Perdita was unable to force her bandaged feet into her walking shoes.

Scarlet with frustration, she looked up at her tormentor. 'Can't you go away?' she cried. 'You are quite without a sense of decorum. You should not be in a lady's bedchamber.'

'I hadn't realised that I was,' he said rudely. 'I had the impression that I was in the room of a foolish child, who will have her way if it kills her.'

Perdita was on the verge of tears. 'The others are expecting me back,' she stormed. 'My sister will wonder what has happened.'

'That is easily remedied. Ellen, will you ring the bell? Jenkins will return to Gunter's with a message for your sister. She must be reassured that you are resting quietly. Under no circumstances is she to interrupt her plans for the day. There is not the slightest necessity for her to do so.'

Perdita heard a snort of amusement from her old nurse and it angered her further. 'You take too much upon yourself, my lord. I could have sent that message myself.'

'Then why didn't you do so?'

This was unanswerable. To make matters worse, Rushmore was gazing down at the battered slippers which Ellen had succeeded in slipping upon Perdita's feet.

'Charming!' he murmured smoothly. 'Tell me, did you embroider these dear little rabbits yourself?'

Perdita did not answer him.

'I must study some further examples of your skill…a sampler, perhaps?' With a maddening air of interest he strolled about the room, examining the framed work upon the walls. 'These homilies are most uplifting,' he announced brightly. 'Did you choose them yourself? How suitable they are. I like this one in particular: ''Pride goeth before a fall''. I could not have imagined a better had I tried.'

'They are not mine,' Perdita ground out.

'Indeed not, my lord! Miss Perdita has never been able to set a stitch to save herself.' Ellen smiled at the forthright gentleman who seemed to have the measure of her troublesome charge.

Perdita closed her eyes. With Rushmore and Ellen in league against her there was nothing more to say. She gave a theatrical groan.

'I believe that I shall rest, after all,' she told them in a faint voice. 'Leave me now. I may be able to sleep.'

Rushmore laughed aloud. 'Never try for the stage, my dear Miss Wentworth. You would find yourself the target of rotten eggs. You are not the least convincing. Come now, can't you stand a little teasing? I had suspected you of having a sense of humour. I should be sorry to find that I was wrong.'

This brought Perdita upright. She glared at him, but she did not speak.

'That's better!' he encouraged. 'Now, what are we to do with you? You will not wish to stay in your room all day. Shall you care for a drive in the Park?'

Ellen spoke up before Perdita could answer him. 'My Lord, that will not do,' she said quietly. 'It would give rise to gossip if you took Perdita up in your curricle.'

'Quite right, Ellen. There is no room for a chaperon. Suppose I carry her down to the salon whilst we await the return of her parents? You might sit with us whilst we enjoy a hand or two of cards, or discuss the latest affairs of the nation.'

Perdita was about to refuse his offer, but the thought of the alternative was a strong deterrent. She had finished her book and had found no opportunity to visit Hatchards in Piccadilly for the purpose of changing it. Possibly one or other of her many admirers might call, but the offending slippers would give rise to anxious enquiries and the need for explanations which she had no desire to give.

Rushmore watched her in some amusement, guessing that she was torn between accepting his offer, and giving him a sharp set-down. He was banking on the hope that common-sense would reassert itself, and he was not disappointed.

'You are too kind!' she said stiffly.

'Am I to take it, then, that you agree?'

Perdita nodded.

'Very well, then.' Rushmore bent down towards her. 'If you will slip your arms about my neck I shall be able to carry you in perfect safety.'

Perdita glanced at Ellen, expecting further protests from her old nurse. She was somewhat disconcerted to note the look of approval upon Ellen's ruddy face.

Not for the first time it occurred to her that Rushmore had the most irritating habit of ingratiating himself with her nearest and dearest. Ellen might at least have insisted that two of the footmen carried her young mistress. The reason for her complaisance was not far to seek. She believed that Rushmore saw Perdita as a wilful child.

Perdita was given no further opportunity for reflection. Rushmore gripped her wrists and put her arms about his neck, lifting her as if she were the child that Ellen thought her. Then he made his way towards the head of the staircase.

He was but halfway down the second flight when a commotion in the hallway heralded the return of Perry and Elizabeth. For just a moment her parents stood transfixed.

Perdita's sense of humour got the better of her, and it was only with the greatest difficulty that she kept her countenance. How would Rushmore explain the fact that he was descending from Perdita's bedchamber with that lady in his arms? She could not blame her mother and father if they wondered at it.

Rushmore was, as always, equal to the occasion. He bowed and addressed Elizabeth directly.

'Ma'am, your daughter has met with a slight accident. Nothing to worry about, I assure you, but her feet are very painful and she finds some difficulty in walking.' He saw the look of alarm in Elizabeth's eyes. 'New shoes, ma'am,' he announced with a twinkle. 'They can be the very devil. Now, if you will show me where I might set her down?'

Elizabeth gave a sigh of relief. Then she led the way into the salon and waited until Rushmore had settled Perdita upon a sofa.

'How came you to rescue Perdita a second time, my lord?' she said at last.

'Pure chance, ma'am. I was at your door when she arrived from Gunter's.'

'Perdita, where are the others?' Perry came over to take his daughter's hand.

'I had to leave them, Papa, but his lordship has sent a message to them saying that they are not to give up the rest of the day as I am quite all right.'

'I am in your debt, my lord.' Perry spoke with some reserve. He was not best pleased by the scene he had just witnessed, much as he admired the Earl of Rushmore. He turned back to Perdita. 'How are your feet, my darling? Do they need attention? Perhaps we should send for Doctor Forbes?'

Perdita blushed. 'Really, Papa! All I have done is skin my toes. It was my own stupid fault. I should have known better than to walk for so long in my new boots.' She gave her father a loving smile. 'They will be better by tomorrow.'

Rushmore gazed down at the enchanting little face, and his heart turned over. When Perdita smiled the room lit up. He would have given much to have won such a smile from her on his own behalf. He turned to Elizabeth.

'I was on my way to speak to your husband and yourself, ma'am. The Duke has not yet released me from my duties, so I cannot get away. It occurred to me that some further discussion of our plans might be useful.'

Perdita pricked up her ears. Plans? What plans? She could think of no possible connection between her parents and this arrogant creature who stood before her, clearly perfectly at ease.

Elizabeth nodded and her lips twitched. 'I agree, my lord. One omission, at least, has been troubling me. Perry, will you show his lordship into the study? Just give me a moment to remove my cloak and bonnet before I join you.'

She waited until the men had left the room before she spoke again.

'Well, Perdita?'

'It is just as his lordship said, Mama. There was nothing amiss. Ellen was with us at all times.'

'Great heavens, Perdita! Do you think me a complete fool? The Earl would scarce attempt to ravish you in your own home and attended by a houseful of servants. I must hope that you were polite to him.'

'I did as he asked...eventually...' Perdita admitted. 'I wanted to rejoin Amy, but he wouldn't hear of it.'

'You'll agree that it would have been difficult, since you cannot walk?'

'Yes, he was right. It seems to be a habit of his.'

Elizabeth glanced at her daughter's face, but she made no further comment, though she was much amused. She had guessed correctly that Perdita found Lord Rushmore's attitude infuriating. He simply would not take her seriously. Well, it would do the child no harm, but peace must be restored if her girls and Rushmore's ward were to deal amicably together.

That thought was foremost in her mind as she entered the study.

'The omission, ma'am?' For once, Rushmore was not quite at ease.

'Why, my lord, you have not given me the name of your ward. I had intended to speak of her to both my girls, but I couldn't do so. Doubtless they will know her. Miss Bedlington's is not a large establishment.'

'I beg your pardon. Her name is Louise Bryant. As I understand it she has not been long at the school. The plan was that she should join her father at Brussels, but naturally, after Waterloo she was deprived of any such opportunity.'

'Poor child! She is Amy's age, is she not?'

'A little older, I believe. She must be seventeen or so by now.'

'And what would you have us do?' Perry was ready to throw himself wholeheartedly into any plan which might ease the suffering of a hero's orphan.

'My hands are tied for the moment. I must wait upon the Duke's pleasure. Hopefully, it won't be long before he will release me. I have written to Louise, of course, telling her of your kindness. I wonder…will the Misses Wentworth make themselves known to her? If she could feel that she had at least two friends to support her in the coming Season…? Her father felt that she was very shy, so it is certain to loom as an ordeal.'

Perry cast aside all his reservations about the Earl of Rushmore. The man was sensitive, after all.

'Pray, my lord, don't trouble yourself further,' he said warmly. 'Put it down to partiality if you will, but I don't know of two better-hearted girls than Amy and Perdita. They will be only too happy to befriend your ward.'

Elizabeth was not so sure. Rushmore had ruffled the feathers of both her daughters, and she had quickly become aware that they were in league against him. Even so, she felt that they would not continue that vendetta against a lonely girl who had been so cruelly deprived of her sole remaining parent.

Her belief was confirmed later that day when she called the girls to her boudoir.

'Do you know a girl called Louise Bryant?' she asked without preamble.

Perdita shook her head, but Amy nodded.

'You left before she arrived,' she told her sister. 'And I don't know her well. She is the quietest creature in the world, always hanging back. Why do you ask, Mama?''

'I want you to befriend her. It is a tragic story. Her father died at Waterloo. She has no other relatives.'

Perdita clenched her fists until the knuckles whitened. She could not imagine life without her beloved father.

'Mother, you need not ask,' she said quietly. 'We'll do all we can to help her.'

'I hope so, my dear, especially when you hear the rest of the story. Louise's father was the Earl of Rushmore's closest friend...Louise is now his ward...'

A silence followed this startling piece of information, but Perdita spoke at last.

'All the more reason to befriend her,' she cried. Then she caught her mother's eye. 'I mean...unless she knows his lordship well, she may find him difficult to understand,' she amended hastily. 'He is not in the least conciliating.'

'As far as I know she has not yet met the Earl,' her mother replied. 'But why, may I ask, should he trouble to be conciliating? The opinion of a schoolgirl cannot possibly be of interest to him.'

Perdita was silenced. She was, she understood only too well, included in that particular group of people to whose opinion Rushmore need pay no attention. It was of little comfort to realise that had she been the most powerful woman in the land her views upon his conduct would have influenced him just as little. The man behaved as if he were a law unto himself. It was an accusation which had been levelled in the past at Perdita herself. Now she was beginning to see just how uncomfortable such behaviour could be to others.

'Perdita, are you paying attention? You seem to me to be woolgathering again.'

'Sorry, Mama! I was just thinking...when is Louise to come to stay with us?'

'At the first opportunity, my dear. It is unfortunate that your father and I must be out of the country for the next few months, but once we return I shall invite Louise. Meantime, I trust that you will both do your best to befriend her. I shudder to think of how she must have suffered in these past few months, without a soul to turn to. Miss Bedlington, I fear, is not the most tender-hearted of women.'

Perdita gave her the ghost of a smile. 'I won't argue with that, Mama.'

Little though she relished the idea of being connected in any way with the Earl of Rushmore, she was conscious of a feeling of relief. He had not, after all, found further reason to object to her behaviour and had sought out her parents on quite another errand.

Honesty compelled her to admit that few people could be more in need of friends than the unfortunate Louise. She was willing to play her part, and a moment's reflection convinced her that the girl was unlikely to be favoured with many visits from her guardian during her stay in Bath. She doubted if he would trouble to seek out the company of the schoolroom misses he had dismissed so casually at Almack's.

He had been quick to hand over the care of his ward to her own mama. Naturally, he could not have refused the last request of a dying man, but she could not think that he would take a serious interest in Louise, other than to see her married as soon as may be, and off his hands.

Possibly he was already casting about him for a suitable candidate. Her mother's next words did nothing to dispel that notion.

'I'm sorry that I shan't be able to meet Louise just yet,' Elizabeth said quietly. 'But you girls must be my proxy. I want her to feel comfortable with the idea of coming to stay with us. Rushmore tells me that she is a considerable heiress, and there are those who make it their business to find out about such matters. You must be her watchdogs. She must not form any unsuitable attachments.'

'At Miss Bedlington's?' Amy was incredulous. 'No gentleman is ever allowed across her doorstep unless he is a relative and even then Miss Bedlington is not at ease. From her expression one would think that all members of the male sex should be confined behind bars.'

Elizabeth smiled. 'I did not imagine that anyone would force an entry into your schoolroom, Amy, but sometimes a stranger will attempt to strike up an acquaintance at a concert, or the play. You will guard against that, I hope.'

'Mama, there are *no* young men in Bath. You should see Aunt Trixie's beaux. They are carried to see her in sedan-chairs and to climb the steps they need two sticks. All they talk about is that filthy, disgusting water, and the wonders it does for all their ailments. Her bosom-bows are just as bad. To hear Mrs Larwood, one must wonder that she is still alive.'

'Even the elderly have nephews, Amy, and grand-sons too. I am sorry to say it, but sometimes they cultivate their failing relatives for the worst of reasons.'

'Oh, Mama, you won't forbid us to go about at all?' Perdita asked anxiously. 'I could not bear it.'

'Of course not, my dear. It is just that I would advise you to be cautious in your choice of friends.'

Amy threw an arm about her mother's neck. 'You don't need to worry about Perdita,' she said solemnly. 'No gentleman has suited her to date, and as for me, I don't intend to marry within the next six months.'

Elizabeth chuckled. 'I'm glad to hear it, but do pray heed my words, No harm must come to Louise.'

'We'll look out for her,' Amy promised. 'I had intended to ask you if I might be a day girl for this last term and stay with Perdita at Aunt Trixie's, but I shall become better acquainted with Louise if I continue to board.' She dropped a kiss upon her mother's cheek. 'I wish you will not worry so,' she said cheerfully. 'As I recall, Louise is so shy that she would flee if a stranger tried to speak to her.'

Elizabeth smiled at both her girls. 'I would not have you think me a fuss-pot, my dears, but I am conscious of the responsibility for Louise.'

Perdita felt rebellious. 'Mama, you have not taken her in charge just yet. Surely it is the Earl of Rushmore who should be concerned.'

'He is, Perdita. That is why he applied to me. He is aware that an unwed military man can have no notion as to how to go on in bringing out a young girl. I wish you will forget your dislike of him, my love. It is Louise who needs our help at present.'

She expressed the same sentiments to her husband when he and she were alone.

'You look troubled, Lizzie.' Perry slid an arm about her waist. 'What is it, my love?'

'Oh, I don't know… I am wondering if we have done the right thing, I suppose, though I don't see how we could have refused to help Rushmore's ward.'

'Out of the question!' Perry replied firmly. 'But do you fear that she will be a trouble to you?'

'No…it isn't that. From all I hear she is a quiet and biddable girl, but both Amy and Perdita have taken the Earl in such dislike…'

'Need that concern you? If I am not mistaken, his lordship will not visit Bath more than is strictly necessary. To me he does not look like a man in need of healing waters.'

Elizabeth smiled at that, but then she gave him a reproachful look. 'I wish you will be serious, Perry. The very sight of him is enough to light Perdita's fuse.'

'I can't say that I blame her overmuch. I was taken aback myself to find her in Rushmore's arms today. Perdita looked as if she could have killed him.'

'Their encounters have been unfortunate, my dear. He is inclined to ride roughshod, you know. Perdita is more accustomed to being placed upon a pedestal by her hopeful swains.'

Perry's face darkened. 'You can't mean that Rushmore thinks of throwing his handkerchief in Perdita's direction? If I thought that, he would not enter this house again.'

'I thought you admired him.'

'I do…but he isn't for Perdita. She's just a child and he is old enough to be her father.'

'Nonsense! He can't have reached the age of thirty, and Perdita is no longer a child, my dear. It can't have escaped your notice that she has grown into an exceptionally beautiful woman.'

'She's still very young,' he growled.

'Now don't get upon your high ropes,' his wife advised. 'We are all aware that there isn't a man alive whom you would consider good enough for her. I can only put it down to a father's partiality.' She twinkled at him. 'What a pity that my own father didn't share your views. He couldn't wait to hand me over to you.'

Perry grinned at her. 'He recognised my sterling worth.'

'And also the fact that you sailed aboard an English warship and were able to spirit me out of a war-torn Italy.'

'Not so!' Perry told her stoutly. 'He'd already offered me your hand before then—'

'And for the same reason. Sadly, you refused that offer. I confess that it has always been the most lowering thought.'

'Minx!' Perry slipped a finger beneath her chin and raised her face to his. 'Tell me that you regret it, and I'll release you from your vows at once.'

'Never! You shan't escape so easily!' Confident in her love, Elizabeth offered him her lips. Then she slid her arms about his neck. 'Do you suppose that all will be well?' she whispered. 'If only I could be certain that Perdita will not come to dagger-drawing with the Earl if they should chance to meet in Bath.'

'Don't trouble your head about it, Lizzie. Dagger-drawing I can tolerate, but I won't have Rushmore throwing out lures to Perdita. I thank heaven that she *does* dislike him. She will find a dozen ways of hinting him away. Should you mention it to Aunt Beatrice?'

'No...I believe not,' Elizabeth said slowly. 'I don't even wish to put the notion into her head that Rushmore is to be considered a prospect for Perdita. Aunt Trixie is so romantical.'

Perry had the grace to blush, but he stuck to his argument. 'Did you not assure me that they are at odds whenever they meet? You can't have it both ways, Lizzie. If they quarrel so, neither can have a *tendre* for the other.'

To her credit, Elizabeth did not challenge this statement, though memories of her own wooing rose at once to mind. She and Perry had crossed swords from the very moment of their meeting. It had not stopped them from falling in love.

'You may be right,' she said without conviction. Under the circumstances she found herself wishing that her proposed voyage to Gibraltar might have been postponed. She didn't suggest it. Her decision to leave without Perdita had been a disappointment to her husband. She would not add to it by staying behind herself.

Even so, she could not repress a niggling presentiment of disaster. Then she shrugged. She was becoming fanciful. It was high time that she concentrated on everyday matters, rather than worrying about problems before they existed. What was it that Perry always said? 'Don't worry, it may never happen.' How she wished she might believe it.

Chapter Five

Elizabeth was given little time to indulge in further speculation. Within the next few days she and Perry were to leave for Portsmouth, where he was due to rejoin his ship.

Before then the girls must be sent off to Bath, with Ellen in attendance. Thankfully, the Earl of Rushmore did not appear, so she was able to draw up her lists and supervise the family packing without interruption.

Amy had cajoled her cousins into taking her on further expeditions about the capital, but Perdita did not go. Her feet were improving though they were not quite healed, and on the day before their departure she was glad of the excuse to join her father in his study for a companionable chat.

Perry settled her comfortably by the fire. Then he walked over to his strongbox and unlocked it, taking out a thick bundle of notes.

'Here, my dear!' He pressed the money into her hands. 'You must take this roll of soft... Doubtless, you will find a use for it.'

'But it is far too much, Papa!' Perdita stared in awe at the roll of notes. She had never handled so much money in her life.

'I think you will not find it so,' Perry assured her. 'You must pay subscriptions in the Pump and the Assembly Rooms. There will be tickets for the concerts too…' He looked at her a little anxiously.

Perdita caught his hand and held it lovingly against her cheek. 'You must not worry that I shan't enjoy myself, Papa. Aunt Trixie is such a dear, and I shall have Amy close at hand. We shall be able to walk and ride and visit with our friends.'

'That's my girl! My darling, I am proud of you. I should have been disappointed had you fallen into a fit of the sullens.'

Perdita managed a wavering smile, which did not deceive him in the least.

'We shall miss you quite dreadfully,' she said in a low voice. 'These next few months will seem like an age.'

Perry's hand ruffled the fashionably short crop of curls. 'We shall miss you too,' he told her lightly. 'But you will be kept busy, especially in trying to keep Amy out of the shops in Milsom Street. Your mother and I rely on you to prevent her from buying bonnets and other fol-de-rols more suitable for a dowager than a schoolgirl.'

Perdita laughed at that. Amy's longing to be considered an adult had led her to experiment with headgear of terrifying dimensions, none of which she had been allowed to buy. Fortunately her own sense of humour had persuaded her in the end that an excess of cherries, apples and other fruits draped about the brims of some of the latest creations left her open to charges of running a market stall.

'Of course, I don't intend you to stint yourselves,' Perry continued. 'Doubtless you will see items in the shops without which a happy life cannot be sustained.' He had intended only to tease a little, but the effect on his daughter was unexpected.

'Papa, you are much too good to us,' she said in a muffled voice. Then she hurried away before her feelings overcame her.

Elizabeth expressed the same sentiments on the following day as the family's private chaise, accompanied by postilions, set out to take the girls to Bath. Their parents waved it out of sight. Then Elizabeth turned to her husband.

'Well, my dear, how much did you give them?' she asked with a twinkle.

'Oh, just a trifle,' he replied vaguely. 'I have sent Beatrice a draft upon my bank. The girls may apply to her if they find themselves at a standstill.'

'That, I suppose, is why Perdita is clutching her largest reticule as if she expects to be set upon by footpads before they have travelled a mile?'

Perry hugged his wife. 'Why can I never manage to deceive you, Lizzie? She has been very good. You'll agree that she deserves to be rewarded?'

Laughing, Elizabeth looked at him in mock despair. 'What am I to do with you?' she asked.

'I can think of a number of things...' Perry leered at her and twirled an imaginary moustache. 'Beware, my proud beauty! You will rue the day that you defy me!'

'You are impossible!' Elizabeth slipped past him. 'Behave yourself, monster! I have far too much to do to listen to your nonsense.'

'Now give me credit for something, Lizzie! Amy, you know, was determined to travel to Bath in the Mail Coach. Did I not dissuade her?'

'Perhaps we should have allowed it. I fancy she wouldn't care to repeat the experience.'

Amy did not share that belief. As she glanced at the passers-by she began to giggle.

'Our state procession is creating a stir,' she answered. 'That man has taken off his hat and bowed. I think I'll give him a gracious wave. It must be the postilions. He thinks that we are of the first importance...most probably princesses at the very least.'

Ellen gave a scandalised gasp. 'You will do no such thing, Miss Amy. Don't you dare smile at him. Such airs, I do declare! And with your family crest upon this carriage too.'

'No one would have noticed us if we had taken the Mail Coach.' Amy was unrepentent. 'Think of the fun we should have had, travelling with a group of strangers!'

Ellen snorted in disgust. 'Fun, indeed! You'd soon have changed your tune, squashed up as you would have been with a crowd of nasty, smelly folk from the Lord knows where.'

Amy grinned at her old nurse. 'Ellen, you are a snob!' she accused.

'I hope I know what is due to your father's consequence,' came the swift reply. 'Behave yourself, Miss Amy, and come away from that window, else you'll sit between your sister and myself. Then you'll see nothing.'

This dread threat caused Amy to offer an olive branch. 'Have you ever travelled by the mail coach, Ellen? You seem to know a lot about it.'

'Indeed I have, and I may tell you that if you had ever done the same you wouldn't care to do so again. I thought my last hour had come!'

'Were you set upon by highwaymen?' Amy's eyes were sparkling.

'We were not! The guard was armed. He would have seen them off. It was much worse than that...'

'Oh, do tell us about it! It must have been a real adventure.'

'Some adventure!' Ellen sniffed. 'The driver had but one good eye, and his horses were in like case. Had he been sober he might have managed them—'

'He was disguised?' Perdita looked startled.

'Blind drunk is what I'd call it myself. He took a fresh noggin or two at every halt. When we reached Lunnon he fell off the box.'

Both girls shouted with laughter.

''Tweren't funny, I can tell you,' Ellen said darkly. 'I thought we must be overturned. The Lord knows how we came out of it with a whole skin.'

'Well, you did!' Amy patted the old woman's hand. 'Now you have got your wish and can travel without fear.'

'That's as maybe! 'Tis a long way to Bath, and we must stop along the road...'

'But Father sent a man ahead to bespeak a private parlour at the inns. I doubt if anyone will try to abduct us, Ellen, although, of course, they may have designs on you.' Perdita could not resist a little gentle teasing.

She was rewarded with a grim smile. 'Get on with you, miss. You know what I think about men.'

'We do indeed! Ellen, I believe you have some dark and sinister secret in your past. Tell us of the dastardly deed.'

'Miss Amy, you are a complete hand! Now, give over with your teasing, the pair of you! Young ladies should not be speaking of abduction and the like.'

Amy was tempted to suggest that perhaps they should sing hymns. Instead, she turned to the safer subject of Ellen's nephews and nieces. As always, Ellen waxed voluble upon the doings of the younger members of her family, and it was not until they reached the first halt that she felt obliged to offer yet another word of caution.

'Now remember!' she warned. 'You are not to speak to strangers, or acknowledge them.'

'Not even if they drop dead at our feet?' Perdita enquired with a smile.

'There wouldn't be much point if they were dead!' Ellen felt that she had scored a point as she motioned her charges to follow the landlord to their private dining-room.

She did not allow them to waste much time. A long journey still lay ahead of them and she was anxious to reach Bath before nightfall.

In the event it was mid-evening before they arrived at Laura Place, to be greeted with huge delight by Miss Beatrice Langrishe. Two of that lady's most faithful beaux and one of her women friends had joined her in a game of cards, but at the sight of Amy and Perdita she came towards them with outstretched arms.

'Welcome!' she cried. 'My dears, you must be exhausted! Let me ring for some refreshment for you, unless you care to go to your rooms at once. Did you have a pleasant journey? And how are your mama and papa? I can't wait to hear your news.'

Both girls disclaimed the notion that they might be tired, or that they were in need of refreshment.

'Nonsense! You'll take a glass of wine at least!'

To Amy's gratification she was included in this invitation. Miss Langrishe, it was clear, had no high opinion on the restorative properties of a glass of milk or a hot posset. Nor did she feel that it was in the nature of human beings to deprive themselves of the best cuisine that money could buy, and that at frequent intervals. Her chef was a legend in Bath. Now he sent in a tray of appetising morsels including hot oyster patties and tiny vol au vent cases, some filled with creamed mushrooms, others with curried eggs and yet more with shredded ham in a Cumberland sauce.

Perdita noted with amusement that at the sight of food her aunt's companions made no attempt to take their leave and Miss Langrishe beamed upon the assembled company as they took full advantage of her hospitality. An evening spent in the company of her friends represented, to her, the height of civilised living. She nodded her encouragement as Amy helped herself to a second devilled chicken leg.

'That's right, my love. With your slender figure you need have no worries about increasing embonpoint. How I wish that I could say the same.'

This brought immediate protests from her two admirers. The goddesses of antiquity, so they claimed, could present no finer appearance than in Miss Langrishe in the full bloom of her maturity.

The lady chided them for blatant flattery, but she was not displeased, though she accused them of pandering to her vanity.

'I'm a silly old woman,' she said without a trace of affectation when her friends had left. 'The Captain cannot know that certain of his remarks were passed on to me. He described me as gliding across the floor of the Assembly Rooms like a galleon under sail... Well, perhaps I am no sylph, but neither, I hope, do I look like a warship.'

'Dear Aunt, I am sure he meant it as a compliment. Is it not obvious that ships and the sea were his life for many years?' Perdita smiled at her aunt. 'How could he honour you more than by comparing you with what he loves best in the world?'

'That, I fancy, is his stomach!' Miss Langrishe signalled to the footman to pour the girls another glass of wine. 'It will do you no harm at all for just this once,' she said in reply to Perdita's warning glance at Amy. 'You will sleep well this night, and tomorrow you shall tell me all your news.' She had noted the drooping eyelids of her guests and dismissed them to their rooms as soon as they had drained their glasses.

'Ellen will think that we are as drunk as her coachman.' Amy giggled as they climbed the staircase. 'Aunt Trixie is a dear, isn't she? She never makes me feel as if I'm still in the nursery.'

'Well, don't let Ellen know that we had a second glass of wine, or we shall never hear the end of it,' Perdita warned.

Miss Langrishe had foreseen the difficulty. At her express request, Ellen had retired to recover from the rigours of the journey, and it was her own personal maid who attended to the girls.

'Back to the prison-camp tomorrow,' Amy groaned as she climbed into bed. 'How shall I bear it for these next few months?'

'It may not be so bad,' Perdita comforted. 'Let us speak to Aunt tomorrow. We can explain about Louise and she may have some ideas as to how we can win her friendship. She may not be too happy with the idea of being ordered to live with a family of strangers.'

'Ordered?' Amy said blankly.

'Oh, yes! I don't suppose that the Earl has used much tact. Most probably he sent her a couple of lines making his wishes clear. As far as I know he hasn't even met her yet.'

'That's hardly his fault,' Amy protested. 'The Duke would not release him—'

'Stuff! He might have asked for leave of absence upon compassionate grounds.'

Amy sighed. 'Oh dear! Let's hope that Louise does not take him in the same dislike as you do.'

'He may be sent away again,' Perdita said hopefully. 'There must be trouble somewhere in the world where his obnoxious character would be useful.'

Privately, Amy thought it unlikely, but Perdita was asleep before she could pursue the subject.

Miss Langrishe was not an early riser. She was in the habit of receiving favoured guests in the comfort of her bedchamber as she sipped her morning chocolate.

There, resplendent in an embroidered silk robe and a matching cap of fetching design, she smiled at the girls as they came to wish her a good morning.

'Now, my dears, how do you go on? You slept well, I trust? I confess that I can't wait to hear your news of London and the family.'

She was an excellent listener, with the rare gift of giving each speaker her full attention without feeling the need to interrupt with comments of her own.

Perdita realised that this was part of the secret of her great-aunt's charm. She brought out the best in her companions, making them feel that their own opinions were of value and worthy of serious consideration. In her presence even the most stupid of creatures felt themselves cleverer and wittier than in fact they were.

She and Amy related all the family gossip, and as much as they knew of the topics uppermost in the minds of polite society during the Season. Miss Langrishe knew of all the latest scandals, thanks to her very efficient grapevine, but she didn't betray that fact. She exclaimed over the meeting with the Duke of Wellington, and teased Amy over her evident devotion to her hero, wondering as she did so if her nieces would trust her enough to discuss a matter that was clearly troubling them.

When they hesitated, she decided to offer a little encouragement. Her approach was gentle.

'Perdita, I won't insult you by pretending that I don't know why you are here,' she said. 'Your mother explained matters when she wrote to me. She mentioned the Earl of Rushmore... Now, my love, may I beg you never to look back? We cannot change the past, but we can look to the future. You must put that episode behind you.'

Perdita was silent. It was Amy who spoke.

'We should like nothing better, Aunt. If only we might be sure that we should never see him again. He's a hateful creature.'

Miss Langrishe looked at the mutinous faces. 'I know the name,' she observed. 'I think I met his father long ago. An arrogant rakehell, if I ever saw one...killed on the hunting field, I believe, but with more charm than any man I ever met.'

'His son has not inherited that quality,' Perdita said stiffly.

'But why let it worry you, my dear? I doubt if you will see him again. From all I hear, it is highly unlikely that he will come to Bath for the waters.'

'He will come for another reason, Aunt. His ward is at school with me. She is to come to live with us next year to share my Season.' Amy was unenthusiastic.

'But why? Has she no relatives?'

Both girls began to explain the situation.

'Of course, we are sorry for her, Aunt. We can't begin to imagine the pain of losing her father, but if only someone else had been her guardian!'

'Don't dwell upon it, my dears. Louise must be our first concern. Amy, do you know her well?'

'No! That is another worry. She is so very quiet...not exactly unfriendly, but not the life and soul of any gathering.'

'Would there be room for two of you, Amy?' Her aunt's lips twitched. 'We must all get to know her better, I think. Now, what do you say to bringing her to see me? I shall procure tickets for the next concert at the Assembly Rooms. I believe we shall all enjoy it.'

'Miss Bedlington may not approve, Aunt Trixie.'

'You may safely leave Miss Bedlington to me. Perdita and I will accompany you when you return to school this afternoon. I shall speak to the lady then.'

'But, Aunt, I can't! She said that I was never to darken her doors again.' Perdita had the grace to blush.

Miss Langrishe gave her a grim smile. 'How dramatic! That sounds like a remark from a bad play. There will be no difficulty, I assure you.'

She spoke no more than the truth. When she walked into the Academy later that afternoon Perdita was reminded forcibly of the description of her aunt as a galleon under full sail.

Miss Langrishe had chosen her toilette with care. Her flowing garments owed nothing to the present fashions, but they became her imposing figure well. The most casual observer would have been aware of the cost of the fabulous silk brocade of her voluminous cloak and of the jewels nestling in her towering turban.

She winked at the girls. 'Nothing like full fig for intimidating the opposition,' she announced. 'I believe we shall have no problems with Miss Bedlington.'

She was right. Beside the tall figure of their aunt, Miss Bedlington looked insignificant, and the girls were surprised to see that she looked a little nervous. Amy she welcomed with as much warmth as it was in her nature to show and even Perdita was greeted with a stiff bow. However, it was the formidable Miss Langrishe for whom the owner of the Academy reserved her most fulsome welcome.

Miss Bedlington was no fool, and in the imposing figure of the woman before her she could see unlimited opportunities. Her Academy was her livelihood, and Miss Langrishe had the entrée to the highest circles in Bath. Her elderly friends might not have daughters of their own, but they had granddaughters and nieces, and a word of recommendation would go far.

She exerted herself to be accommodating, agreeing that young ladies on the verge of their come-out must be exposed by degrees to the pleasures of the adult world.

Miss Langrishe settled herself in the largest chair in the room. To Perdita it seemed as if she were seated upon a throne, graciously accepting a glass of ratafia.

'I have never believed it wise to take young girls from the schoolroom and throw them into Society untrained,' Miss Langrishe announced. 'They must appear gauche. It can do their prospects no service.'

'Quite, ma'am, quite…although they do receive some training here.'

'I'm sure you do your best, Miss Bedlington.' Miss Langrishe was at her grandest. 'I cannot fault your academic standards, but among the *ton*, you know…?'

Miss Bedlington understood her visitor perfectly. Miss Langrishe intended to have her way. If it wasn't blackmail, it came close.

'What do you suggest, ma'am?' she asked politely.

'Why, with your permission, of course, I think that the girls must be allowed to come to me as much as possible. Louise Bryant, I understand, is to share her Season with my niece. I plan a programme of concerts for them…nothing too extreme, of course.'

'A splendid idea!' Miss Bedlington's voice lacked conviction, but Beatrice Langrishe did not appear to notice.

'Then, of course, there will be small dinner-parties... I plan one for tomorrow evening. Shall we say that the carriage will collect the girls at six?'

Miss Bedlington felt unable to disagree, and Perdita looked at her aunt with awe as she left the Academy for Laura Place.

'How do you do it, Aunt?' she asked. 'Miss Bedlington agreed to everything.'

Her aunt looked a little conscious. 'Perhaps I should not tell you this, but I look for the Achilles' heel, my dear. Miss Bedlington is aware that my recommendation can help her. She won't set up her will against me.'

Perdita smiled. 'What a dangerous creature you are, Aunt Trixie! I am not tempted to enter the lists against you.'

'Why should you, my love? After all, I am on your side.'

Perdita felt comforted. It was such a boon to be surrounded by uncritical affection. Her parents loved her dearly, but the relationship with her aunt was different. With Beatrice Langrishe she could speak of things which she could never mention to them. She wondered why that was. Possibly because they were not so closely bound by ties of blood? Possibly not. She was unable to decide, but in the meantime she could bask in the loving affection of the older woman.

*   *   *

She had had to confess that she was curious about Louise, and when the two girls arrived on the following evening, she realised that Amy's assessment of the girl's character had been correct.

Tall and fair, Louise was no beauty, but there was intelligence in the fine grey eyes and a pleasing regularity in her features. Her manners were beyond reproach, but there was an air of reserve…a barrier…which discouraged intimacy.

Miss Langrishe appeared to be unaware of it. Before the arrival of her guests she appealed to the girls for help.

'My guests are new arrivals here,' she told them innocently. 'I wonder… They are bound to feel a little ill-at-ease. Could you possibly help them out…ask them about themselves…their families…their interests? It is so daunting to be forced to dine with strangers, and Miss Murray, in particular, is very shy.'

It was enough to enlist their help and even Louise felt enabled to play her part. In thinking of others, she had forgotten her own shyness. Miss Langrishe had nothing but praise for her co-hostesses.

'Well done!' she smiled. 'We shall have you leading your own salons before next year is out… It isn't difficult, is it, if one remembers that a favourite topic of conversation with most people is themselves?'

Three beaming faces agreed with her. The girls had done well, encouraged by the compliments and the old-fashioned courtesies which they had received from the other guests. Elderly shoulders had been straightened and moustaches twirled at the sight of these fresh young creatures.

Miss Langrishe too came in for her share of praise.

'Well, m'dear, I can't say when I've enjoyed an evening more,' Captain Merton told his hostess. Then he turned to his friends, but recently arrived in Bath. 'Did I not say that you would find the town far from dull?' he said. 'All this nonsense about it being a dead-and-alive hole! How can that be so when we are invited to enjoy the company of such charming ladies?'

They were quick to agree with him, and departed expressing the hope that they might be allowed to return such delightful hospitality, and enquiring if Miss Langrishe meant to bring her party to the next concert in the Assembly Rooms.

'Indeed! We should not miss it for the world,' she smiled.

It was enough to send Amy and Louise back to the Academy quite reconciled to another week of study before their next outing.

Miss Langrishe rang for her tea-tray before she and Perdita retired for the night.

'No need to ask if you enjoyed your evening, my dear,' she said warmly. 'I was proud of you. You made my guests feel welcome.'

'They were interesting people, Aunt. It was a pleasure to speak to them.'

'Most people are, if one takes the trouble to draw them out. Shall you be able to make a friend of Louise, do you suppose?'

'I hope so, though it may be difficult to get to know her…she is so quiet and shy.'

'She is more reserved than shy, I fancy, though she did well enough tonight.'

'She must be feeling the loss of her father, Aunt. I'd like to have spoken of him to her, but it is difficult to know what to say that could possibly be of any comfort. Don't you find it so?'

Miss Langrishe considered for several moments. 'We human beings have a curious attitude to death,' she said at last. 'I have never understood why it should be found embarrassing. I suppose it is thought an unwelcome reminder of one's own mortality, but the subject should not be avoided with the bereaved. Above anything, they need to be encouraged to remember their loved ones and to speak of them.'

'But surely that is distressing?'

'It helps, my dear, and as to words of comfort, well, I have my own philosophy.'

'Which is?'

'A simple one, Perdita. I believe that our loved ones never die as long as we remember them. They live on in our hearts.'

'That is beautiful!' Perdita raised her aunt's hand and held it against her cheek. 'I shall remember it all my life.'

Beatrice Langrishe patted the dark curls. 'Have you any plans for this week?' she asked.

'I am at your disposal, Aunt. Shall you wish me to attend you to the Pump Room?'

Miss Langrishe gave a hearty laugh. 'Never think that I take the waters, my love! Nasty-tasting stuff! In my opinion a good burgundy is much better for one's health.'

Perdita was tempted to giggle. 'So you don't visit the Pump Room? I thought that everyone did so.'

'They do, my dear. I would not miss the morning gathering for the world. How else would one learn the latest gossip?' Miss Langrishe gave Perdita a sly look. 'The waters have their uses. They encourage the potted plants to flourish.'

Perdita could not keep her countenance. The thought of her aunt disposing of the medicinal offerings into the nearest plant pot was too much for her, and her shoulders shook with laughter. Her stay with aunt Trixie promised to be much more entertaining than she had at first imagined.

That lady's dry sense of humour was a source of great joy to her, and she had the ready ability to convulse Perdita at unexpected moments. It was difficult to keep a straight face on the following morning when Miss Langrishe surveyed the decrepit occupants of the Pump Room. 'As you see, Perdita, we are gay to dissipation!' she announced, as she turned to greet an aged gentleman who came to them with all the speed he could muster.

Miss Langrishe engaged him in conversation, using him as a shield as she tossed the contents of her glass over the roots of the nearest plant. In spite of her ironic remarks, she enquired most kindly about his health and appeared to be enthralled as he related the most intimate details of his digestive processes. It was enough to put Perdita off her nuncheon until she managed to thrust the conversation from her mind.

'Aunt, will you tell me something?' she asked as she helped herself to a plate of cold meats and sallets.

'Certainly, my dear, if I can. What is it you wish to know?'

'Don't think me forward, but, well…I wondered why you choose to live here…in Bath, I mean?'

'You think it unsuitable for me?'

'Not exactly, I suppose, but there are so many old people.'

Miss Langrishe smiled at her. 'What a delightful compliment, my love. You forget that I am not in the first bloom of youth myself.'

'But you don't behave like an older person, and you don't think in an elderly way… Would you not prefer to live in London?'

'Not in the least, Perdita. I have always loved this city and the surrounding countryside. For me there is as much to interest here as in the capital. It is possible to study a smaller canvas with as much enjoyment as a larger one.'

'You mean the people?'

'I do. It is the most absorbing subject in the world. One learns as much about oneself as one does of others.'

'I wish I could feel the same,' Perdita said slowly.

'Look outwards, my love! That way it is possible to forget oneself and one's own troubles.'

'I haven't any troubles, Aunt,' Perdita said impulsively. 'I am so happy here with you.'

'That's my girl!' Miss Langrishe patted her head. 'Now, what do you say to some shopping in Milsom Street? I must not disgrace you at the concert.'

Perdita thought this highly unlikely, and that opinion was confirmed as the days passed and her aunt added to her already vast collection of jewels, scarves and headgear. She also bought gifts for the girls, dismissing their protests with a smile.

'Now you won't rob me of the pleasure of giving you these trifles?' she asked. 'I have no children of my own, so this is an unexpected joy for me.'

It was as they were preparing for the concert in the Assembly Rooms that Amy took Perdita aside.

'Can we talk?' she asked.

'Now? We haven't much time, you know.'

'This is important!' Amy looked troubled.

'Then tell me...'

'It's Louise. I don't want to betray a confidence, but...well...she has an admirer.'

'What!'

'Oh, don't fly into the boughs, Perdita. She hopes to marry him.'

'She must be mad!' Perdita said with conviction. 'How on earth did she meet him? She's still at school.'

'It was after she heard the news about her father. She was sitting in the park and, well...she was distressed. He asked if he could be of service to her.'

'Oh, Amy, does she know anything about him? It can't be right that he would offer for her in this way. Rushmore will go mad!'

'He isn't here!' Amy said stubbornly. 'I, for one, don't blame her. Who else has offered her sympathy and comfort?'

'I'm sure he meant it kindly, but this can't be right. Does Miss Bedlington know?'

'Of course she doesn't.'

'Then how did Louise...? I mean, how did she come to be allowed out on her own?'

'She just walked off. She's so quiet that Miss Bedlington didn't miss her.'

'But this man? Who is he, and where does he come from?'

'He lives in Bath. He has connections here.'

'Well, I think he might have waited before proposing to Louise. She could have been in no condition to consider.'

'Oh, don't be so prosy! He didn't offer on that day, you goose. She has known him for some weeks.'

'That will please Rushmore.' Perdita's ironic tone was not lost upon Amy.

'Why should he not be pleased? He wants her to marry, doesn't he? After all, she'll be off his hands.'

'I think you'll find that he doesn't take his responsibilities so lightly.' Perdita left it there, but her sister's news had cast a cloud upon her spirits. Rushmore's appearance in Bath could not now be long delayed. She shuddered to think of his reaction.

His arrival was unexpected, but she sensed his presence halfway through a concert. She glanced round and her heart sank. That thunderous expression boded ill for both Louise and her admirer. Perdita was in no doubt that the connection was already known to him.

Chapter Six

Under the cover of a particularly spirited passage in the music Perdita nudged her sister.

'Rushmore is here,' she whispered. 'He is standing by the door. Don't turn your head! I believe he has seen us already.'

Amy waited for a moment or two. Then she stole a glance in his lordship's direction.

'Oh, Lord, just look at his expression! He must have murder on his mind... shall I tell Louise?'

'Wait until the interval,' Perdita hissed. 'I doubt if he will approach us in the middle of the recital, but I think we should warn Aunt Trixie.'

Very little escaped that lady's notice. 'Yes, I have seen the Earl,' she announced. 'It is impossible to mistake him. He is the image of his father, and sadly he wears the same unfortunate look. Don't allow it to worry you, my dears. His ill humour can have nothing to do with you.'

Minutes later the music stopped and the players retired for refreshments. To Perdita's relief, Miss

Langrishe and her party were surrounded at once by a group of her friends. With any luck they would stay throughout the interval, making it impossible for Rushmore to approach them.

She was mistaken. The crowd parted as if by magic to allow his lordship through. His bow to Miss Langrishe was stiff in the extreme.

'My name is Rushmore, ma'am. I am sorry to break in upon your party in this way, but—'

'No need for formality, Adam. My dear boy, I knew you when you were in leading strings. What a pleasure to see you again! Come, sit by me and tell me all your news. I was sorry to hear about your father.'

His lordship was nonplussed. Whatever reception he had expected, it was most certainly not to be greeted by this affable smiling elderly lady as if he were barely out of the nursery.

'Thank you, ma'am!' He bowed again to acknowledge the expression of sympathy. 'You are very kind. However, if you will forgive me, I have come to find my ward. Miss Bedlington assured me that I should find her here.'

He bent his gaze upon Louise with such a stern expression that she quailed and shrank closer to Perdita.

'You have not met, I think,' Miss Langrishe said in an equable tone. 'Louise, my dear, you must make your curtsy to your guardian.'

Louise rose to her feet, curtsied, and resumed her seat.

'I think we must go before the music starts again,' Rushmore said sharply. 'I have much to say to you—'

'But not at this particular moment, I must hope.' Miss Langrishe was in full command of the situation. 'My dear boy, I can't allow you to steal my guest away in this hurly-burly manner. Louise does not know you. I cannot allow her to leave here with a man who is a stranger to her.'

'Must I remind you that she is my ward, madam?'

'You have already done so.' Miss Langrishe beckoned Colonel Waters to her side. 'Here is Rushmore's boy,' she said. 'Is he not the living image of his father?'

The Colonel agreed. Privately he considered that the likeness was astonishing, even down to the ugly look upon his lordship's face.

Miss Langrishe appeared to be unaware of it. She knew quite well that Rushmore was at a standstill. He could hardly drag Louise from the Assembly Rooms by main force.

'Do sit down, my dear,' she begged. 'You know both Amy and Perdita, I believe. They must be happy to see you here in Bath.'

Perdita's gasp of disbelief at this astonishing statement apparently went unnoticed by her aunt, but it brought a grim smile to his lordship's lips. He did not argue further as he took a seat beside her.

She could not resist the opportunity to taunt him further.

'Are you fond of music, sir?' she asked. 'I hear that it is said to soothe the savage breast.'

'At this moment I feel savage,' he told her coldly. 'I might have known that I should find you somewhere in this plot.'

'Which plot is that, my lord?' Perdita gave him her sweetest smile. 'Does someone plan to assassinate you?'

'Don't raise your hopes, Miss Wentworth. You won't be rid of me so easily. I am speaking of this unfortunate attachment. You must have known that Louise is embroiled in an unsuitable affair.'

'You are well informed, sir, especially as you have not met Louise before this evening.

'I am well informed because she wrote to me herself. Good lord, she even thought that I'd be pleased to give my permission as it would take her off my hands!'

'Pray moderate your language, sir! You shock me!' Perdita raised her fan, revealing nothing of her face except a pair of sparkling eyes. She was enjoying herself hugely.

'I'll do more than shock you! I'd like to put you across my knee!'

'Great heavens, my lord…such violence! It can only recommend you to the female sex. We are said to prefer the company of undesirables, you know.'

'It's God help the man who takes you on,' he snarled.

'The feeling is mutual, sir.'

Rushmore was about to reply when the musicians returned. A request for silence was met with a hush from the audience and he was forced to listen with all the patience at his command until the concert ended.

He was on his feet at once, and he addressed Miss Langrishe direct.

'Ma'am, I believe you can have no knowledge of what has been taking place in secret, as far as my ward is concerned. I must insist—'

'You may insist to your heart's content, my dear Adam, but this is hardly the place. Louise and my nieces stay with me this evening. I would suggest that you return to Laura Place with us. Then you may explain yourself.'

Perdita hid a smile. Miss Langrishe had wrong-footed this angry young man. Now he was to be asked to account for his own behaviour, rather than criticising that of others. It did not improve his temper.

Her aunt swept into her salon and ordered tea. 'Wine for you, my lord?' she asked.

'No, I thank you, ma'am. Now, if I might explain the reason why I am here in Bath?'

'Yes, I think you should do that.' Miss Langrishe sat back in her chair, prepared to give him her full attention. She had known from the first that something was sadly wrong. Even Rushmore's son would not have appeared with a face like thunder, prepared to remove his ward without a by-your-leave. None of this showed in her expression.

'May I not speak to Louise in private?' Rushmore said stiffly.

'Oh, we are all friends here, my dear. We have no secrets from each other.'

'Ma'am, I think you will find that that may not be the truth of it. This morning I received a letter from Louise, in which she expressed her intention to be married.'

Miss Langrishe was unable to hide her astonishment. She turned to the shrinking girl. 'Is this true?' she asked.

'Ma'am, there was nothing underhand,' Louise whispered. 'I wrote to my guardian at once, asking his permission for me to wed. I thought he would be pleased.'

'Did you, indeed?' Rushmore was barely in control of his temper. 'How old are you, miss? Not yet seventeen, I fancy. What age is that to make a decision for life?' He stood over the girl until she cowered away from him.

'You are being unfair,' Perdita told him. 'Have you met the man to whom Louise is betrothed?'

'Louise is not betrothed,' he said darkly. 'Nor will she become so, for the next year or more.'

'You haven't answered my question.'

'With all respect to your aunt, Miss Wentworth, this matter need not concern you—'

'But it *does* concern us,' Perdita flashed back. 'Louise is a dear friend of ours.'

'You surprise me! Since the welfare of our friends must be of importance to us I had imagined that you would advise her of the folly of her action, rather than supporting her against me—'

'They have not done so,' Louise told him in a faint voice. She was on the verge of tears. 'Miss Langrishe and Perdita know nothing of this, and I told Amy only yesterday.' A sob escaped her lips.

'Perdita, I suggest that you and Amy take Louise to her room. The Earl and I will discuss this matter further...' Miss Langrishe waited until the door had closed behind the girls. Then she turned to Rushmore.

'Well, Adam, have you taken leave of your senses? This is no way to go on. You have frightened Louise half out of her wits. Take care or you may push her into an elopement.'

'I think not, ma'am.' His lordship's voice was cold. 'She will leave Bath with me tomorrow. From now on I don't intend to let her out of my sight.'

'That may be difficult for you. Where will you take her? To your London house to be locked in her room? It seems a somewhat Gothic course of action and it won't enhance her reputation, or your own, unless of course, you intend to wed her yourself.'

'What!' The Earl's roar of anger could be heard throughout the house. 'Allow me to inform you, ma'am, that nothing could be further from my mind.'

'I'm glad to hear it. In any case, I doubt if she would take you. Now, do sit down, my dear, instead of behaving like a nincompoop. It may surprise you to hear that I am entirely of your opinion in this matter, but it is always a mistake to indulge in dagger-drawing with the young. Nothing is more likely to harden their opposition to your wishes, especially when a supposed grand passion is involved.'

Rushmore was strongly tempted to swear aloud, but he restrained himself from doing so. 'Grand passion, indeed! Louise is a schoolgirl, ma'am. I am at a loss to understand how she came to be allowed the freedom to become acquainted with this fellow. Miss Bedlington has much to answer for.'

'Have you thought of this from Louise's point of view?'

'I have not, Miss Langrishe.' Rushmore threw himself into a chair. 'An understanding of young girls is quite beyond me.'

Miss Langrishe reflected privately that this statement most probably included his lordship's understanding of women in general, but she did not say so.

'Louise must have been very lonely,' she said gently. 'Not even her schoolfriends were at hand to comfort her, and Miss Bedlington, though an excellent teacher, is not the warmest of creatures... I lay no blame on you, my dear boy. I know that your time is not your own, but can you wonder that Louise would be affected by an offer of affection?'

'I suppose not,' Rushmore admitted grudgingly. 'But what am I to do? Your nieces already regard me as an ogre, as I'm sure they have informed you. I can expect no help from them.'

Miss Langrishe regarded him thoughtfully. 'I think you may be mistaken in that belief. The girls are not as gullible as you might suppose. Naturally they will defend their friend, but it won't have escaped their notice that this young man, whoever he may be, has done Louise no service in attempting to attach her affections in such an underhand way.'

Rushmore said nothing, though clearly he was unconvinced.

'They will know, of course, that he should have sought a proper introduction to her, through her connections, and asked her guardian for permission to address her.'

'Well, at least we are agreed in that respect,' the Earl said heavily. 'Louise is an heiress, ma'am, and a tempting target for any gazetted fortune-hunter, especially as she is so young. I blame myself, you know. I promised her father that I would take good care of her.'

'And you will do so, Adam. You shall not think that you have let her down. Now, we must consider what is to be done. A fresh start is needed, I believe.

Why not call upon us tomorrow when we may have a sensible discussion with Louise?'

'I still think it would be best to take her back to London—'

'Nonsense! Will you make a martyr of her? We must consider a more subtle approach. Let us speak to her about the young man. Then, at least, you will be in a position to make enquiries about him. And do try not to scowl at her, my dear. More flies were caught with honey than with a blunderbuss.'

She was rewarded with a reluctant smile.

'That's better!' she approved. 'Use your charm, my dear. Louise is an intelligent girl. If you reason with her sensibly, she will understand your concerns.'

His lordship looked at her and his gloomy expression lifted. On an impulse he kissed her hand. 'What a diplomat you are!' he said admiringly. 'You should be in government, ma'am.'

Miss Langrishe laughed at that. 'Not all of my views would be welcomed in political circles,' she said cheerfully. 'Where are you staying, Adam?'

'I am at the York House, ma'am.'

'For several days, I hope?' Her look was full of meaning.

He threw up his hands in surrender. 'It shall be as you wish. I promise not to drag my unwilling charge back to London tomorrow.'

'How sensible! Believe me, all will be well, if you allow a little time to straighten out this muddle.'

He left her then, but he had barely gained the street before Perdita returned to her aunt's side. She was clearly ill at ease.

'Was I wrong to speak out as I did?' she asked anxiously. 'The Earl seemed about to threaten to beat Louise...'

'His lordship had had a shock, my dear, as had we all.'

'I know, but he might have spoken more gently instead of flying into the boughs as usual.'

'It was understandable, my love. Even your father, tolerant though he is, would have found such behaviour unacceptable. Don't you agree?'

Perdita nodded. 'I know that it was wrong,' she admitted. 'But, Aunt, she felt so sad and lonely...'

Miss Langrishe patted her hand. 'Has she told you anything about this man? I have been wondering why he did not approach her guardian first.'

'He is a visitor to Bath, Aunt Trixie. He knew no one who might have provided him with an introduction to Louise. He spoke to her on impulse, I believe, when he found her weeping in the park. That was kind, you will agree.'

'It was, my dear, and might have been forgiven if matters had gone no further, but you will not tell me that he proposed on that occasion. There must have been clandestine meetings. Why did Louise agree to that?'

'She knew that Miss Bedlington would forbid her to see him.'

'In this instance, Miss Bedlington would have been right. Louise was in her care. How could she countenance a friendship with a stranger of whom she knew nothing?'

Perdita was silent for several moments. 'What does the Earl intend to do?' she asked at last. 'I suppose he will punish Louise by sending her to Yorkshire, or some such place.'

'Not at all,' her aunt said mildly. 'Naturally, his lordship wishes to have a sensible discussion with Louise. That would be wise, I think, don't you?'

Perdita grimaced. 'Do you think him capable of a sensible discussion, Aunt? For my part, I do not. He is too accustomed to issuing orders and having them obeyed. Doubtless he will storm and rave, or try to crush Louise with his unpleasant sarcasm.'

'Shall we wait and see what happens before we condemn him out of hand? And, my dear, do try to persuade Louise not to be a watering-pot. Few gentlemen can cope with tears, and when they are at a loss they become irritable. If Louise will exercise a little self-control…?'

'I don't expect it would make much difference if she were as calm as the Sphinx,' Perdita told her bitterly. 'The Earl regards Louise as a tiresome schoolgirl, which she is not. She is my own age, after all, and will make her come-out next year. Girls of seventeen are often wed at the end of their first Season.'

'And a great mistake it is, for the most part. Is it not wiser to gain a little experience of the world before making such a serious decision? You must have thought it so. I know you have had offers, my dear.'

Perdita smiled. 'I can lay claim to no great wisdom, Aunt. It's just that I was never tempted to accept, and Mother and Father would not force me.'

Miss Langrishe was satisfied. As she had long suspected, Perdita, although impulsive by nature, had great strength of character. If Rushmore could win her to his side, she would bring her influence to bear upon Louise.

With this in mind, she was at pains to leave Rushmore and Perdita alone together on the following day.

'Am I too early for Miss Langrishe?' his lordship asked as he was shown into the salon 'Perhaps I mistook the time.'

'My aunt will not be long, sir. She felt it best to visit Miss Bedlington with Amy and Louise to ask that the girls be allowed to extend their stay here.'

'An excellent idea,' he said stiffly. 'Your aunt, at least, will keep an eye upon my ward.'

Perdita was silent, ignoring him as he took a turn about the room. Finally he swung round to face her.

'You are very quiet, Miss Wentworth. Have you nothing to say to me? No comments upon my brutal manner, or my monstrous behaviour yesterday?'

'You frightened Louise,' she said defiantly. 'That is no way to persuade her to confide in you.'

To her astonishment he smiled at her, and that smile transformed his face.

'I lost my temper,' he admitted. 'But for the most part I was angry with myself. I felt that I had failed in my promise to Louise's father. I had not provided the care which she was entitled to expect.'

Perdita's eyes widened. Rushmore's explanation came very close to an apology, and she had not expected it.

'You could not have known what was happening,' she said carefully. 'But I hope that you can understand it.'

Rushmore sat down beside her. 'I can, but I am sorry that she felt the need to seek affection elsewhere. Believe me, I have her best interests at heart. I want to see her happy.'

'Then will you not tell her so, my lord? She is a gentle soul, and will not set her will against yours if it can be avoided.'

'That will be difficult,' he mused. 'She fancies herself in the throes of a great passion, I suppose. I have no experience of such matters. I can't think what is to be done.'

This was another surprise. It sounded like an appeal for help.

'Are you asking for my advice, my lord?' she asked in astonishment.

'I am, my dear.' His eyes were twinkling. 'Even ogres are not infallible. You think highly of your friend, but I do not know her in the least. Won't you help me to win her round to my way of thinking?'

Perdita hesitated. 'What have you in mind? You don't intend to spirit her away and lock her up, I hope?'

'On a diet of bread and water? No, that would be too Gothic, and it would serve no purpose. I'd like her to regard me as her friend. How best shall I persuade her?'

Perdita was in no doubt of his sincerity, but if she agreed to help him it would be a strange alliance. She would be in league with her enemy. Rushmore sensed her indecision.

'We have not been the best of friends, Miss Wentworth, but this is more important than personal antipathy. Louise's whole life may be at stake. Do you agree that we should put her future first?'

Perdita found it impossible to refuse. 'I agree!' She held out her hand and Rushmore took it in his own. Then he raised it to his lips.

'Thank you!' he said simply. 'I knew I could rely on you.'

Perdita blushed and drew her hand away as if she had been stung. There was something disturbing about the touch of that warm mouth against her own flesh. To cover her confusion she spoke sharply.

'There are certain conditions, sir.'

'And they are?'

'You will *not* browbeat Louise, my lord, nor shall you seek to harm her friend, whoever he may be.'

'I had not planned to have him knocked on the head, my dear. As yet I do not even know his name.'

'You agree to my conditions?'

'I do. Now, what is our next move?'

'Sir, I believe that you should speak to Louise, telling her of your wish to be her friend. She is an intelligent person, and will understand your concerns. She will know that you are quite within your rights to make enquiries about her admirer and to seek an interview with him. She cannot object to that.'

'I'd like to wring his neck!' Rushmore said with feeling. 'I wonder how he learned that she was heiress to a fortune?'

'You can't be sure of that,' Perdita scolded. 'Now you are jumping to conclusions.'

'Am I?' Rushmore was unconvinced. 'This has been a havey-cavey game—a chance meeting with a vulnerable girl, a whirlwind romance, with no attempt to contact those who have her interests at heart? No, Perdita, there is something smokey here.'

Perdita did not take her companion to task for using her given name. The force of his argument had confirmed her own suspicions. Now it was important to unmask this fellow, if he was indeed a fortune-hunter.

'It seems a little difficult to believe,' she whispered. 'Are there really men who prey on defenceless women?'

Rushmore took her hand again, holding it firmly in his own. 'For some it is a way of life,' he said. 'But I am determined that Louise shall not fall victim to such a creature.'

Perdita did not draw her hand away this time. It was oddly comforting to be in such complete accord with the complex creature who sat beside her. Had she misjudged him from the first? It would not be the first time she had been mistaken in her assessment of character.

Her mother's words came back to her. Elizabeth advised always to judge by actions rather than words. Well, she would see if the Earl of Rushmore's actions matched his words.

She had not long to wait. A bustle in the hall announced the return of her aunt together with Amy and Louise. At the sight of her formidable guardian Louise shrank back, but he advanced towards her, holding out his hand.

'I hope I see you well,' he said kindly. Then he turned to Beatrice Langrishe. 'I'd like a private word with Louise,' he said. 'May I have your permission, ma'am?'

It was given at once, but it was a cowed Louise who was led into the study.

'Oh, Lord!' Amy pulled a face. 'Will he use his riding crop, do you suppose?'

'He will not,' Perdita said firmly. 'The Earl has promised to listen to Louise. He will not lose his temper. He has given me his word.'

Amy's mouth fell open. 'Given *you* his word? I thought you were at dagger-drawing with him.'

'We were thinking of Louise,' Perdita said with dignity. 'All other considerations must be set aside…for the moment.'

The private interview was short, and when Louise was returned to her friends she had lost the somewhat haunted look which had bedevilled her.

His lordship made no reference to the matter uppermost in his mind. Instead, he promised himself the pleasure of seeing the ladies at a ball in the Assembly Rooms on the following evening.

'Oh, are we to be invited too?' Amy was in transports of delight.

'Why not, my love?' Miss Langrishe smiled benignly upon her companions. 'It is high time that you and Louise were put in the way of things.' She turned to Rushmore. 'Such a mistake to throw these girls straight from the schoolroom into society. Don't you agree, my lord? And this, after all, is Bath…not quite so formal as the London Season.'

'Ma'am, I cannot disagree if I have the choice of three such charming partners.' Rushmore's bow was faultless.

Perdita caught his eye, and was strongly tempted to laugh.

'His lordship is an enthusiastic dancer,' she observed slyly. 'I doubt if he will ever lack for partners. He has a most persuasive way of leading a lady out.'

He gave her an appreciative grin. 'No hard feelings?' he asked in a low voice.

Perdita affected not to hear him. It was too soon to forgive him for her present situation. But for Rushmore, she would now be aboard her father's ship, sailing for Gibraltar and all the delights of a visit to the Mediterranean.

Yet honesty compelled her to admit that he was not the unfeeling creature she had thought him. His concern for Louise was genuine enough. This enforced visit to Bath might be a blessing in disguise. She was now in a position to help Louise out of what might prove to be a dangerous situation. With Rushmore as her ally all might yet be well.

She waited until Amy and Louise were deep in discussion with Miss Langrishe about the coming ball. Then she drew Rushmore aside on the pretext of consulting him about the purchase of a riding mare.

'Have you come to some agreement?' she asked quietly.

'Yes. Louise had given me the young man's name and his direction. I have promised to speak to him.'

'So you did not forbid the marriage outright?'

'No, Miss Wentworth, but let me assure you that it will not take place.'

Perdita did not argue. 'But you will make enquiries about him? That is only fair, I think.'

'Consider it done. Louise has admitted the necessity. I was at some pains to point out to her the difficulties she might face if she has been deceived in him. Her faith in this fellow is absolute, so she has no fear that I shall find anything untoward.'

'You don't share the belief, I know.'

'I don't, but I shall go on slowly. Love is blind, so they say. Proof of his perfidy must be overwhelming before she is convinced.'

'And you will let me know what you discover?'

'Of course. Are you not my ally? Now, smile at me as if I have made some splendid joke. Louise must not think that we are plotting against her.'

Perdita's low laugh sounded false to her own ears, but Amy looked up in astonishment.

It was not until later that day, when the two girls were alone, that she challenged her sister.

'What was his lordship saying to you?' she demanded. 'Suddenly you seem much in charity with him. Never say that you will take his side against Louise?'

'Of course not, but in some ways he is right. It may sound prosy, but you will agree that Mother and Father would not countenance such behaviour from either of us.'

'I know it.' Amy hung her head. 'But Louise is our friend. We must support her, even though we think that...well...the clandestine meetings were wrong.'

'It could be more serious than an offence against propriety,' Perdita told her. 'The Earl has pointed out to me that Louise is a considerable heiress. Suppose this man should be a fortune-hunter?'

Amy's eyes widened. 'I don't see how he could have known,' she objected. 'She does not mention it.'

'Rushmore says that there are certain men who make it their business to discover these things. They live by preying on wealthy women.'

'It can't be true,' Amy said decidedly. 'Matthew Verreker loves Louise for herself alone. He is so tender with her and he sends her such wonderful letters filled with poetry.'

'Letters too?' Perdita looked at her sister. 'How does she receive them? They cannot go to the Academy.'

'No!' Amy coloured a little. 'They have a hiding place. It is a hole in an old tree near the park. Oh, Dita, you won't tell his lordship?'

'No, since from now on everything must be above board. Rushmore is to arrange a meeting with Mr Verreker.'

Amy gasped. 'Oh, Lord! Does Rushmore intend to call him out?'

'Of course not, goose! But he would like to know more about this man. That is not unreasonable, is it?'

'He didn't sound reasonable yesterday,' Amy said darkly. 'I wonder what has changed his mind. Did you manage to persuade him?'

'He has been speaking to Aunt Trixie, I believe.'

Amy's face cleared. 'He did seem calmer today,' she admitted. 'I hope this new mood lasts until Matthew returns from London.'

'Mr Verreker is not in Bath at present?'

'No, he was called away at short notice yesterday…some private family business, so he told Louise.'

Perdita caught her sister's eye. 'It could not be that he had heard of the Earl's arrival in Bath?'

'There you go, believing the worst of him before you know the facts!' Amy was still unwilling to admit that Louise might have been the victim of a confidence trick. 'You sound exactly like the Earl, and I thought you hated him. What has he said to make you change your mind?'

'He told me that he wished to be Louise's friend, and I believe him.'

'Hmm! More likely that he has his eye on her fortune for himself. At his age he must be thinking of taking a wife.'

'Now who is jumping to conclusions?' Perdita felt a sudden spurt of anger. 'Amy, you must not let your affection for Louise lead you into folly. You won't be a party to arranging meetings, or collecting letters, will you?'

'No, I won't do that, but pray don't preach at me! You ain't a model of discretion yourself, you know.'

Perdita laughed at that. 'There's no need to remind me, Amy.' She took her sister's hand. 'We must not quarrel, you and I. Now tell me, are you not excited by the thought of attending your first ball?'

This delightful prospect raised Amy's spirits at once. The details of a possible toilette were discussed at length, though Miss Langrishe had insisted that both the younger girls were to wear simple white gowns.

On the following evening she looked at Perdita enviously, admiring her sister's overdress of pale yellow silk worn over a satin slip. It became the older girl's dark beauty to perfection, set off as it was by the yellow riband which confined her raven curls.

'No one will look at us,' she mourned. 'Louise and I are likely to spend the evening sitting with the chaperons.'

'Nonsense! Rushmore has promised you at least one dance, you know.'

Amy grimaced. 'He'll probably march up and down as if he's on parade.'

'Sourpuss! His lordship is an excellent dancer. Besides, there will be other young men, I promise you... Aunt has taken pains to make sure of it.'

In the event Miss Langrishe might have spared herself the effort. As her party entered the Assembly Rooms they were accosted by a familiar figure.

'Why, it's Thomas!' Amy's face was wreathed in smiles as she held out both her hands to her cousin. 'Oh, I am so glad to see you. Are the boys here too?'

'Large as life, and twice as ugly...' Grinning, Thomas motioned his brothers forward to greet the ladies.

Chapter Seven

Miss Langrishe welcomed her young relatives with open arms. 'With so many young people about me I shall be the envy of Bath,' she cried happily. 'Thomas, where are you staying? There is plenty of room for you in Laura Place.'

'Wouldn't dream of it, Aunt!' Thomas gave her a smacking kiss. 'You've trouble enough with the girls, I fancy. We are putting up at the York House. Can't fault it, I must say.'

Perdita pricked up her ears. The Earl of Rushmore was also a resident of the most exclusive, and expensive, hostelry in Bath. She drew her cousin to one side.

'What made you come to visit us?' she asked. 'I had not thought to see you here. Bath is hardly the most exciting place for a young man on furlough…'

'Promised your father we'd look in on you,' Thomas told her in a tone so casual that it aroused her suspicions at once.

'Then Aunt Trixie did not send for you?'

156

'Good Lord! Why would she do that?' Thomas did not disguise his look of relief and Perdita knew at once that she had asked the wrong question.

'I see. How fortunate that you should find us here on this particular evening. We might have been at the theatre.'

'Oh, no! Rushmore said—' Thomas clapped his hand to his mouth.

'Dammit, Perdita, must you trick a fellow in this way? You weren't supposed to know.'

'So it was the Earl who summoned you here?' Perdita's colour rose as her anger mounted. 'I wonder why he imagines that he has the right to do so? What was his excuse?'

'Now, coz, don't get upon your high ropes! Bless me, if you don't fly off before you give a fellow a chance to explain.'

'I'm listening,' said Perdita coldly. 'And your explanation had better be good.'

'Spitfire! Don't try your tricks on me! I ain't one of these mooncalves who swoons when you look at him. You'd best change your tune, or I shan't explain at all.'

Perdita gave him a conciliatory smile. 'I'm sorry!' she said meekly. 'But I do want to know.'

'Very well, then! Rushmore sent me a note. He thought that if we came to Bath you might cool down a bit.'

Perdita drew herself up to her full height. 'I can't think what he meant by that!' she answered.

'Come off it, Dita! You've been at odds with him ever since you met.'

'Not without reason!' Perdita told him bitterly.

'Well, that's just it, you ninny! It troubled him. Blest if you females don't take a fellow in dislike without a word of explanation. How was he to know that you'd been sent to Bath because of him?'

Perdita looked at Thomas in dismay. 'Oh, you did not tell him, did you? I would not give him that satisfaction.'

'It wasn't of much satisfaction to him. In fact, he looked...er...nonplussed. He had asked Aunt Elizabeth to overlook that scene at Almack's—'

'And you believed him? Well, he can be plausible, I suppose.' Perdita frowned. She was lost in thought for several moments. 'Thomas, do you understand him?' she asked directly. 'Why should it matter to him if I think well of him or not?'

'It don't!' her cousin told her bluntly. 'His ward is his concern, and you and Amy are her friends. He felt that you might set her against him.'

Perdita's colour rose. 'I hope I should not be so foolish, Thomas. On one point at least the Earl and I are in agreement. We wish her a happy future.'

'Yes, I can understand it! There is something about her, isn't there? Some quality? I can't think what it is, but it sets her apart from other girls.'

Perdita was startled. She had never seen Louise in quite that light, but there was a look in her cousin's eye which she could not mistake.

'Louise is a schoolgirl,' she told him slowly and deliberately. 'This is the first occasion on which she and Amy have been allowed to attend a ball. Dance with her if you will, but pray don't try to turn her head.'

'I doubt if I could. Look at those eyes! She looks as though she can see into a person's heart.' With a charming smile he invited Louise to dance.

'They make a handsome couple, don't they?'

Perdita spun round to find the Earl of Rushmore standing by her side. She nodded briefly, still annoyed by his lordship's temerity in summoning certain members of her family to Bath.

His eyes rested for a moment on her profile. 'Thomas, I take it, has been unable to hold his tongue? Well, ma'am, I expected it. Are you at odds with me once more?'

'Naturally, I am delighted to see my cousins.' Perdita gave him a steady look.

'Yes, I thought you would be. Do you care to dance, Miss Wentworth? On this occasion I'm sure that you won't turn your ankle.' His smile was intended to rob his words of all offence, but Perdita's colour rose.

'I have no wish to dance with you,' she told him coldly.

'A wise decision! It will be difficult for us to talk in such a crowd.' He looked at her with twinkling eyes. 'But perhaps you have no wish for conversation either?'

'We have nothing more to say to each other, my lord. I am sorry if you thought that I should set Louise against you. Unlike yourself, I don't propose to interfere in matters which are none of my concern.'

Rushmore grasped her firmly by the elbow and led her to a secluded alcove. 'Dear me! Was it not only yesterday that you assured me that your friendship for Louise made her welfare your concern?'

'I wasn't referring to that!'

'I know it, you prickly creature! Come now, let us be honest with each other. You hoped to keep the reason for your visit to Bath a secret from me, isn't that it?'

'I see no reason why it should interest you.'

'But it does, my dear, since I am to blame for it. It was not intended, I assure you. Do you still regret the loss of your visit to Gibraltar?'

Perdita did not answer him for a time. She was never less than truthful, and now she was struggling with conflicting thoughts.

'I wanted to go,' she said at last. 'But now, I can't think it important. Tell me, sir, have you learned anything of this Matthew Verreker?'

Rushmore's face darkened. 'I'd hoped to meet him today, but the fellow is nowhere to be found.'

'He is gone to London, I believe. Louise told Amy that he'd been called away on family business.'

'How convenient! When did he leave, I wonder?'

Perdita gave him a demure look. 'He left on the day that you arrived, my lord.'

Rushmore caught her eye, and they both began to laugh.

'We are on the right track, I think. Give me a few days, Perdita. I have made *some* enquiries about this man of mystery. He's unknown at any of the hostelries in Bath, so he must be in private lodgings. He isn't a subscriber here at the Assembly Rooms, and neither the Master of Ceremonies nor such of the visitors I have spoken to know him by name.'

'Verreker is a visitor to Bath himself, so Louise told Amy. He has no connections here who might give him an introduction into Bath society.'

'Poor fellow! A worthy object of compassion to Louise, I must suppose.' He looked up as she approached, accompanied by Thomas.

Anxious to intervene in what he suspected might develop into an awkward confrontation, Thomas handed Louise to a seat beside her guardian. Then he turned to Perdita. 'You promised me a dance,' he said. 'I've come to claim it.'

As she reached out a hand to him, her companion rose to his feet. 'Miss Wentworth is promised to me,' he told the young man with a smile. He took the outstretched hand in his own, and tucked it beneath his arm.

Perdita was tempted to giggle at the look of astonishment on her cousin's face. Then, to her consternation, she heard the first notes of the waltz.

'What is it?' Rushmore sensed her hesitation. 'You *do* waltz, Miss Wentworth, don't you?'

She nodded, but it was with the greatest reluctance that she allowed him to take her in his arms. His hands were gloved, as were her own, but she could sense the pressure of the powerful arms about her waist as he swung her into the dance.

All her misgivings vanished as she surrendered to the movement and the music, and Rushmore smiled down at her.

'Aren't you glad that I persuaded you?' he whispered.

'You did not *persuade* me, sir. You brushed aside my offer from another partner, as usual, and dragged me on to the floor. If you go on like this I shall become a wallflower. No one will dare to approach me.'

'You? A wallflower?' He threw back his head and laughed. 'I dare not leave your side, Miss Wentworth. I shall not see you for the rest of the evening.'

She smiled, but she did not answer him. Then, as she looked about her, she realised that many of the other couples had stopped dancing and were grouped by the side of the floor, even though the music had continued.

'My lord,' she whispered, 'we are the only couple left. Pray let us sit down.'

'Are you tired?' he teased.

'No, but…we are making an exhibition of ourselves.'

'We are giving a demonstration, Perdita. It is all thanks to you. You are an excellent dancer.'

She coloured and shook her head, but she was too embarrassed to continue, and after another turn about the room, Rushmore led her to a seat beside her aunt.

'That gave us all such pleasure, my dears!' Miss Langrishe beamed upon them. 'What it is to have such grace and energy!'

'But not less than your own, I'm sure, ma'am.' Rushmore bowed to her. 'May I engage you for the next waltz?'

'Good gracious! A woman of my age? Go on with you, my boy… It is a kind thought, but—'

'Miss Langrishe, were you not the belle of the London Season? Your graceful dancing is still a legend. You cannot have forgotten it.'

'Well, no, but…it is so many years since.'

'But you have not lost your interest? Confess it, ma'am, you have given in to temptation. You may not have waltzed in public, but I suspect that you have learned in private.'

'Wicked creature! How did you guess? Have you been speaking to the Colonel?'

'No, Miss Langrishe, but once a dancer, always a dancer. Now, do I have your promise?'

His request was supported by the girls. 'Dear Aunt, we wish to see you enjoying the ball,' said

Amy. 'Your toes are tapping when the music starts, and his lordship is an excellent partner, as Perdita will assure you.' She gave her sister a look which was filled with meaning.

Miss Langrishe needed no further persuasion, and when she and Rushmore took the floor the girls were startled into silence.

Like many large people, Miss Beatrice Langrishe was light upon her feet. Somehow her massive bulk was forgotten as she floated across the floor in perfect time with her partner.

Amy leaned towards her sister. 'Rushmore is making himself agreeable this evening,' she observed. 'He looks like the cat that has found the cream. Has he unmasked Verreker? That is his intention, surely?'

'He hasn't yet met Mr Verreker, as you know. You told me yourself that he is gone from Bath.'

'Well then, why is he so pleased with life this evening?'

'Must he have your permission to enjoy himself?' Perdita's tone was cooler than she had intended.

'Oh, hoity-toity! Here's a change! Are you defending him, Dita? I tell you what! You have spent too much time in his arms. First at Almack's, then when you blistered your feet, and now tonight. Take care, or I shall think that you have a *tendre* for him.'

Perdita glared at her. 'If this were not a public place I'd pull your hair, you little monster! The Earl is worried, though he does not show it. No one seems to know the name of Verreker. What has he told Louise about his family...his parents?'

'They were killed in a carriage accident.'

'And other relatives...aunts, uncles, brothers, sisters, cousins?'

'He has none.' Amy looked at her sister. 'I didn't mean to snip at you, but don't you see? I know that it sounds strange, but he and Louise have so much in common, being orphaned as they are... It is another bond between them.'

'But curious, Amy. How many people do we know who have not a relative in the world?'

'Not many,' Amy admitted cheerfully. 'Though some would be glad to have it so. I can think of a few myself.'

'So can I, and one of them is sitting beside me!'

'You don't mean it, Dita. Now confess it...you ain't quite so set against the Earl as you once were.'

'No, I'm not, but I cannot like his assumption that he may do exactly as he wishes.'

'Well, it takes one to know one,' Amy teased. 'How many times have I heard Mama accuse you of the same thing?'

'This is different,' Perdita said with dignity. 'I, at least, do not attempt to order other people's lives, but, well, he has convinced me that he wishes to protect Louise.'

'And he has chosen you for his ally?'

'You too, Amy. He knows that we are fond of her. Has she no idea when Mr Verreker will return?'

'I don't think so. I'll admit that it is a little odd that he should go away just now, leaving her to face the Earl alone.'

'It was the action of a coward.'

'Well, you know, he may have hoped that the news of her betrothal would be less surprising if she explained it to Rushmore herself.'

'Then he's either a fool or a scoundrel!' Perdita cried hotly. 'It would have been more honourable to seek out the Earl and ask permission before addressing himself to an innocent girl.'

'Keep your voice down, Dita! You may be misjudging Mr Verreker. Louise is convinced that he will make himself known to his lordship as soon as he returns from London.' She grimaced. 'I wish that I may not be there. The Earl of Rushmore is not the man to cross, I fancy.' She looked up as her cousin Henry came to claim her for the next dance.

'It's a cotillion,' he said a little doubtfully, 'and with complicated steps, as I recall. Would you prefer to wait for a country dance?'

'Not in the least,' Amy told him grandly. 'I know the steps of the cotillion as well as you do. Of course, I should have preferred to waltz.'

'No chance!' her cousin grinned. 'I don't want Aunt Trixie on my case. You ain't out yet, so you can forget the waltz.'

'A stickler for the proprieties, are you, Henry?' Rushmore's deep voice broke into the conversation.

'I must say that I hadn't noticed it before this evening.'

Henry blushed and looked an appeal at Miss Langrishe. 'I don't mean to be a spoilsport,' he said in an injured tone. 'But—'

'You are quite right to consider your cousin's reputation,' she assured him. 'But you must not tease her.'

Henry's sunny smile returned. 'Old Amy don't mind, do you, coz? Blest if she don't look as fine as a fivepence tonight.' He held out his hand to lead her into the dance, and, mollified by the compliment, she took it.

As she passed him, Rushmore bent to whisper in her ear, 'What do you say to a turn about the anteroom later, Miss Amy? No one will see us there, and you may waltz to your heart's content.'

Amy was startled, but after a quick glance at her aunt to seek the lady's approval, she smiled and nodded.

'Amy will be your slave for life,' Perdita teased. Rushmore's whisper had been loud enough for all to hear. 'Is this your way of making her your ally too?'

Rushmore slipped into a seat beside her. 'I had no ulterior motives,' he said quietly. 'It is just that...well...she looked so disappointed.'

'It was good of you to wish to please her.' Perdita gave him a long look. He had surprised her once again. She was beginning to suspect that beneath his autocratic manner he had a kind heart.

'You are the person I wish most to please,' he remarked in a conversational tone. He had half-turned to look at her and saw at once that he had gone too far. Her colour rose and the easy camaraderie which he was beginning to enjoy so much vanished at once. He changed the subject swiftly.

'I need your advice,' he said. 'If Matthew Verreker is indeed a fortune-hunter, it may not be enough simply to discredit him. Where their affections are engaged I find that women are prepared to forgive even the most villainous behaviour. Do you agree?'

'I cannot help you, sir. I have not met a villain, and my own affections have never been engaged.' Perdita's tone was cool, and her manner was stiff, as she sought to hide her confusion. Why should Rushmore announce so calmly that he wished to please her? It had been said in a casual way, but she had sensed at once that it marked a change in their relationship. Amy's words came back to her. Was she indeed developing a *tendre* for this arrogant creature who sought her companionship at every opportunity? She pushed the thought aside as Rushmore continued.

'I have thought about this matter carefully. Louise was an easy target as she was so much alone. She has had so little pleasure. Perhaps if we were to show her a little more of life beyond the Academy?'

'My aunt agrees with you. That is why she allowed both Amy and Louise to attend the ball this evening.'

'It is a start,' he mused. 'Louise has made some friends and your cousins have been more than gallant. What I hope is that she will realise that her happiness does not depend on Verreker alone.'

'What do you have in mind?' Perdita asked cautiously.

'I wondered if we might undertake an expedition into the countryside. The weather is holding well, and a picnic is always popular.'

Perdita was undeceived. 'A picnic, sir? Is that something you enjoy?'

He gave her a rueful smile. 'No, it isn't! I don't care to share my food with insects. I had enough of that in the Peninsular War, but I am prepared to suffer in a good cause.'

'Very noble of you!' Perdita had recovered her composure. 'The girls would delight in it, and my cousins too.'

'And you?' Again there was something in the question beyond polite enquiry.

'Of course, but there may be difficulties. You must ask my aunt's approval. She may not care to allow it.'

Perdita was mistaken. Miss Langrishe was happy to agree to the expedition, although she begged to be excused from joining the party.

'Picnics are for the young,' she announced. 'I am too advanced in years to think of dining other than at a table. Bless me, if I sat down upon the ground, I might never get up again!'

'You could sit in your carriage, Aunt.'

'No, no! You shall not persuade me, Perdita.' Miss Langrishe turned to Rushmore. 'You understand, my lord?'

The Earl bowed. 'I can't accept your reference to advancing years, ma'am,' he said gallantly. 'But as to the rest, I have already explained to Miss Wentworth that alfresco dining is vastly overrated and only to be undertaken upon special occasions.'

'And this is a special occasion, Adam?' The old lady's eyes rested briefly on his face.

'Yes, ma'am, I think so. If possible, I'd like to change the direction of Louise's thoughts…to show her that Verreker need not be the centre of her world. She needs young friends, and laughter, and other occupations for her mind.'

'You are right, of course. Have you seen Miss Bedlington? If Louise is to spend more time away from the Academy, you should speak to her.'

Rushmore's face darkened. 'I have not paid her a visit yet. I could not trust myself to speak in any civil way about her lack of supervision. Such neglect is monstrous! Bath has its share of villains, I imagine. I can't believe that she allowed my ward to wander unattended, at risk of insult or the attentions of some cut-purse, aside from striking up a friendship with a stranger.'

Perdita was alarmed. 'Oh, please!' she whispered as her aunt's attention was distracted by the arrival of the Colonel. 'I beg that you will say nothing of that friendship to Miss Bedlington. She does not know of it, and it will only stir up trouble. She hates men and…well…I think her a vicious creature.'

'Because she hates men? I thought you hated them yourself!' Rushmore's eyes were twinkling as he looked down at her, and she was relieved to see that his angry expression had disappeared.

Perdita knew that he was teasing her, but she would not be drawn. 'I can't imagine how you came by that idea, my lord,' she said sedately. 'I have the highest regard for my father and my uncles and my cousins.'

'That wasn't quite what I meant, Perdita. You told me earlier that your affections had never been engaged in any particular way. Why is that, I wonder?'

She was spared the need to reply to this impertinent question by the arrival of Amy, who was bursting with excitement. She addressed Rushmore direct.

'Sir, the next dance upon my card is a waltz, and you did promise, if you recall…'

'So I did!' His lordship rose to his feet. 'Come, Miss Amy, let us remove ourselves from the public gaze.' He tucked her hand within his arm and led her into an adjoining salon.

Thomas stared after them in astonishment. Then he spoke to Perdita. 'Should Amy be wandering off like that, alone with Rushmore? That ain't the refreshment room, you know.'

'Don't make a cake of yourself!' Perdita replied with some asperity. 'Amy longs to waltz, and she can't do so in public. His lordship offered to give her a turn about the salon.'

Thomas grinned at her. 'He's putting himself out for you ladies tonight. I've never seen him quite as affable. What have you done to him, Perdita?'

'This is merely an example of his good manners,' she replied in a lofty tone. 'You might study them yourself.'

'Ouch! I'll hold my tongue in future.' Thomas turned to Miss Langrishe. 'Aunt, do you care for a glass of wine? I've promised to find a table for Louise and the rest of our party.'

'Well, do you go on, my boy. I expect that you are starving. It is a common complaint with the young men of my acquaintance. Your brothers will bring us along to join you.' Miss Langrishe eyed him fondly as he ushered Louise away.

'Such a dear creature, isn't he, Perdita? Will you think me a meddlesome match-maker if I say that Louise could do much worse?'

'Than Thomas, Aunt?' Perdita was startled. 'Why, he's just a boy.'

'He's five years older than you are yourself, my dear, and he is not a boy. Have you not noticed how he looks at her?'

'Calf-love!' Perdita announced scornfully. 'Oh, I know that he was with Wellington's army, but he has no thought of marriage. If you could but hear him on the subject!'

'Opinions can change...sometimes overnight. However, let us say no more of it. When do you plan to go upon this picnic?'

'Quite soon, I think. Rushmore believes that the weather will hold for the next day or two. You see no objection?'

'Oh, no, my love! Your cousin will take good care of you, and Rushmore will accompany his ward. The carriage is at your disposal, naturally, but I imagine you will prefer to ride?'

'Oh, yes, I've missed it so. We were out each day in London, riding in Rotten Row. Shall we be able to hire good mounts in Bath?'

'Most certainly, Miss Wentworth.' Rushmore was standing by Perdita's side. 'Will you leave it to my discretion?'

'Only if you promise not to mount me upon a slug,' she said mischievously.

He laughed at that. 'I should not dare,' he replied as he offered Miss Langrishe his arm. 'Shall we join the others?'

Rather to Perdita's surprise, Thomas had managed to secure the best table in the refreshment room. Now he was awaiting their pleasure with the offer of small savouries, a selection of patties, ices, and beverages ranging from tea and coffee to lemonade, orgeat, and wine.

Miss Langrishe accepted only a glass of wine. 'Lord preserve us from the efforts of the cook here,' she whispered to Perdita. 'All his offerings taste like sawdust.'

Perdita smiled. 'You have high standards, Aunt. Will you not try a pastry boat? The filling is delicious.'

Her aunt shuddered. 'I have too much regard for my digestion, Perdita. Your cousins must be blessed with stomachs of cast-iron. Look at their plates, my dear.'

Perdita giggled. 'Perhaps it's time that we discussed the picnic...otherwise, between the three of them, they are likely to clear the tables.' She turned to Rushmore. 'Sir, I wonder if you will explain what we have in mind.'

The Earl kept his suggestions brief, but they were received with undisguised pleasure. Only Louise looked a little hesitant.

'What is it, my dear?' Miss Langrishe was all concern.

'It is just that...well...I am not the most experienced rider in the world,' Louise confessed. 'I could not manage a spirited mount.'

'But there is not the least need for you to do so,' Thomas assured her quickly. 'We shall choose a steady mare for you and you may ride at your own pace. Henry and I will be beside you in case you feel a little nervous.'

He could not have made his feelings more obvious if he had shouted them aloud. Perdita frowned at him, but then she caught Rushmore's eye. Noticing his bland expression she was strongly tempted to give him a sharp set-down. He shook his head at her.

'Never interfere with the blossoming of young love,' he whispered sententiously. 'It is a fragile thing.'

Perdita felt a little spurt of anger. 'I fancy this is all a game to you,' she said furiously.

'No, Perdita, you are quite mistaken. This is not a game to me. I have my objectives, certainly, but I don't propose to tell you of them here and now.'

'More mysteries?' she said scornfully. 'What an exciting life you lead, my lord!'

'I hope to make it even more exciting in the future, my dear. However, at the moment we are discussing our expedition to the countryside. To date, I am required to find three horses for you ladies, one of which, I am warned, must not be a slug.'

'Make that two!' Perdita told him crisply. 'Amy will not thank you for finding her some ancient nag incapable of breaking into a trot.'

'It may surprise you to hear that I had not thought of doing so.' Rushmore refilled his glass in a graceful toast to her. 'What an astonishing family you are! I had thought your sister merely a jolly school-girl.'

'And now?'

'Now I find that she has a head upon her shoulders. It is a refreshing change.'

'Pray don't attempt to patronise her, sir.' Perdita was furious.

'I had no intention of doing so. It was meant as a compliment. You are both a credit to your parents, Perdita, as I told your mother.'

'She did not say so,' Perdita answered doubtfully.

'No, she was cross with you at the time.'

'And you were not?' she challenged.

'No, I had a curious mixture of emotions.'

'Of which amusement was uppermost, I must suppose?'

'No, it was not. I was surprised, I will admit. I had expected to encounter yet another simpering miss. You disabused me of that idea.'

'I...I have a hasty temper, sir, and your remarks—'

'Were unforgivable, I agree. You were right to give me a set-down. I deserved it.' Rushmore smiled down at her. 'We began at odds with each other, my dear. Since then I have been trying to recover my character in your eyes.'

'My opinions can be of no great interest to you, my lord.' Perdita felt once again that they were reaching dangerous ground. She rose and gave her hand to Crispin, the youngest of her cousins, overriding his objection that he was the worst dancer in the world.

'Then you must learn,' she assured him. 'You won't improve by standing about like a statue. It takes practice, that is all.'

'A strong-minded lady!' Rushmore observed as the young couple walked away. 'With that face one might expect her to trade upon her looks alone, but she does not.'

'She is very dear to me,' Miss Langrishe replied quietly. 'It is Perdita's passion for justice which gets her into scrapes. Appeal to that and you will always have her by your side. Like her father, I cannot see it as a fault.'

'They are a delightful family, are they not, ma'am?'

'They have great charm. Partly it is their openness and their interest in other people. One can always be sure that the girls will tell the truth, however painful it may be for them.'

'I don't doubt it.' Rushmore's eyes had never left Perdita as she and Crispin circled the floor. 'You will think me foolish, Miss Langrishe, but I would describe her as ''lion-hearted''.'

'I don't think you foolish, Adam. I won't insult your intelligence by pretending that I have not understood you, but are you quite sure?'

'I was never more certain of anything in my life. I love Perdita. I think I've done so from the moment

I set eyes on her. I want to ask her to be my wife, but there may be obstacles in the way.'

'Such as?'

'The gap in age…her parents may not like it. Unlike some others, they are sure to consider her happiness before all else.'

'As you will do, if you love her, but this is non-sense, my dear. There cannot be ten years between you. She would not be marrying a greybeard.' Miss Langrishe studied his face. 'Is Perdita aware of your feelings for her?'

'No, ma'am. Unlike Mr Verreker, I shall not make her an offer without her father's permission.'

'I expected nothing less of you, but you will have a lengthy wait, I fear, before Perdita's parents return to this country.'

'It is no matter, ma'am.' Rushmore's smile trans-formed his face. 'It will give me time to plan my campaign.' He gave his companion a rueful look. 'What do you suppose would be her answer if I were in a position to offer for her now?'

'She would think you had run mad,' Miss Lan-grishe told him bluntly. 'Go slowly, Adam! Per-dita's pride will be offended if she believes that you are making game of her. First persuade her to be your friend before asking more of her. Her love may come unbidden.'

Rushmore took her hand and raised it to his lips. 'I must hope that she will be as good a friend as you are, Miss Langrishe. At least you do not frown upon my hopes.'

'Of course not! You will make a vastly entertaining couple, sir, though I have no doubt that battle will be joined at regular intervals. You have my blessing, but I warn you. Perdita must not be hurt. I make as strong an enemy as a friend, you know.' Her look was filled with meaning.

He laughed at that. 'Another strong-minded lady? I don't doubt that either.' Then he grew serious. 'You need have no fears on that account. I would defend Perdita with my life.'

Chapter Eight

As Rushmore had predicted, the weather continued to hold fair and two days later the party assembled at Laura Place for their expedition.

Perdita inspected her mount with unaffected pleasure. As he had promised, the Earl had chosen the best of what the local livery stable had to offer, both for herself and for Amy. Blaze was a mettlesome chestnut and his half-brother slightly darker in colour except that he lacked the distinctive white flash which had given Blaze his name.

'Well, Miss Wentworth, will they do?' The Earl was smiling down at her.

'We could not wish for better,' she announced warmly. 'May I take Blaze? He seems so friendly.' For an instant she rested her cheek against the horse's massive head, and he made no move to pull away. 'Amy, shall you be happy with his brother?'

'Will I not!' Amy was already in the saddle. 'Is this not the best scheme in the world? How I've missed our rides in London.' She bent to pat her horse's neck. 'Lancer is so fresh...he's longing for a gallop.'

'But not through the town, I beg of you, Miss Amy!' Rushmore's smile robbed his words of all offence. 'Let us take it slowly until we reach the open country.'

Amy laughed. 'It shall be as you say, my lord. Our cavalcade will proceed with all decorum.' She glanced behind her. 'Lord, what a crowd we are! Do we need quite so many grooms?'

The Earl regarded her gravely. 'Miss Langrishe's chef is on his mettle,' he announced. 'Though he disapproves in general of eating out of doors he intends to prove the haute cuisine is not beyond his powers even there...'

Amy giggled. 'So we have a full staff for our alfresco picnic? I wonder if he has sent along the family silver?'

'I should not be the least surprised. I suggested that the White Hart could well provide sufficient for our needs in the way of food and drink, but I was turned down out of hand.'

'A new experience for you, my lord?' Perdita observed mischievously.

'On the contrary, Miss Wentworth. It has happened all too frequently in recent weeks.' He was laughing down at her and she blushed, turning away quickly before he could offer to help her to mount, and accepting the assistance of one of the grooms.

Amy led the way, accompanied by Henry. She knew Bath well, and took the road to the north-west, out of the town. The gradient was steep, but they rode at a leisurely pace until they reached the heights above. There Amy stopped and threw out her arm in an extravagant gesture.

'I love this place,' she cried. 'Is it not a perfect jewel, set in the bowl of the hills? It was so clever of the Romans to discover the warm springs. Did you know that they called it Aqua Sulis?'

Her enthusiasm brought a smile from the rest of the party, though Henry could not resist the opportunity to tease her. He grimaced.

'Are we to have a history lesson?' he cried. 'Lord, Amy, I hope you ain't got your heart set on going to see the ruins.'

She gave him a disarming grin. 'Not today, you Philistine! Come on, I'll race you to that far copse of trees!'

Henry needed no second challenge and they set off at a speed which made Louise turn pale. With Thomas on one side of her and Crispin on the other she was minding instructions from the two young men as to how best to control her horse. From that height it seemed a long way to the ground. She longed to close her eyes to shut out the distance she might fall, but determination won the day and her fears soon lessened as the mare walked on at a steady gait.

'Well done, Miss Bryant! You are a natural, I believe.' Thomas voiced his encouragement.

Louise managed a rueful smile. 'You flatter me, Mr. Wentworth. I fear I am a nervous rider. I had a bad fall as a child and would not try again. I am not so brave, you see.'

'I don't agree!' Thomas said stoutly. 'You didn't refuse to join our party, though you had every reason for doing so. It takes courage to do the thing you fear.'

'I'm told it is the only way to conquer those fears,' she said quietly. 'I'm glad I came. It is so pleasant to be out of the town and in the fresh air, enjoying this lovely countryside.'

'And also the company of your friends, I hope?'

She coloured a little. 'Of course! I do not need to tell you that. Amy and Perdita have been so kind to me, and I cannot speak too highly of Miss Langrishe.'

'I'm glad of it,' Thomas said simply. He caught his brother's eye and saw that Crispin was longing to join his cousins in their gallop. 'Miss Bryant, do you feel confident enough to ride with me alone if Crispin leaves us?'

'Oh, yes!' Her warm look caused his heart to skip a beat. 'I feel quite safe with you.'

Crispin kept a commendably straight face, though he winked slyly at his brother and ignored the answering frown. A jerk of Thomas's head sent him off at a gallop to the distant wood to join Amy and Henry.

'We are losing our party one by one,' Rushmore observed. 'Do you long to try out Blaze, Miss Wentworth?' He and Perdita were bringing up the rear of the party. 'I have sent the grooms ahead to our destination, but at this pace it will take some time for us to reach them. Please don't feel that you must stay behind to keep me company.'

Perdita gave him a suspicious look. Was he teasing her? 'I don't!' she announced in withering tones. 'I am thinking of Louise. She must not be made to feel that she is the only female who cannot ride her horse at speed.'

'Very commendable, my dear!' Rushmore's eyes were twinkling. 'May I hope that your charitable intentions will extend to me today?'

'Certainly, my lord! I should not dream of urging you to venture more than a trot. The consequences of a fall must be uppermost in your mind!' She was baiting him deliberately. The Earl was a noted horseman, as she well knew.

'True! It would be disastrous, especially in view of my advancing years. I will try to keep my seat, but there are other ways of suffering a heavy fall, Miss Wentworth. I fear that your advice has come too late.'

Again Perdita was aware of some hidden meaning behind his words, but she refused to acknowledge it. Was Rushmore attempting to flirt with her? She would have none of it.

She changed the subject hastily. 'Has Mr Verreker returned to Bath?' she asked. 'I had hoped that he might have been to see you.'

'I have heard nothing yet. Louise cannot give me his direction. She does not know it. I have been wondering how she and this creature keep in touch, if she cannot send to his lodgings.' Rushmore frowned. 'Surely she cannot be receiving letters at the Academy? Miss Bedlington would know of it.' He glanced at Perdita's face and was suddenly enlightened. 'Won't you trust me?' he asked gently. 'I believe I have the right to know.'

Perdita flushed with embarrassment. 'Oh, it's all such nonsense, sir! It sounds like the plot of some Gothic novel...'

'Well?'

'Well, I'm afraid that they leave letters for each other within a hole in some tree-trunk in the park.' Perdita looked away, expecting an explosion of rage. Instead, she heard a shout of laughter.

'Oh, no! And she takes this mountebank seriously? That is the outside of enough! Gothic indeed! How right you are to think it nonsensical!'

'I expect she felt that she had no choice,' Perdita told him quietly.

'There is always a choice, Perdita.' Rushmore's face grew serious. 'She might have insisted that Verreker spoke to me before allowing matters to go so far. This underhand way of going on merely confirms my opinion of him.'

'But you don't know what pressures have been brought to bear on her. He sounds a plausible rogue. Doubtless he convinced her by an appeal to her affections.'

'So you are coming round to my way of thinking?'

'Yes, my lord. I cannot think it right to behave as he has done. If he has used Louise's love for him to persuade her into folly, it is a shameful thing.'

'I doubt if he knows the meaning of the word, my dear.' He was silent for a time, and then Perdita broke into his thoughts.

'Is there nothing we can do?' she asked.

'We can wait. If Verreker is the type of man I think him, his return will not be long delayed. His absence might cause Louise to think more carefully, or to seek the advice of her friends. If Verreker is to win his heiress he must not lose influence over her. He may also have another consideration in mind.'

'And that is…?'

'These charming rogues spend most of their time in dun territory. I should not be surprised to learn that he is penniless and deep in debt. His need for a rich wife may be of the utmost urgency.'

Perdita considered his words. 'Then, sir, why not ask Louise to leave a note for him? She could explain that you have agreed to see him, and it might…er…flush him out.'

'An excellent idea! My worry has been that he would persuade her into further folly, such as an elopement.'

'Oh, no!' Perdita stared at him in horror. 'That would ruin her in the eyes of all her friends. She would not be received…'

'It could happen, especially if he believes that I shall oppose his suit. You know her better now, Perdita. Tell me, would she agree to such a course of action?'

'Oh, no!' Perdita said decidedly. 'Louise is a gentle soul, but she has a stubborn streak, and she does know right from wrong. She is already a little ashamed of what has happened…not of falling in love, of course…but of not informing you about Verreker from the first. I think she was overtaken by events. Everything happened so fast.'

'A whirlwind romance, in fact?' The Earl's tone was dry. 'I am not surprised. Speed is of the essence with these fortune-hunters. They can't afford anyone the time for close scrutiny of their lives.'

'We may still be wrong about him,' Perdita said cautiously.

'I don't believe that, and nor do you, I think?'

'No!' she admitted. 'The more I hear, the more convinced I am that you are right.'

She was rewarded with a brilliant smile. 'Am I to believe my ears?' he teased. 'The redoubtable Miss Wentworth offering an olive branch?'

'I hope I am not so foolish to disagree with you for the sake of disagreement, sir. In this case I believe that you are right.' Without waiting for his reply, she spurred her horse ahead to ride alongside Louise.

They were almost at their destination, and in the distance they could see the well-known vantage point which had been chosen as their picnic site. The snowy cloths were already laid upon the ground, with rugs beside them. As they watched, the grooms began to unpack the hampers.

'No tables or chairs?' Amy exclaimed. 'I confess, I feel deprived. All that is offered is food and wine, and none too much of that.'

These facetious remarks were treated with the contempt which they deserved. The grooms withdrew to a respectful distance, leaving the rest of the party to enjoy their meal.

As a picnic it went far towards restoring the status of alfresco dining. Guided by Miss Langrishe, her chef had taken the comfort of the assembled party much to heart. Devilled legs of chicken were surrounded by paper collars to avoid the danger of greasy fingers. Tiny pastry cases held an assortment of delicious fillings. Paper-thin slices of fine York ham were rolled around asparagus spears and stout containers held salads of every kind.

'May I?' Rushmore advanced towards Perdita, bearing a bottle of the finest Burgundy.

'Take care, my lord! On the return journey I have no wish to fall from my horse.' Perdita smiled at him as she held out her glass.

'Fall? Not you!' Rushmore served the rest of the company and then he returned to stretch out on the grass beside her with a sigh of satisfaction.

'Well, sir, do you still tell me that you have no time for picnics?' Perdita said in a rallying tone.

'Allow me to assure you, ma'am, that this is not in the least like a bivouac in the Peninsula.'

'Tell me about Spain,' she said suddenly. 'Was it very dreadful?'

'It is always hard to lose one's friends,' he told her slowly. 'You will have heard of the famous battles—butchery for the most part...but there were other trials for our Commander. His allies let him down...promised supplies of both materials and men did not arrive...' Rushmore lapsed into silence. When he spoke again it was with admiration in his voice. 'We were fortunate in the Duke. He is a consummate diplomat.'

'Amy would love to hear you say so,' Perdita told him. 'He can not have a more fervent admirer.'

'There are those who would disagree with you,' he told her with a smile. Then he looked about him. 'Dear me!' he said. 'We are deserted once again. It must be our venture into politics, Miss Wentworth. The subject is inclined to cause the eyes of most young people to glaze. Where are they going, do you suppose?' His eyes rested briefly on the departing figures in the distance.

'I think they intend to climb to the top of yonder hill. Do you care to join them, sir?'

'Not in the least, my dear. I can imagine nothing more comfortable than to be exactly where I am at this particular moment.'

Perdita blushed. He had made his meaning all too clear. She stole a glance at his face and froze. His expression had changed completely.

'What is it?' she asked.

When he spoke his words seemed to come with difficulty.

'Stay where you are!' he ordered in a low voice. 'Don't move a muscle!'

Perdita gazed at him in astonishment. 'What on earth…?' she began. Then her eyes followed the direction of his gaze and the words died in her throat. An adder was sliding through the heathland within inches of her foot. There was no mistaking the distinctive pattern on its skin. Sheer terror held her rooted to the spot. Her heart was pounding in her breast and her mouth was dry.

Then Rushmore's hand closed about his riding crop. He struck just once and killed the snake outright.

'I…I…' Perdita swayed. Then she found herself in Rushmore's arms, clutching his coat and shaking uncontrollably.

'There!' he soothed as he stroked her hair. 'You are quite unharmed, my dear.'

Perdita found that she was babbling. 'I thought it was going to strike! I was never so frightened in my life. Oh, let us go away from here…there may be more of the creatures in the undergrowth!' For the moment it had escaped her notice that she was gathered to his lordship's brawny chest, and in spite of his reassurances he had shown no disposition to release her.

Instead he shook her gently. 'The snake would not have killed you,' he observed mildly. 'You are a healthy young woman and well able to survive a bite. Besides, for all we know, it could have been a grass snake.'

'It was not, and well you know it, sir. I can recognise an adder when I see one, and they are venomous.'

She heard a chuckle. 'You are well informed, Perdita. Now where, I wonder, have you seen such a reptile before? Are they to be found at Almack's?'

'No!' she retorted sharply as she began to recover her composure. 'The only snakes at Almack's walk about on their own two feet.' She managed a wavering smile. 'If you must know it, I have seen an adder at the zoo.' She shuddered. 'I had to turn away. The mere sight of the creature reduced me to a jelly. It was so…so silent and so slithering.'

'It hadn't any option but to crawl, my dear.' Rushmore rested his head against her hair. 'Adders have no legs. Now tell me, how many people do you know who have died of snakebite?' Purposefully, he kept his tone light, but in truth he was keeping his own emotions on a tight rein.

He hadn't lied to Perdita. It was unlikely that an adder bite would have killed her, but certainly it would have made her very ill. He dared not think of those few heart-stopping moments when she had been in serious danger. He could only be thankful that she had obeyed his order to keep still. That had taken courage of a high order. If she had screamed and run towards him or fainted upon the spot the reptile, feeling itself threatened, must certainly have struck. His blood ran cold at the thought of it and his arms tightened about her.

Perdita made no attempt to release herself for a moment or two. She was still trembling, and it was a comfort to be held so closely to his lordship's breast. No harm could come to her within that strong embrace. Then distant voices recalled her to the impropriety of her situation. She looked up to see the rest of the party returning from the summit of the hill, and Amy, in particular, looked dumbfounded to find her sister in Rushmore's arms once more.

Perdita struggled to free herself, and began to offer a halting explanation when the Earl forestalled her. He gave a brief account of the incident in the most casual of tones, sending the three young men in search of the snake, which he had tossed into a nearby patch of scrub. They could not wait to see it.

'Oh, Mr Wentworth, pray take care!' Louise begged faintly. 'The creature may not be dead.'

'No doubt about it,' Thomas cried in triumph. He found a stick and lifted the lifeless snake on to the path. 'I ain't seen one so close before. I didn't know they were so small. Look at the markings! The thing is beautiful in its own way.'

'You are right!' Amy had joined him and was regarding the snake with interest. 'I wonder if there are any more around this place?''

This artless question was enough to bring a low cry from Louise, who had grown pale. Even Perdita glanced about her nervously. It was enough to bring a sharp remark from Rushmore.

'Thomas, you are frightening the ladies,' he reproved. With a lifted arm he signalled to the grooms. 'Let us mount up and be on our way. The men will follow us, but I'll send Dent ahead to the nearest inn to bespeak a private parlour.'

'Oh, do we need...?' Thomas caught his lordship's eye and lapsed into silence. It had not occurred to him that the female members of the party might wish to attend to their toilettes and to use certain other facilities which only an inn might offer.

Rushmore's thoughtfulness was not lost upon Perdita. What a spectacle she must present, she thought ruefully. The fashionable shako which matched her dark-green riding habit was still lying upon the ground. She had removed it before the picnic. Fashionable it might be, but the day was over-warm to be wearing a hat for hours.

Now she regretted removing it. Her hair had become disarranged in the Earl's embrace, and her clothing was sadly crushed. She looked across at him and saw that he had read her mind.

'I am in like case,' he whispered. 'My lapels have suffered…'

Perdita flushed with mortification as she examined the ruined coat. In her terror she had clung to the Earl with such force that she had almost destroyed the loving efforts of his fashionable tailor.

'Don't worry!' he chuckled. 'I have another coat, and consider that I lost this one in a good cause.'

'You are too kind!'' she said stiffly. The warmth in his voice was raising eyebrows, and Amy, in particular, was giving her a look that was full of meaning. Perdita ignored it, but when she was in the saddle again she took care to remove herself as far as possible from Rushmore's side, leaving him to ride with Thomas and Louise.

'Come on, Dita, you ain't given your mount his head today!' Henry and Crispin were ready to offer her a challenge, but she shook her head. 'Amy will go with you,' she said.

'No, I won't! Off you go!' Amy waved her cousins on ahead. Then she turned to her sister. 'Did you arrange that encounter with the snake on purpose?' she demanded mischievously.

'Of course not!' Perdita did not pretend to misunderstand her meaning. 'I…I did not mean to…er…find myself in his lordship's arms, but I was frightened. You would have felt the same yourself.'

'I doubt if I'd have clung to him as if my very life depended on it,' Amy replied drily. 'He'd killed the adder by then. There was no further danger… I can only think that you enjoyed it. After all, you must by now be getting accustomed to his embrace.'

'Now you are being stupid!' Perdita did not trouble to hide her annoyance, which was all the sharper because it was dangerously close to the truth.

'Am I? You have no *tendre* for him, then?'

'Amy, you know my feelings about the Earl. We are allies for the moment, but only to help Louise. Beyond that we do not have a single thing in common.'

'I doubt if his lordship would agree with you. Are you blind, Perdita? Did you not see his face when you were in his arms? When we came up to you I thought he must have made you an offer upon the spot!'

'That proves how little you know about him,' Perdita said sharply. 'He thought me a fool to be so frightened, and he laughed about it.'

'It did not prevent him taking you in his arms...unless, of course, you hurled yourself at him?'

'I don't know why I listen to you, Amy. I had forgotten that you are just a silly schoolgirl with a vivid imagination.' Perdita spurred her mount into a fast trot. Then she allowed him to lengthen his stride until she was galloping fast towards her cousins in the distance.

Amy was about to follow when she realised that Rushmore had come up beside her. His eyes were fixed upon Perdita's disappearing figure, and he was chuckling.

'Well, Amy, what have you said to send her off riding like the very Devil?' he asked.

'Oh, did you not overhear our conversation, sir? How did you know that she was cross?'

'Intuition, my dear, and a certain familiarity with the set of her head when she finds herself in a serious disagreement.'

'You are growing to know my sister well, my lord.' Amy smiled at him, but she did not answer his question.

'I hope so, Amy.' Rushmore gave his companion a steady look, and she could not mistake his meaning.

Greatly daring, she ventured a little further. 'You think highly of her, sir, I believe.'

A smile touched the corners of his mouth. 'Is it so obvious? I had thought to have kept my feelings hidden for the time being. It is too soon…and I have no wish to drive Perdita away.'

'She has not noticed, I assure you.' Amy grinned at him. 'Whenever I broach the subject, she flies into alt.'

'I see. She feels that you are giving rein to your imagination?'

'That's it!' Amy told him candidly. 'But I see more than she does. No one takes much notice of a schoolgirl.'

'A formidable schoolgirl, if I may say so, Miss Amy. Have you nothing more to tell me?'

'Well, yes, I have, my lord. Have you noticed that we are being followed?'

'The gentleman silhouetted against the skyline? Yes, I spotted him some time ago.'

'And do you recognise him?'

'No, but I can make a guess that Mr Verreker has returned to Bath.'

'Then why does not he come up to us and make himself known to you?'

'That is a mystery we have yet to solve. Perhaps he fancies himself invisible. He cannot be a military man. He would make a perfect target for a sniper, out in the open and without cover.'

'Are you tempted?' she asked slyly.

'Strongly tempted, you minx! Unfortunately, I am unarmed. Ah, I see that we are coming to the inn. I wonder if the gentleman will join us?'

'I thought we were to have a private parlour?'

'That's true. It need not stop him sending up his name.'

The mysterious stranger did not satisfy their curiosity, but later they saw him in the stable-yard chatting to the ostlers. A glance at Louise told Amy all she needed to know. Her friend went red and white by turns. She seemed about to stop as she passed the man, but he turned aside and walked into the inn without a sign of recognition.

Amy eyed him closely. Then she nudged Perdita. 'That is Matthew Verreker, I'm sure of it,' she whispered. 'If you doubt me, look at Louise.'

Their friend was having difficulty in controlling her emotions. The tears welled up as she followed Matthew with a despairing glance.

Amy seized her hand. 'That's Matthew, isn't it?' she said without hesitation. 'Louise, you can't go on like this. He *must* speak to your guardian.'

'Of course…I know it…and he will do so…but this is neither the time nor the place. I know that well enough.'

Perdita made her way to Rushmore's side. She was having the utmost difficulty in hiding her disgust. 'When will he come into the open, my lord? To put Louise in this position is the outside of enough.'

'We shall not have long to wait, I think,' he told her quietly. 'Louise is a gentle soul, but even she is beginning to see that matters have gone far enough.

She must get in touch with Verreker and insist upon his meeting me.'

'I shall tell her so without delay.' Perdita was incensed. It was one thing to offer to help Louise, but another to support her in what appeared to be blind folly.

Whatever was said, it served to stiffen Louise's resolve. She was quieter than ever as the party returned to Bath.

On the following evening a message was brought up to Rushmore's apartments at the York House.

'A gentleman, you say?' Rushmore paused in the act of tying his stock.

'Well, sir, I do not know him, but he claims to have business with you.'

Rushmore smiled. Trust a servant to place his unexpected visitor at his true place in society. 'You had best send him up,' he said as he put the final touches to the arrangement of his neckcloth. Then he allowed his valet to help him into his coat, dismissing the man with the assurance that he must not wait up. His lordship might be late to retire that evening.

Now he eyed his visitor with interest. At the inn on the previous day a single glance had told him much of what he needed to know. Clearly, Matthew Verreker's looks were his stock-in-trade. Tall and fair, his features were cast in a classic mode. Dark blue eyes showed to advantage against his tanned skin, as did his perfect teeth, glimpsed when the generous mouth curved into a smile.

He was smiling now, as he held out a hand to Rushmore.

His lordship's eyesight seemed to be failing. For some reason, he appeared not to see the proffered hand.

'I beg you will sit down, Mr Verreker,' he said with the utmost courtesy. 'What may I do for you?'

'You may grant me my heart's desire!' the gentleman cried in ringing tones. 'My life is in your hands, my lord.'

'Quite a responsibility!' the Earl observed mildly. 'Tell me…upon what does your survival depend?'

Verreker gave him a wounded look. 'Pray, sir, do not torture me. Louise…Miss Bryant…must have told you of our strong attachment. She promised that she would do so.'

'She kept her word. And now…?'

Verreker was nonplussed. He had been dreading this interview with Louise's guardian, but his lordship's manner was unexpected. He knew of Rushmore's reputation. He had made it his business to find out, and had expected a stormy scene, and invitation to a duel, or, at the very least, to be refused admittance to the Earl's presence. On the contrary, this quiet gentleman seemed prepared to be reasonable. True, he had refused an offer to shake hands, but that might be the way of these haughty aristocrats.

Possibly Louise was right in thinking that Rushmore would welcome the opportunity to be rid of all responsibility for her. He'd doubted her, of course. In his experience, no sane person would refuse control of a handsome fortune, especially if its owner was little more than a child. He gave the Earl a solemn look.

'Now, sir, I am come to beg for your indulgence. Give me leave to pay my addresses to your ward.'

Rushmore leaned back in his chair and regarded Verreker with half-closed eyes. 'I thought you had already done so.'

There was a hint of menace behind the quiet words and his companion picked it up at once. He hung his head, but when he looked up at last his blue eyes were filled with guileless innocence.

'That was ill done of me,' he admitted simply. 'But if I might explain the circumstances? When I met your ward she was alone, bereft of friends, and visibly distressed. I felt obliged to offer her my help.'

'Quite the Good Samaritan, in fact! Naturally, you had no idea who she was?'

'Of course not!'' Verreker bridled at the thought. 'She was just a young girl, quite unprotected, and possibly at the risk of unwelcome attentions—'

'Including your own?'

'Miss Bryant was grateful for my help,' Verreker assured him. 'I saw her safely back to the Academy.'

'For that, at least, I must be grateful, sir. What I cannot accept is your behaviour from then on...clandestine meetings, the exchange of letters, and finally this suggestion of a betrothal.'

'It is not a suggestion, my lord. We are betrothed.'

'Let me assure you that you are not, and nor are you likely to become so—' Rushmore caught himself in time. He must not refuse this creature out of hand. Nothing would be more likely to drive Louise into his arms. 'You will understand my position,' he continued. 'I cannot countenance an attachment undertaken in this underhand way.'

'I have no excuse except that our love struck like a bolt of lightning.'

'Then let me advise you not to get burned.' There was something in Rushmore's eyes which struck terror to the heart of his companion, but the look was swiftly veiled.

Verreker was at a loss. He was beginning to understand the Earl, and he knew in his soul that this man was his enemy. Rushmore would never allow Louise to marry him.

He was tempted to cut and run, but he had too much at stake. His pockets were to let, and his creditors were gathering like sharks about a wounded fish. Within weeks, or possibly even days, they would close in on him and consign him to a debtors' prison. Only the certain prospect of a marriage to a wealthy bride would hold them off.

He made a last despairing appeal to Rushmore. 'Sir, would you break Louise's heart?' he asked in a low voice.

'My ward is seventeen years old. Better a little unhappiness now than to suffer a lifetime of misery.'

'But I would make her happy...I swear it.'

'How? I know nothing about you, Mr Verreker. You have not mentioned your past life. Where do you come from? Who are your parents? What are your prospects? You have said nothing of these things.'

'I come from the north of England, sir. Sadly, my parents are dead. They cannot speak for me. As to prospects, well...I have influential friends...I think of entering politics.'

'Do you, indeed? And what settlements would you make upon my ward?'

Verreker glared at him. Then his eyes fell. 'I...I have nothing to offer her but my love...but surely that is beyond the price of rubies?'

'Possibly, but it will not put a roof above your head, nor fill your larder. Louise cannot help you. The control of her fortune is in my hands.'

'Her fortune?' Wide-eyed and innocent, Verreker stared at him. 'My lord, I had no idea! Do you tell me that she is an heiress? Well, I suppose that that must be the end of me.' Apparently crushed, he rose from his chair and prepared to take his leave. 'I see

now why you are against me. You think me a fortune-hunter.'

Rushmore gave him a lazy smile, but his knuckles
whitened. He was strongly tempted to thrash
Verreker within an inch of his life. The man must
think him a fool!

'And I am wrong, of course?' he mocked. 'Now,
sir, let me warn you. There will be no more clandestine meetings, nor an exchange of letters. You
may see Miss Bryant for one last meeting. Miss
Langrishe, I am sure, will allow you to present yourself at Laura Place. I shall speak to Louise myself.'

'She will defy you,' Verreker cried hotly. 'We
are tied together by the bonds of love.'

'Oh, spare me your histrionics!' Rushmore eyed
his companion with distaste. 'You should consider
a career upon the boards, sir. I shall tell Louise that
she must wait...at least until she has enjoyed her
London Season.'

'I see!' Verreker looked at him with undisguised
hostility. 'You hope that someone more suitable will
offer for her?'

'She is unlikely to be approached by anyone *less*
suitable,' his lordship suggested with a pleasant
smile. 'In a year's time, who knows? If she is still
of the same mind...well...we'll see.'

Silently, Verreker cursed him to perdition. He
could not afford to wait a year and he suspected that
Rushmore knew it.

Chapter Nine

After ridding himself of his unwelcome visitor, Rushmore strolled round to Laura Place. The walk gave him time to think. A shrewd judge of men himself, he had seen Verreker for what he was…a handsome fly-by-night, living on the fringe of society, and always with an eye to the main chance.

Doubtless the fellow had a pack of creditors after him. That had been all too clear when the Earl had insisted upon a delay. With any luck he would be thrown into a debtors' prison before he could carry his plans much further.

The Earl frowned. That would not do, he decided. He must not make a martyr of Matthew Verreker. Louise would feel obliged to stand by him out of loyalty, if for nothing else. Could she really be so naive as to take the fellow at face value? With a sigh, his lordship realised that she had done so. Perhaps he could expect little else from a seventeen-year-old.

As always, his thoughts strayed to Perdita. Would she have been so gullible? A smile curved his lips. Perdita was all woman…capricious and sometimes unreasonable in his eyes. Fondly he recalled how she had clung to him after he had killed the adder. It was a very feminine reaction, but in his heart he knew that behind that lovely face lay a strong reserve of common sense.

He was assured of it when she greeted him in the salon at Laura Place. Perdita looked at him intently.

'Something has happened,' she insisted. 'Won't you tell me what it was?'

'Verreker has been to see me,' he told her as he drew her towards the window-seat.

'And what did you make of him?'

'I thought him false in every respect, Perdita. All he could offer me by way of recommendation were high-flown sentiments.'

Perdita chuckled. 'Those will carry no weight with you, I think.'

'You think me impervious to the softer feelings. I assure you that I am not, my dear, but in this case I found it impossible to believe him. He claimed not to know that Louise had any expectations.'

'That could be true,' Perdita said slowly. 'She does not flaunt her prospects…'

'I think she had no need to do so. If I am not mistaken, this fellow knows her worth down to the last penny.'

'But what can you do, my lord? You can't force her to give him up.'

'I hope I should not be so foolish as to consider it. I have asked Verreker to wait for a year. If Louise is still of the same mind after her London Season, then we'll see.'

Perdita looked at him. 'Remind me not to take up any cause against you, sir. Verreker durst not wait a year, if your suspicions are correct.'

'Louise does not know that. It is my hope that she will see my views as sensible.'

'She will…as long as you don't fly into alt, my lord.'

'Now, would I do that, Perdita? I am the most reasonable of men. If she will but listen to my arguments, all may yet be well. Don't you agree?'

Perdita was tempted to argue the point. Did Rushmore truly believe himself to be the most reasonable of men? The notion made her want to laugh. Then a glance at his face told her that he was deeply worried. The interview with Matthew Verreker had confirmed his worst suspicions.

Now he was in a quandary. Outright condemnation of the man would persuade Louise to fly to his defence, but he could not pretend to give his blessing to the match. The situation needed careful handling.

'My lord, it is not for me to give advice,' she told him slowly.

'But I have asked for it, my dear. I'd welcome your thoughts on how I should proceed. I have no wish to drive Louise away.'

'Then speak to her of her father. Tell her how happy you are to fulfil his wishes in becoming her guardian and that you will never regard it as an unwelcome burden upon you.'

'Do you think I should? I have avoided the subject of her father's death, fearing that it would cause her pain.'

'Perhaps it will, but it may also bring relief. My own feeling is that we need to speak of those we have lost. It keeps their memory alive and somehow it brings them closer to us.'

Rushmore took her hands in his. 'You have wisdom beyond your years, Perdita.' Something in his tone brought the hot colour rushing to her cheeks.

'My lord, we should rejoin the others. This private conversation must give rise to comment and I would not have Louise believe that we are plotting against her.'

He released her hands at that and strolled over to Miss Langrishe, who was deep in conversation with the girls.

'Your pardon, ma'am, but may I steal my ward away from you for a few moments? I have something to discuss with her in private.'

Louise paled and threw a hunted look at Thomas. This was the moment she had dreaded. Matthew must have been to see his lordship. Now she had to learn her fate.

'Use the study, Adam.' Miss Langrishe nodded encouragement to the shrinking girl. 'Go along, my dear!'

Louise walked to the door with lagging footsteps, and Thomas watched her with a frown. He made as if to rise to his feet, but a look from Miss Langrishe stopped him.

'Leave it, Thomas!' she ordered. 'You must not interfere. The Earl has every right to speak to his ward alone.'

A silence fell upon the assembled company. Only Crispin and Henry were unaware that momentous decisions were being made in the other room. Perdita and Amy fell prey to speculation, and Thomas wore a thunderous expression.

Miss Langrishe called him to her. 'Don't make a cake of yourself, my boy,' she advised. 'Rushmore will not eat Louise, nor threaten to beat her.'

'He had best not do so,' Thomas muttered darkly. 'Else he'll have me to deal with. She is afraid of him, you know.'

'Then she is a very foolish girl, and you are not much better. You know the Earl...you have served with him...I thought that you admired him.'

'I do, ma'am. He is the best of men, but Louise don't know it, you see. Have you not noticed how she quakes whenever he appears?'

'Thomas, you could change all that. In your company Louise seems perfectly at ease. I think she sees you as a friend. Why not speak to her about the Earl? She may trust your judgement.'

Thomas brightened. 'Do you think I should?'

'I am convinced of it, my dear boy. It is of great importance that Louise learns to have faith in her guardian.'

Thomas glanced towards the door. 'What can be taking them so long?' he asked impatiently. 'I hope he ain't laying down the law as if Louise is one of his captains.'

Miss Langrishe laughed. 'I doubt if he'll do that. Now, are we in agreement, Thomas? You will try to persuade Louise to feel more in charity with the Earl?'

'It depends...I don't know what he's said to her. If she is in tears again he will have lost my good opinion of him.'

Fortunately his lordship was spared this dreadful fate. Louise looked perfectly composed when he led her back into the room and the sigh of relief from all her friends was almost audible.

Normal conversation was resumed at once, but the subject of the interview was carefully avoided.

It was not until the gentlemen had departed and the young ladies retired to their rooms that their curiosity was satisfied.

A tap at the door brought Louise to join her friends in their bedchamber.

'Well, what happened?' Amy could not contain her excitement. 'Did Matthew go to see his lordship?'

'Yes. I believe they spoke together for some time…'

'And did Rushmore call him out? Is there to be a duel?'

'Of course not, Amy… What a ghoul you are!'

'No, I'm not, but I've never seen a duel. It always happens at dawn, you know. I thought if we could find out where it was to be held we might rise early and go to watch. We could have hidden behind a tree.'

'Be quiet, you wretched little monster!' Perdita glared at her sister. 'You can't wish to see a man get killed.'

'That doesn't always happen,' Amy told her stoutly. 'Sometimes they delope…that is, they fire into the ground or up in the air. I don't see the point myself.'

'Shut up!' Perdita cried. 'Don't you see? You are upsetting Louise—'

'No, she isn't. There is to be no duel. His lordship was not too hard on Matthew about the way we met, nor of our assignations and the letters. He was more concerned as to Matthew's background and his prospects.'

'Well, that sounds reasonable enough,' Perdita announced. 'After all, he takes his promise to your father very seriously. Your papa would have done the same, I'm sure.'

'The Earl reminded me of that. He spoke so kindly of my father. They were the best of friends and he feels the loss...' For a moment her lip quivered. 'Now he wants me to go on as my father would have wished.'

Perdita threw an arm about her shoulders. 'You would agree to that, I'm sure. And in caring for you, your guardian must feel that he has not lost his friend completely.'

Louise smiled at her through misty eyes. 'That is almost exactly what he said. I think I have misjudged him. He has a generous heart.'

'So, are you to be allowed to go ahead with your betrothal?' Amy was all impatience.

'Not for the moment, though the Earl did not dismiss it out of hand. He pointed out that your own mama has kindly promised to sponsor me for the coming Season. All he asks is that I wait until I have made my come-out with you, Amy.'

'And you don't mind waiting?' Amy was bewildered. 'It will be almost a year.'

Louise managed a faint smile. 'His lordship admitted that at seventeen a year can seem a lifetime, but he told me too that true devotion would stand up to the test.'

'So you have agreed?'

'Yes, I have.'

'But what will Matthew say?'

'I expect he will be disappointed, but I am to be allowed to see him and to explain. That is, if Miss Langrishe will allow me to receive him here. He is to call tomorrow... Certainly he cannot object to the Earl's suggestion.'

Louise was mistaken. When Matthew Verreker was shown into the study at Laura Place, it took him less than a minute to learn that all his plans had been foiled. His soulful expression disappeared to be replaced by one of fury as he listened to her.

'My darling, you can't have agreed to this!' he cried. 'Oh, cruel...cruel! How are we to bear it?'

'I believe it is what my father would have wished, my dearest. I am not yet out, you know...and, well...his lordship is convinced that true devotion will stand the test of time.'

'He's a liar!' Verreker shouted. 'He hopes that you will forget me...I know his thinking...he made it clear enough.'

Louise laid a placating hand upon his arm. 'Will you not wait for me?' she begged. 'We have pledged our troth for a lifetime...is a year so long?'

It was only with the greatest difficulty that Verreker managed to control his rage. He looked in disgust at the innocent face of the girl beside him. What a vapid creature she was...swayed by the latest argument to reach her ears. Once he'd welcome the compliant nature...now it had turned against him. He assumed a mournful expression.

'I told the Earl that I was unworthy of you,' he muttered. 'I should never have attempted to attract your interest, but this is a bitter pill to swallow. I see it all now. I was mistaken. You do not care for me with the passion which I have for you.'

Louise's face was twisted in pain. 'Don't say that!' she pleaded. 'I have risked everything for you. I knew quite well that we were wrong in behaving as we did.'

'Ah, is our love to be measured by convention? I had thought better of you.'

Gentle though she was, Louise was growing impatient. For the first time it occurred to her that her lover had a tendency to declaim as if he were acting in a third-rate play. She turned away and that slight movement sounded a warning.

Verreker pulled himself together quickly. At this stage in his affairs he could not afford to lose her. She was his last hope. Without her there would be no time or opportunity to restore his fortunes before the duns moved in. Tenderly he slipped an arm about her waist.

'Forgive me, my dear one!' he murmured. 'You are my life, my only love. We have been so close these last few weeks. I have learned to look for you each day, to offer you my heart, and to bask in the warmth of your affection. Have we not been everything to each other? We have laughed and cried together, sharing our troubles like good friends. Is that not so?'

'I won't deny it, Matthew.'

'Then listen to me, dearest. Rushmore is my enemy. I don't know why, but he has other plans for you. For all we know he may intend to wed you himself.' As Louise gasped he stopped her with a lifted hand. 'Don't discount it, I beg of you—'

'But this is nonsense,' she protested. 'He was my father's friend.'

'So he claims, but what do you know of him? Did he come to see you as soon as he returned to England from the continent of Europe? Has he shown you any affection? No! It was not until you announce your intention to be wed that he arrived in Bath. I think you should beware of him. The Earl is not all he seems.'

'I think you are misjudging him. I did so myself at first, but he has spoken so kindly of my father. All that concerns him now is that I shall be happy.'

She heard a snort of disbelief.

'He has a curious way of showing it. Don't you care that he has ruined all our plans?'

'He has asked us to wait, that is all.'

'That is all?' Verreker's face was ashen. 'He has broken my heart. Tell me, are we to be allowed to meet during this waiting time?'

Louise was silent.

'Just so!' Verreker cried in triumph. 'And letters are forbidden too?'

'All he said was that we should not meet in secret. If you write to me I must show the letters to Miss Langrishe.'

'Splendid! What pleasure she will derive from reading private correspondence! No, thank you! You had best make up your mind, Louise. We are to be parted for ever. Rushmore is a heartless brute!'

'I don't think so,' Louise said quietly. 'All he asks of me is to do as my father would have wished.'

Verreker cursed beneath his breath. Rushmore was a clever devil! He had seized upon the one argument which would sway this girl. He decided upon a final throw of the dice.

He took Louise's hand in his. 'He is right, of course,' he told her with a winning smile. 'And what would have been your father's first consideration? That must have been your happiness, my dear. Will you send me away like this? I won't believe that you have played me false. I believed your love to be as strong as mine. Did we not say that we were two halves of one whole?'

'I haven't played you false,' she whispered. 'But—'

'But you lack the courage to trust me?'

'Of course not.'

'Then listen to me carefully. Rushmore intends to part us, but there is a way to force his hand.'

'I don't know what you mean.'

'We must elope, my love. Once we are wed he can do nothing. Even he cannot come between husband and wife.'

Louise snatched her hands away. She was deeply shocked. 'You must be mad!' she cried.

Verreker threw his arms about her. 'Of course I'm mad…mad with love for you… Believe me, this is the only way if we are ever to make our dreams come true.'

'I can't do it…and I won't!' Her face was set.

Matthew Verreker knew when he was beaten, and now he too was shocked. Who would have suspected that this gentle girl had such a streak of stubbornness in her nature? Now disaster loomed before him. His creditors would not wait, and money he must have before the month was out.

The idea of abduction crossed his mind. One night alone with this stupid creature would still all objections to their marriage. She would be damaged goods, especially if he took care to let the circumstances be known to all her friends and acquaintance.

He was unaware that his expression had changed, but Louise glanced up at his face and was afraid.

'I must go,' she said. 'I'm sorry, Matthew, but I could never agree to such a plan. Will you not trust *me* to wait for you?'

'You must do as you think best,' he told her coldly. 'I shall not contact you again. If you change your mind, a letter will find me.' He looked at her bent head, and knew then that the letter would not come. He bowed and left her.

Pale with fury, he strode off into the town contemplating the ruin of all his hopes. His careful plans had come to naught, but she'd seemed such an easy target, and finding her alone in the park had been a heaven-sent opportunity. He'd seen at a glance that she was gentry. It had been so easy to offer her his sympathy, and later, when he had made enquiries as to her background, his love.

Fatherless and vulnerable, she'd fallen into his hands like a ripe plum until the arrival of the Earl of Rushmore. Slow-burning hatred for his enemy consumed him as he walked along. The Earl was a powerful man, but he would learn that he had met his match in Matthew Verreker. There were other ways of gaining possession of the funds he needed.

Abduction? It might be worth a try, but Louise no longer walked in the park alone. And Rushmore? Matthew did not underestimate his enemy. If he made Louise his wife, it was more than likely that she would soon become a widow. Rushmore had killed in battle. If he was given just cause, it was more than likely that he would kill again.

But there was another way. In the past he had always made contingency plans in case certain of his schemes fell through. This time he hadn't thought it necessary, but an idea crossed his fertile mind and he began to chuckle.

The scheme was not his own. He had heard of it some years ago. It had been tried in this very place. True, it had not met with much success, but the intended victims had been an elderly couple. Now, in the case of a young girl...? As he considered all the possibilities he knew that it could not fail.

Unaware of the plans being made for her, Louise had sought the company of her friends. Amy was bursting to know the outcome of her interview with Matthew Verreker, but, cautioned by Perdita, she held her tongue until Louise should choose to speak of it.

'I expect you want to know,' Louise said at once. 'I have explained to Matthew that we must wait.'

'What did he say to that?' Perdita asked. She suspected that she knew the answer to the question before her friend could reply.

'He was disappointed,' Louise told her in a low voice. 'He thinks the Earl a monster...and...well... I'm afraid we quarrelled about it.'

'He will come round,' Amy assured her cheerfully. 'When gentlemen are crossed they fly into the boughs, but they get over it and then forget what they have been quarrelling about.'

Louise gave her a sad little smile. 'This was not quite the same as your differences with your cousins, Amy. Matthew says that he will not contact me again. If I change my mind, I am to write to him.'

'Change your mind?' About what? Perdita was seized with a feeling of dread. 'Surely he does not expect you to go on meeting him in secret and hiding letters in the park?'

'No, he doesn't, but he is convinced that his lordship means to part us for ever.'

Amy took her hand. 'Are you very unhappy about it?' she asked. 'Perhaps if we spoke to the Earl he might agree to you meeting Matthew in company.'

'I said as much, but Matthew will not have it. It is not enough for him…' She turned her head away and gazed through the window, fighting back her tears.

Perdita moved to sit beside her. 'Is there something more?' she asked. 'I hate to see you so distressed. You say that Mr Verreker wishes you to change your mind? What has he suggested to you?'

Louise began to sob. 'He…he wishes me to agree to an elopement,' she gasped. 'I can't! I can't!'

'Of course you can't!' Perdita's anger threatened to overwhelm her. 'What kind of man is he even to suggest such a thing?'

'He must be mad! Doesn't he realise that the Earl would follow you? I believe that I shall offer to go with him, Louise. You will need a friend when he catches up with Mr Verreker.' Amy's eyes were gleaming with excitement.

'Amy, if you can't be sensible you may leave the room. Louise has no intention of eloping with Mr

Verreker.' Perdita turned to her friend. 'How have you left things with him?'

'It is as I told you. I must make the decision whether or not to see him again.'

'Let him suffer for a while,' Amy advised. 'That is, if you truly wish to see him again.'

'Do you, Louise?' Perdita cast a searching glance at her friend's face. 'I think you cannot have suspected that he would stoop so low.'

'I don't know! I'm so confused. Matthew seemed different somehow. He's always been so kind, but today I saw another side to his character.'

'Well, now you have plenty of time to consider how you should go on.' It was with a feeling of relief that Perdita heard a bustle in the hall which heralded the arrival of all three of her cousins, together with the Earl of Rushmore.

'Girls, I beg you will not speak of this to his lordship,' Louise begged anxiously. 'It can only give him a poor opinion of Matthew.'

Amy and Perdita nodded. A horse-whipping would be the likely outcome and that would serve no purpose except to relieve the Earl's feelings.

Rushmore was too circumspect to question Louise directly. Her dead father's wishes would be uppermost in her mind, he knew. Now he felt he could trust her to follow his own advice.

Miss Langrishe beamed at him, and made no objection when he suggested that the young people might enjoy a stroll in the park. She had turned down his invitation that she join them.

'Bless you, my dear boy, I can think of nothing more exhausting. Why do you think I live here in Laura Place, rather than in the Royal Crescent? I am all for convenience, you know, and here I need struggle only a few yards to the shops.' She chuckled. 'My feet do very well as long as I don't punish them too much.'

'Then you might prefer to drive in a barouche, ma'am?'

'Not this morning, Adam, I thank you. I have much to do, and the Colonel intends to call upon me with tickets for a subscription ball. Now, off you go…the girls will enjoy the outing.'

Her charges needed no further encouragement. Both Amy and Louise knew that their return to the Academy could not be long delayed, and they intended to enjoy their freedom to the full.

They hurried ahead with Thomas and his brothers, leaving Perdita and the Earl to follow at a slower pace. Perdita gave her sister a suspicious look. It seemed almost as if Amy was at pains to throw her together with his lordship.

Then she dismissed the idea. Amy was merely giving her the opportunity to discuss Rushmore's plans for Louise.

He did not leave her long in doubt.

'Verreker has been to see Louise?' he asked.

'He came this morning, my lord.'

'Oh, I wondered…' He looked ahead to the party of young people strolling happily in the sunshine. 'She does not seem to be overly distressed…I must hope that she made my wishes known to him.'

'She did.'

'And what was his reaction?'

Perdita considered her next words carefully. She had promised not to speak of Verreker's plans for an elopement, but there could be no harm in mentioning his anger.

'He was not best pleased,' she admitted.

She heard a suppressed laugh. 'Perdita, I shall regard those words as a masterpiece of understatement. Confess it now—he was furious?'

'Well, yes, he was, but he could not sway Louise. You may not think it, but she *was* distressed. They had a serious quarrel, and he went off in a rage, saying that they must part unless she changed her mind.'

'Really! This is good news indeed, except that you are keeping something back from me, I think. What was she to change her mind about?''

Perdita was silent.

'Well?'

'Sir, I cannot betray a confidence. Louise insisted that she must do as her father might have wished.'

'I see. And it was enough to cause him to withdraw his suit? You surprise me! I had not thought that he would give her up so easily.'

Perdita felt that she was on dangerous ground. She tried to hurry ahead towards the others, but a large hand closed about her wrist and Rushmore drew her arm through his.

'Don't run away, my dear!' he said. 'I won't ask you to break your word, but we are speaking of a dangerous man. He is at *point non plus* and he cannot afford to let Louise escape. As I see it, he has few choices open to him.'

Perdita averted her face. In seconds her shrewd companion would have the secret out of her, and that might lead to disaster.

Rushmore strolled on, apparently unaware of any tension.

'Yes,' he continued, 'few choices. One, I fancy, might be to suggest an elopement.'

Perdita gasped and tried to withdraw her arm from his, but he would not release her.

'Louise, I fancy, would not agree to that,' he mused. He looked down at the lovely girl beside him, and then he smiled. 'Don't worry, my dear, I shall neither call him out nor horse-whip him. Perdita, has anyone ever told you that your face is the mirror of your thoughts?'

She coloured deeply and turned her head away.

'No, I shall not make a martyr of this creature,' he continued. 'He is safe enough for the moment. Louise herself must see him for what he is, and she may not have long to wait.'

'Sir, what can you mean?'

'Verreker is facing ruin, I believe. I should not put it past him to have considered abduction—'

'Oh, no!' Perdita's hand flew to her mouth. 'He could not be so wicked.'

'Needs must when the devil drives…' Rushmore considered for some moments. 'I have no wish to frighten her, but she must not be left alone.'

'But if you set a guard on her she will think that you don't trust her.'

'She won't suspect my guard.' Rushmore chuckled.

'But who?'

'I was thinking of your sister, Amy. Shall we take her into our confidence?'

Perdita sighed with relief. 'Sir, you could have thought of nothing better. Amy will guard Louise and consider it an adventure. Why, she was planning to attend the duel if you had challenged Verreker.'

'She has much to learn,' he said softly. 'Verreker is not a gentleman. I could not have challenged him.'

There was something in his tone which caused Perdita to look up at him. She was startled. This was not the laughing, teasing man she knew. There was murder in his eyes. She shrank away from him.

Rushmore sensed it at once and when he spoke again it was in a rallying tone. 'Your sister is a jewel.' He laughed. 'She was prepared to rise at dawn to attend us on some blasted heath or other? Where was she to hide?'

'Behind a tree, I think. Her greatest worry was that you would delope, or miss each other in the fray.'

'Good heavens! I see that I am unlikely to be lucky in my ally. Remind me not to offer her a pistol. We shall have bodies everywhere.'

'Pray be serious, sir.' Perdita returned to the matter in hand. 'Matthew Verreker would be foolish in the extreme to attempt to abduct Louise. He must surely know that you would follow him?'

'He won't have forgotten that possibility. He may hope to ruin Louise before we catch him.'

Perdita blushed, but she did not pretend to misunderstand him.

'Of course, it will avail him nothing.'

Again, she saw the bleak look in his eyes.

'It won't happen,' she assured him earnestly. 'Let us speak to Amy and to Aunt Trixie. Louise must not be left alone. Shall we tell Thomas and the boys?'

The suggestion brought a reluctant smile from Rushmore. 'I think not. If Thomas were to learn the facts, Amy might get her duel after all. It could serve no purpose, except to cause a scandal in which Louise might be named, and rouse sympathy for Verreker if he should be wounded.'

'I'd shoot him myself!' Perdita said fiercely.

'Yes, my love, I know you would, but there are other ways to bring him down. I have set matters in train…enquiries are being made here and in

London. The man must have a past. This cannot be his first attempt to secure an easy living for himself.'

If Perdita was startled by the endearment she gave no sign of it. She walked along sedately with her companion.

'And how do you find Bath?' he asked with an easy grin. 'Not quite as boring as you had at first imagined?'

'Not in the least,' Perdita shuddered. 'This will teach me not to yearn for excitement. I have had enough to last a lifetime.'

'Oh, I hope not, my dear.' Rushmore twined her fingers in his own. 'You have your life ahead of you. I hope…I mean, I am certain that you will find it interesting and fulfilling.'

Perdita allowed her hand to rest in his. 'It's difficult, isn't it?' she said frankly. 'I mean, one does not know what lies ahead.'

'But that is the beauty of it. Imagine if some seer told you! Would you wish to know? There would be no surprises.'

'Most of my surprises have turned out to be unpleasant recently,' she told him with a rueful smile.

'Ah, yes, but you must not give up hope! All this will change—' Rushmore caught himself in time. He must not speak of love just yet, or even attempt to attach Perdita to him. Let her grow to know him as a trusted friend. That must be enough for now.

Chapter Ten

Amy made an excellent co-conspirator. Once taken into the Earl's confidence she was even able to face the dismal prospect of returning to the Academy as a boarder with a certain degree of equanimity.

Her eyes sparkled at the thought of becoming Louise's bodyguard, though she objected when Rushmore refused to lend her a pistol.

'But suppose we are attacked?' she cried. 'We should fight, of course, but we'd be no match for a group of ruffians.'

'An attack is highly unlikely if you stay together,' Rushmore told her. 'All I'm asking is that you make quite sure that Louise does not go out alone. You girls are allowed to walk in Bath, I believe?'

'Only in a stupid crocodile! We look like a group of schoolgirls.'

With commendable restraint the Earl refrained from mentioning that that was exactly what they were.

'But you are able to go into the shops to make small purchases?'

'Only in company with each other.'

'Good! I may be imagining danger where none exists, but it would be foolish to take a risk. Take care that you don't get separated and, whatever the temptation, don't stray into alleyways or lonely streets.'

Amy's eyes widened. 'Then you do fear an attempt at an abduction, sir?'

'Only if an opportunity were to present itself. I am certain that Louise will be watched, but once it is seen that she is never left alone such plans would be abandoned.'

'But I thought you said that Verreker was desperate?'

'He is. I don't underestimate him, but it is difficult to arrange an abduction in a crowded street. He would need help...a closed carriage...and the knowledge that he could spirit Louise away without detection.'

'You are well informed, my lord. Have you ever considered abduction yourself?' Amy gave him a teasing look.

'I have been tempted, my dear.' The Earl's eyes strayed to Perdita. 'To date I have managed to resist that temptation... Now, let us change the subject. You will attend the subscription ball?'

Perdita threw him a look of gratitude. Amy, she knew, would be alert for danger. Pray heaven she would not take her new responsibilities to extremes. She was capable of challenging Verreker herself.

Later she said as much to Rushmore, but he persuaded her to set aside her fears.

'Amy has a good head upon her shoulders,' he assured her. 'She sees the need to follow my instructions to the letter. I have pointed out that everything she does must be low-key. Louise must not become aware that we are worried about her safety…' For a few moments he was lost in thought. 'Verreker has not returned?'

'No…and it is the strangest thing, but Louise is not as crushed as I had expected. After all, she fancied herself in love with him, else she would not have agreed to the betrothal.'

'She was vulnerable,' Rushmore said slowly. 'At the time she would have fancied herself in love with anyone who showed her kindness.'

'Then you think it was merely infatuation?'

'Possibly not even that. Of course she may have believed herself to be in the grip of some grand passion…'

Perdita gave him a curious look. 'You sound as if you have no time for sentiment, my lord. Do you believe all love to be an illusion?'

Perdita had caught him unawares. He swung round to face her with an expression that made her catch her breath. His eyes had an inner glow. Then he turned away and walked over to the window, staring across the busy expanse of Laura Place as he fought to control his voice.

Then he turned and smiled at her. 'No!' he said 'I believe in love…as I'm sure you do yourself. It is not the same thing as infatuation.'

'It must be very difficult to know the difference, sir.'

'You have experienced neither feeling?'

'No…have you?'

'Not infatuation, certainly.'

'And love?'

'You ask too many questions, my dear. Gentlemen are shy in speaking their innermost thoughts. Had you not noticed?'

'Oh, I beg your pardon, my lord. I had not intended…I mean, I have no wish to pry.'

'I know that, Perdita. And I am wrong in fighting shy of your questioning. These matters should be discussed among friends.' Even so, he did not pursue the subject.

'Have you heard from your parents?' he asked.

'Mother wrote from Portsmouth before they sailed. Now I expect that we shall have a lengthy wait before the next letter.'

'You must miss them sorely.'

'We do, but Aunt Trixie has been the solution.' Perdita twinkled at him. 'Letter writing is her passion. She will have no dealings with crossings and re-crossings in the interest of economy. She is happy to pay the cost of her outpourings and of ours. We

write a little each day, with details of how we spend
our time. Then at the end of the week the letters are
sent off. I had thought that the news must be stale
by the time they reached their destination, but the
Colonel has the matter in hand.'

'Carrier pigeon?' Rushmore teased.

'Not exactly, but the Colonel has connections
with a number of naval men. It is his boast that no
service is more expeditious than that to Gibraltar
through his friends.'

Neither of them knew it, but Miss Langrishe had
been taking full advantage of this service. Since
Perdita was in her care she had felt obliged to write
to Perry and Elizabeth with her views upon the appearance of the Earl of Rushmore. As yet she had
had no reply.

Now she resolved to tell the Earl about the content of her letter.

'Was I wrong?' she asked. 'I feel as if I am *in
loco parentis* to Perdita. I thought it best to tell Perry
and Elizabeth what is happening here.'

'Nothing is happening,' Rushmore assured her
firmly.

'But that is nonsense, my dear boy. Any fool can
see that you are falling deeper in love each day.'

'Perdita does not see it, and I have done nothing
to persuade her.'

'Adam, I respect you for your honourable behaviour, but there may come a time when your feelings

overcome you. Can you wait until her parents return? Is it not best to let them know of your desire to wed Perdita?'

'I have written to them myself. Perhaps I was a little premature. Perdita has given me no encouragement—'

'Give her time!' Miss Langrishe begged. 'You have gained much ground with her. I noticed how she listened carefully when you spoke to Amy of your plans.'

'A military man is expected to be in command of strategy,' he said lightly. 'I still have far to go, ma'am.'

She nodded and did not argue the point. 'Amy will obey your wishes?' she asked.

Rushmore nodded.

'I cannot say that I like the situation, Adam. I had hoped to take the girls out shopping into Milsom Street when next they come to visit me.'

'Then you must do so, Miss Langrishe. As I explained to Amy, you cannot possibly be in danger in the centre of the town.'

Later he was to recall those words, and so did his companion. For the moment they had no idea of the perils which lay ahead.

'There is one other matter,' he said at last. 'May I ask you to undertake a commission for me?'

'Gladly, my dear boy! What do you have in mind?'

'It is Louise's birthday next week. I should like to give her some token...a brooch...a bracelet possibly. Had her father been alive he would not have let the occasion pass unnoticed.'

'You will not accompany her to the jeweller yourself?'

'No!'' For once he looked a little ill at ease. 'I would not have her think that I am trying to buy her friendship.'

Miss Langrishe shook her head. 'I shan't deny that the gift has come from you, my dear, but you misjudge Louise. Have you not noticed? She is gaining in confidence by the day. She no longer sees you as an ogre.'

'I have Thomas to thank for that, I believe.' He cocked an inquisitive eye at the old lady. 'Do you see a match there, ma'am?'

'Should you have any objection, Adam?'

'Not in the least. Louise could not do better. That young man is sound to his backbone.'

Miss Langrishe smiled. 'You must not make it too easy for them.'

'That is unlikely to happen. Thomas must soon be recalled to his duties, and I want her to have her Season before taking such an important step. She has seen nothing of the world.'

'A wise decision!' Miss Langrishe frowned. 'I wish we could be certain that Matthew Verreker has given up all hope of her.'

'So do I, but Louise is well protected now. I must return to London soon myself. The Duke will wish to see me...' He was lost in thought for several minutes.

'What is it, Adam? You are still not easy in your mind?'

'No!' he told her frankly. 'I don't trust Verreker to lose his prize without a struggle. I need to know more about him. This cannot be his first attempt to capture a wealthy wife. That in itself is not a crime, but he struck me as a confidence trickster. If only we had some evidence against him he could be given in charge and prosecuted. It would put an end to his activities.'

'But you have already made enquiries and found nothing, so you tell me.'

'He's expert at covering his tracks. I hear no word of him in Bath. That leaves London. He must seek the company of the wealthy, so possibly my men will have some news for me.'

'When will you leave?' she asked.

'Within a day or two. It won't be easy.' He gave her a rueful smile. 'I shall leave my heart behind.'

'But not for long, I fancy. We shall miss you, Adam.'

'I wonder!' Rushmore was seized with doubt. Perdita might welcome his absence with a sigh of relief. At worst she would not give him another thought.

*   *   *

He was mistaken. Rather to his surprise, the news of his imminent departure brought a chorus of protest from Amy and her cousins. Even Louise asked to know when he would return.

Perdita said nothing. Her face was in shadow, so it was difficult for him to read expression. Had she welcomed the news? He looked at her, praying that he would not see triumph in her eyes. From the first she had seen him as her enemy, though of late she had become his unwilling ally.

He joined her on the window-seat. 'Have you nothing to say to me?' he asked in a low voice.

Perdita kept her eyes fixed on her folded hands. She had been badly shaken by his decision to return to London.

'I had not thought that you would leave us at this time, my lord.' Her tone was cool. He must not guess that she wanted him to stay. 'There may still be danger to Louise.'

'I think we have done all we can, Perdita.'

She made no reply.

'Besides, I think you have forgot. I am a serving soldier, my dear. My time is not my own. The Duke gave me leave to come and see my ward, but I cannot extend my stay by much longer.'

'Of course not!' Perdita rose as if to leave him, but he caught her hand.

'Are you concerned only with Louise?' he asked. 'We have been friends, I think. I shall miss our conversation. Will you not say the same?'

Perdita was very close to tears. She dared not attempt to answer him. It was ridiculous. Why should she be upset by his departure? And why should the prospect of a future without him appear so bleak?

It was Miss Langrishe who came to her rescue. She called Perdita to her with an innocent enquiry about a proposed shopping trip.

'It is Louise's birthday soon,' she whispered. 'We are to choose a brooch or a bracelet for her from the Earl.'

'Is he unable to choose the gift himself?' Perdita snapped. Her nerves were at breaking point.

'He does not know what would please her.' Miss Langrishe wore an imperturbable expression. She had noticed the interchange between Perdita and his lordship, and knew that it had ended in a difference of opinion. Well, it would be no bad thing if Rushmore went away for a time. Perdita might then realise how much she had grown to enjoy his company.

Louise's birthday fell on the same day as the subscription ball towards the end of that week. There was no time to be lost if a suitable gift was to be chosen and engraved for her, so the following morning Perdita and Miss Langrishe set out for the jewellers.

Rushmore had not mentioned price. He would have considered it an irrelevance, so the ladies were free to make their choice from the treasure trove on offer. It did not take them long. They settled upon a slim gold bracelet of classical design, instructing that it should be engraved on the inside simply with Louise's name and the date.

They had intended to go on to visit the largest haberdasher in the town, but as they gained the street again Miss Langrishe stumbled. Perdita was quick to catch her elbow, thinking that her aunt had merely tripped. Then she heard a gasp.

'What is it?' she cried in alarm. 'Aunt Trixie, are you ill?'

'Not really, my dear. It is just a touch of gout, but the pain is severe. Shall you mind if we go back to Laura Place? I need some lace and some gloves, but at this present time I cannot think…'

'Of course we must go back. Aunt, you should have told me. Have you anything to ease the pain?'

Miss Langrishe nodded, but it was not until she was safely back at home and had taken the draught prescribed by her own doctor that she felt herself again. She even managed a chuckle.

'My chickens are come home to roost!' she admitted. 'This complaint is the result of a surfeit of good living.'

'Have you had it before?'

'Just a touch of it in a single finger. This time it has affected my right hand.'

Perdita looked down at the swollen knuckles beneath the reddened skin. 'It looks extremely painful,

Aunt. Will the draught make you sleepy? Perhaps if you were to rest?'

Miss Langrishe nodded. 'I shall feel better later in the day. Then we shall finish our shopping.'

'You must not think of it. The girls will be here this afternoon. You shall commission us to buy whatever you need.'

'I don't know, Perdita. His lordship warned of possible danger in the town.'

'But not if we stay together, and, if you wish it, Ellen shall go with us.'

'I wish you would ask Rushmore or the boys.'

Perdita laughed. 'Gentlemen hate shopping, Aunt, as well you know. Now you shall not worry about us. Bath is crowded, and we shall not stray from the main street.'

Miss Langrishe was still doubtful, but at last she gave a sleepy consent and was persuaded to retire to her bedchamber.

Released from their studies, both Amy and Louise were happy to fall in with her plan later that afternoon. Mindful of her aunt's wishes, Perdita allowed a grumpy Ellen to accompany them.

Their purchases took longer than she had expected. Both Amy and Louise were in need of new white gloves for the ball. Then they became distracted by a display of artificial flowers and gaily coloured ribbons.

Perdita called them to her. 'Help me to choose,' she begged. 'Aunt is in need of several yards of lace for trimming. It is so very expensive and I don't want to make a mistake.'

'We could change it if she doesn't like it,' Amy pointed out.

Louise was fingering the lace. 'It is truly beautiful,' she said wistfully. 'Miss Langrishe could not fail to like this cobweb pattern.'

'But it is white and she wanted black. I wonder if they have it...' Perdita called an assistant to her, and the girl went into the rear of the shop.

They were unprepared for the scene which followed. As the assistant returned she was confronted by the furious owner of the store.

'How dare you leave your post?' he shouted. 'Idling your time away and leaving customers unattended. I should dismiss you on the spot.'

Perdita looked at the shrinking girl, who grew red and white by turns. There was nothing of her. She looked badly undernourished, and clearly it was fear of losing her post which brought the first few stammered words.

'Sir, I did not mean to—'

'Silence! Get your things and go—'

'One moment, please!' Perdita was at her most imperious. 'At my request, this lady went to make enquiries about some lace for me.'

The man swung round and stared at her. Then he too went red. 'I beg your pardon, madam. I did not know.'

'And you didn't trouble to find out, did you, before behaving in this disgraceful way?'

By this time they had an interested audience, and the man was aware of it. He glared at the rest of his staff who had drawn near. Then he turned back to Perdita, containing his anger only with great difficulty. He was unaccustomed to being taken to task, especially by a chit of a girl.

Perdita saw his sneering expression and knew that it was only the presence of other customers in the shop which kept him from insulting her.

'May we not discuss this matter in private, miss?' he asked.

'No, we may not. You made your comments in public. They shall be answered in public. Allow me to inform you that I do not expect to be treated to such a display of ill temper when I bring my custom to a shop.'

'It was not directed at you,' he muttered.

'Kindly go away,' Perdita told him coldly. 'This young lady will serve me. She, at least, is courteous.'

He had no option but to slink away, but all the pleasure had vanished from their shopping expedition. Perdita was tempted to cancel all her purchases and stalk out of the shop. It was concern for the assistant which caused her to change her mind. In the event she bought far more than she had intended.

'Will you be all right?' she asked the girl.

'Yes, miss, thanks to you.'

'Come then, girls!' With her head held high, Perdita swept out into the street.

Beside her, Ellen sniffed. 'There you go again!' she muttered. 'Behaving like a duchess.'

Perdita stopped and turned to face her. 'And was I wrong?' she demanded. To her astonishment the old woman smiled.

'Not this time, my pet. That poor critter was ready to faint clean away when she was dismissed.'

'I hope we have prevented that, Ellen.' Perdita looked ahead to see that Amy and Louise had stopped. To her alarm they seemed to have been accosted by a young man. There was something familiar about him.

Perdita hurried towards the little group. Then she realised with a sigh of relief that the young man had served her in the haberdasher's store on a previous occasion. He was the son of the owner.

'Is something wrong?' she asked.

'I don't think so, madam, but we are missing a length of lace. It may have fallen into this young lady's reticule by mistake...' His eyes rested on Louise.

'Oh, do you think so?' Louise was untroubled. 'I did leave my reticule open on the counter. I was not paying attention, I'm afraid.'

'Then, Miss Bryant, if I might ask you to look?'

Louise was perfectly willing to do so. The packet of lace was there, and she handed it over with a puzzled look.

'And if I might have your direction, miss?'

'You have our direction,' Perdita said coolly. 'We live in Laura Place. Our packages are to be sent there.'

It was a curious incident, but no member of the party gave it another thought. It was not until later that day that Perdita found herself wondering how the young man knew Louise by name. It did not matter. The incident might have happened to anyone. She did not trouble to mention it, either to Rushmore or Miss Langrishe.

They had other news to occupy their minds. Thomas had been recalled to London, and his brothers had decided to accompany him.

Their imminent departure cast a cloud over preparations for the ball, although they were not to leave beforehand.

And Rushmore too was soon to leave them, Perdita thought in despair. He must have convinced himself that the danger to Louise had passed. Verreker had not been seen in Bath, and he had neither written to Louise nor been to see her. Possibly he was pursuing some other wealthy prospect.

Perdita took herself to task. Her fears for Louise's safety had been groundless. Why, then, was she still a prey to doubt? It was dispiriting and she vowed to pull herself together. Her lowered spirits might be due to the fact that her cousins were to leave them short of dancing partners and young company. As for Rushmore...well...it must be a relief to be spared that sardonic presence for the next few months. In her heart she knew that she was being unfair. The Earl did not sneer at her, nor was he mocking or bitter. Sardonic was not a description which might be applied to him.

It was not until the evening of the ball that she realised the truth. That night she was looking at her best in a gown of creamy spider gauze over a matching satin slip. Her only ornament was a string of river pearls.

Rushmore had engaged her for the waltz. This time she had no reservations so she gave herself to the pleasure of the dance. Her enjoyment communicated itself to him.

'Happy?' he asked quietly.

'Of course, my lord!' Perdita gave him a brilliant smile.

'I'm glad of it! In these last few days I have found you a little...er...preoccupied.'

'I know. It's just that...well...this resolution of Louise's problem seems too easy. Do you not agree?'

'I've been surprised,' he admitted. 'But you have noticed nothing untoward?'

For a moment Perdita considered telling him of the curious incident when the lace was found in Louise's reticule, but she dismissed the notion. That could have nothing to do with Matthew Verreker. She shook her head.

'Then put these worries out of your mind. You are in famous looks tonight, my dear. I am the envy of every man in the room.'

Perdita blushed. 'Sir, I wish that you would not…'

He gave her a tender look. 'You must be the only woman in the world who does not care to be complimented upon her appearance.'

'It is not the most important thing,' she told him in a low voice. 'I can think of worthier reasons for a compliment.'

'So can I!' Suddenly the Earl forgot his promise to himself. After all, he had written to Perdita's father, stating his intentions, and Miss Langrishe knew of his feelings for her. He was doing nothing underhand. Before he left for London he must tell Perdita of his love.

'Do you not find it warm in here?' he asked. 'Let us find a place where we can talk.'

'But this waltz is not over,' she protested.

'We can waltz again later,' he told her firmly. 'This is important, my dear.'

Unsuspecting, she allowed him to lead her to a sofa in the adjoining anteroom. He took a seat beside her, but he was silent for so long that she was seized with dread.

'What is it?' she cried. 'Are you keeping something from me? Does this concern Louise?'

Rushmore took both her hands in his. 'I have been keeping something from you, but it does not concern Louise. Can you not guess, Perdita?'

She drew her hands away. 'You are speaking in riddles, sir. I cannot read your mind.'

'How I wish that I could read yours. Tell me, shall you miss me when I leave for London?'

To her horror, Perdita felt her colour rising. She tried to smile. 'You are certain to be missed, my lord. When you and my cousins leave, we shall be bereft of half of our company.'

'Don't torment me, my dear one. That was not what I asked you.'

Perdita tried to rise, but he slipped his arm about her waist, and held her to him.

'Don't be afraid,' he whispered, 'I love you. I want you to become my wife... I have written to your father asking his permission to address you.'

Perdita was too shocked to answer him. His offer had been totally unexpected and it startled her.

'You have written to my father?' she asked in disbelief. 'How dare you, sir? Are my own wishes not to be considered?'

'They are of the first importance, but your parents must be consulted, as you know.'

'Kindly remove your arm,' she said stiffly. 'You said once that I planned to become a Countess. Let me assure you that nothing is further from my mind.'

Rushmore released her at once. 'So nothing I have done or said since that unfortunate evening has changed your opinion of me?'

'I won't lie to you, my lord. I was wrong in thinking of you as I did. We have been allies, you and I, but only in regard to Louise. You have been kind to her...but that does not make us friends.'

'I see! You have not learned to trust me?'

'I have, but I will not be your wife.'

'Won't you reconsider? You might offer me some hope. I can wait, Perdita. Only say that you will think about my offer.'

'Sir, it would be useless,' she told him firmly. 'I have no wish to wed you, and that must be an end of it.'

Rushmore dropped his head in his hands, but at that moment another couple entered the room. Their curious look brought Perdita to her feet.'

'Please take me back to my aunt,' she said in a low voice. 'We are giving rise to speculation.'

On their return to the ballroom Rushmore surrendered her to her cousin Henry. Then he took a seat beside Miss Langrishe.

'Well, my boy? You look as if Napoleon has escaped.'

'I've ruined any chance I might have had, ma'am. I hadn't meant to speak so soon, but tonight I couldn't hide my feelings…'

'So Perdita has refused you?'

'Yes, she offers me no hope. She will not even think about my offer.'

'You moved too fast. She is still so young, my dear.'

'In some ways…I agree…but not in others. Sometimes she surprises me.'

Miss Langrishe smiled to herself. Perdita had not planned it so, but it would do the Earl of Rushmore no harm to be forced to struggle for her affections.

'Go away!' she advised. 'When you return, Perdita may have changed her mind.'

Rushmore shook his head, convinced that he had lost his only love, but Miss Langrishe had her own beliefs confirmed.

For the next few days Perdita was subdued. Rushmore's offer had come as a surprise and must, of course, be refused, but she could not be easy in her mind. Had she been unkind? The look on his face returned to haunt her. His lordship had looked stricken to the heart. How unworthy it had been to remind him of the casual remark he'd made at Almack's. After all, he had offered her his heart and she could not doubt his sincerity. At last she told her great-aunt.

'Don't worry about it, Perdita!' that lady advised. 'After all, gentlemen cannot always have their way. You did not wish to marry him, and you told him so. That is fair dealing, so it seems to me.'

'I suppose so,' Perdita said reluctantly. 'It is just that...well...I might have been more tactful, but he caught me unawares.'

'The Earl is a man grown. This is a disappointment for him, but in my experience gentlemen do not suffer overlong. All the fond mamas in London will regard him as a catch. He won't be deprived of female company. When next we hear of him it is likely to be in the society pages of the *Gazette* with news of his betrothal.'

For some strange reason this did nothing to reassure Perdita. As the days went by she found herself wondering how the Earl was spending his time. He did not care for Almack's, that she knew, but there were other diversions, such as military reviews and balloon ascents, to say nothing of the daily parade of beauties in Rotten Row.

He was welcome to them, of course. It was just that she seemed unable to rid herself of the habit of looking for his tall figure everywhere she went and searching other faces for that same quizzical smile. There seemed to be a curious flatness in the conversation of those about her. She had grown to enjoy the Earl's challenging banter, but even that could not account for the fact she felt so lost without him.

'I knew it!' Amy announced. 'It has turned out as I thought it would. You are in love with Rushmore!'

'Don't be stupid, Amy! What on earth gave you that ridiculous idea?'

'Only the fact that you've been mooning about like a love-sick calf ever since he went away. I tell you, Dita, I long to find a place where *no one* is in love. Between Louise, who quotes Thomas and his perfections until I tire of hearing her, and you, who have not a word to say to anyone, I find the whole thing overrated, especially for a bystander.'

'I'm sorry! I have been finding Bath a little dull of late. It was much more interesting when the boys were here.'

'But not, of course, the Earl of Rushmore?' Amy's tone was teasing, but then she saw Perdita's face crumple. 'Oh, love, I didn't mean to distress you. I thought he must have spoken before he went to London.'

'He did,' Perdita whispered in a broken voice. 'But I refused him…'

'Well, that is not so very dreadful,' her sister soothed. 'He will come back. I can't think why you did it, though. You deal so very well together, and he is besotted with you.'

'He won't come back. I told him that he must not hope. I was unkind, and now I am regretting it. It was just that… Oh, Amy, I did not know just how much I cared for him. I wouldn't admit it, even to myself. Now I have lost him and I don't know how to bear it.' A little sob escaped her lips.

'Cheer up!' Amy advised. 'Don't forget that the Earl is a military man. Even now he is planning his campaign to win you.'

'Or to win someone else.' Perdita would not be comforted.

'Don't be such a watering-pot!' Amy's reply was scathing. 'You are suffering from boredom as much as anything. Let us ask Aunt if we may hire the horses for another ride into the country. The grooms could escort us. We must do something or we shall fall into melancholy.'

'Would that be wise? We promised the Earl that we would stay in town.'

'The men could be armed in case of an attack upon Louise. *That* would provide a diversion for you.' Amy's eyes were sparkling.

'It isn't one that I should welcome. I believe that we should stay in Bath for the present. We know that Louise is safe here.'

Perdita was wrong, but she did not know it at the time.

Chapter Eleven

Miss Langrishe was not an early riser, so Perdita was startled to receive an urgent summons to her room whilst she was still abed the following morning.

Throwing on her robe, Perdita hurried along the corridor, expecting to hear that her aunt's attack of gout was worse.

'Are you ill, ma'am?' she asked anxiously. 'Must I send for the physician?' The old lady's pallor was alarming.

Miss Langrishe shook her head. 'He can do nothing in this instance.' With a shaking hand she held out a letter to Perdita. 'This was delivered at first light.'

The letter was addressed to Louise.

'You have not opened it?'

'No, my dear. Clearly it is a private correspondence. Oh dear, it must be from that dreadful creature, Verreker!'

'It could be from his lordship.' Perdita scrutinised the writing. 'It is not a woman's hand.'

'Adam would have sent a letter by the post and franked it in the usual way. It would have borne his seal. He would not have sent some urchin to the door to hand it in.'

'Then Thomas?'

'Your cousins have returned to London, as you know. And Thomas would not write without asking permission first. Oh, my dear, I hoped that we had heard the last of Verreker.'

'It could be a letter of farewell,' Perdita comforted. 'He may have given up all hope of Louise. Possibly he has found another target.'

'I hope you may be right.' Miss Langrishe was unconvinced. 'I shall not rest until I know the contents.'

'Louise will show it to you, Aunt. She knows that she must do so. The Earl was most insistent on that point.' Perdita handed back the letter, disturbed by the older woman's agitation. 'The girls will be here this afternoon, so do try not to worry. Louise has changed, you know. She is no longer quite so gullible, and she does not speak of Verreker as she was used to do.'

'You are right, my dear. She does not go about as if she is wearing the willow, but who knows what that creature has in mind?'

'It may not even be from him.' Perdita managed a brief smile.

'Who else would write to her? It *is* from him, I know it.'

'Even so, you do not need to fear for her. She will do nothing foolish. Adam…his lordship…has persuaded her that she must behave as her late father would have wished.'

'How sensible you are, my dear! I am a foolish old woman, seeing danger behind every bush.' The colour was returning to her cheeks. 'Even so, I shan't be easy in my mind until we know the contents of this letter.' She pushed the offending missive away from her.

Perdita left her then, but her thoughts were troubled. Her words of encouragement had sounded unconvincing even to her own ears. Verreker was not the man to write a noble letter of farewell. He must have some other plan in mind.

She was unprepared for the magnitude of the shock which awaited her that afternoon.

'I have no secrets from you, ma'am.' Louise blushed a little when Miss Langrishe handed the letter to her. 'Please open it yourself.'

'No, no, my dear, though I must admit that we are mighty curious. The letter did not come by the post, you see. Now, pray don't keep us in suspense…'

She waited expectantly as Louise tore the missive open and scanned the contents. Then she heard a gasp. Louise was swaying and would have fallen if Amy had not slipped an arm about her waist.

'What is it, my dear? Oh, do sit down! Perdita, will you ring the bell? Bates must bring some brandy—'

'No, please! I am all right. It is just that I did not expect…' With a trembling hand Louise held the letter out to the old lady.

It was brief, but Miss Langrishe paled as she read it aloud. 'Your friends and acquaintances will wish to know how you came by the piece of lace stolen in Bath some days ago. This unpleasantness may be easily avoided, for a certain consideration. You may signal your compliance by visiting the cathedral to-morrow at eleven…alone. Failure to do so will result in charges being laid with the magistrates. There were several witnesses to this theft.'

Miss Langrishe was as white as the ribbons which trimmed her gown. 'What is all this, Louise?' she asked. 'I have heard nothing of it.'

'It didn't seem important enough to tell you, ma'am. It was all a mistake. We bought your lace, and then the man came running after us in the street. He said some lace was missing.'

Amy looked confused. She was still trying to grasp the enormity of what was being suggested.

'But that could have nothing to do with you,' Miss Langrishe protested.

'He found the missing lace in Louise's reticule,' Perdita told her slowly. 'We wondered why he should ask for Louise's name and her direction. Then we thought nothing more about it.' Anger threatened to consume her. 'This is nothing more than a cheap attempt at blackmail. Verreker must be behind it.'

'No! You are mistaken!' Louise went red and white by turns. 'He was not there. How could he know of the missing lace?'

'I don't know, but it all sounds very smoky to me. An assignation in the cathedral? He mentions consideration, but he must know that you are much too young to be in control of your own fortune.'

'But he has threatened to lay charges with the magistrates.' Louise was close to tears. 'I must keep the appointment, if only to enquire—'

'You will do no such thing,' Perdita told her sternly. 'Nothing can be proved against you. You had best ignore the letter. Throw it in the fire!'

'No! I believe that we should keep it.' Miss Langrishe was insistent on the point. 'How I wish that Rushmore had not left us. He would know exactly what to do.'

'I will go back to the shop,' Perdita told her. 'There is some mystery here. Why ask for a secret meeting? The owner might have come to see you here.'

She thought she knew the answer. The letter bore all the signs of Verreker's hand.

At eleven in the morning the cathedral would be deserted. There were several entrances. What could be easier than to throw a veil over Louise's head and hurry her away by a side door?

'I will go with you,' Miss Langrishe said at once. Her gout was no better, but she was determined to accompany Perdita.

It came as no surprise to Perdita to discover that the owner and his son were absent from the shop in Milsom Street that day. An obsequious male assistant announced that they had been summoned to the funeral of a distant relative.

'I don't believe it for a moment,' Perdita fumed. 'They must be in league with Verreker.'

'Is that likely, Perdita? I detest the man as much as you do yourself, but such a notion seems far-fetched.'

'Perhaps! But once he has Louise and her fortune he could offer them a share of it.'

'They have not reckoned with Adam.'

'No, Aunt, but he isn't here. How clever they were to wait until he'd left for London! They may hope to spirit her away tomorrow. By the time he found them it would be too late.'

It was her aunt's turn to offer comfort. 'That won't happen, my dear. Louise must not keep the appointment.'

'He may lay charges purely out of spite—'

'Let him do so. My name is good enough, I think, to counter any accusations.'

* * *

Miss Langrishe was mistaken. It was an apologetic officer of the law who arrived at Laura Place the following week, but he could not be persuaded from his duty.

'My apologies, ma'am!' The young man was all deference. 'But I am afraid there is no help for it. The young lady must be taken in charge.'

'I wish to see the magistrate,' Miss Langrishe announced in awful tones. 'He is well known to me.'

'As you wish, madam.' The young man was prepared to wait. The charge was clear, and he doubted if this formidable lady would away the decision of his superior. He was right.

'Beatrice, I am very sorry,' that gentleman informed his friend. 'The law is clear in this respect. Miss Bryant must be taken into custody. Naturally, she will not be lodged in the common gaol. The gaol-keeper will take her into his own house.'

'Frederick, she is a child. This is a trumped-up charge.'

'She will be given an opportunity to defend herself, but the law is clear. This is a serious accusation. If proved as Grand Larceny, the penalty could be death.'

'For a scrap of lace?' The old lady's face was ashen.

'It depends on the value. If the value is more than one shilling, which, in this case, it is, the law is severe.'

Miss Langrishe seemed to be breathing with difficulty and her companions became alarmed.

Perdita addressed the magistrate. 'This has come as a grave shock to my aunt. As you see, she is not well. As for me, I cannot believe that you would allow an innocent girl to suffer such a fate.'

'Miss Wentworth, I have the highest regard for your aunt, but the law is clear. Miss Bryant must appear at Taunton Assizes to answer the charges laid against her. I can assure you that, in practice, the sentence is rarely death if the accused is found guilty.'

'What then?'

'A reprieve means transportation to Botany Bay for a period of fourteen years.'

'Merciful indeed!' Perdita faced the guardian of the law with flashing eyes. She was about to say more when a low moan from her aunt brought her to that lady's side.

'Don't worry, Aunt!' she comforted. 'The Earl will know what to do.'

Miss Langrishe was beyond comfort. 'He isn't here,' she whispered. 'Frederick, must you take Louise in charge at once? May she not stay here? I will guarantee that she does not leave Bath.'

'I'm sorry, my dear, but that is not possible. It would set a bad precedent. We should be charged at once with operating one law for the rich and another for the poor.'

'You do that anyway!' Perdita told him rudely.

'Not if we can help it, Miss Wentworth. We are not all corrupt.'

Perdita was ashamed of her outburst. Clearly, the magistrate was uncomfortable in exercising his duty, but he would not be dissuaded. She thought him an honest man.

'Where will you take her?' she asked.

'To Ilchester, Miss.'

'To the Somerset County Gaol?' Perdita was horrified. 'My dear, sir, you would not expose her to those conditions…the company of thieves and murderers and women who are no better than they should be?'

'Of course not!' The magistrate was growing impatient. 'She will be lodged in the gaol-keeper's own house, as I have explained. Now, if you will forgive me, we are wasting time. If the young lady will collect such things as she may require?'

He looked at Louise, but she made no move to follow his instructions. Perdita doubted if she had heard him. Frozen to the spot in shock, she seemed incapable of movement.

Perdita turned to Amy. 'Pack her things,' she whispered. 'For the moment we can do nothing more to help her.'

'I could go with her,' Amy offered. 'With the two of us together, it might be easier.'

This suggestion was turned down by the magistrate, though he tried to soften the blow. 'Naturally, you may come to see your friend as often as you wish,' he announced. Then he turned to Miss Langrishe. 'Beatrice, Miss Bryant will suffer little more than to be deprived of the company of her friends for the time being.'

'Rubbish!' Perdita told him shortly. 'Bath is a positive hive of gossip. How long do you suppose it will be before this sorry tale gets out? Louise is innocent, but tongues will wag. What will this do to her reputation? If nothing is proved against her, there will still be those who believe that there is no smoke without fire.'

'That cannot be helped,' the magistrate said firmly. He was no coward, but he offered a private prayer of thanks that his prisoner was the meek Miss Bryant, rather than this fiery little beauty who refused to be overawed by the power of his office.

Perdita was furious, but anger gave way to pity as a mute Louise was led away. Then she pulled herself together.

'The first thing to do is to write to Rushmore,' she cried as the sound of the carriage wheels died away. 'Aunt, will you do it, or shall I?'

Miss Langrishe seemed to have aged by a full ten years. 'I would do it gladly,' she whispered. 'But I cannot use my hands…' She looked at her red and swollen fingers.

'Then I will write.' Perdita sat down at the escritoire. Her note was brief and pithy, setting out the facts, but it was only when it had been dispatched to London that she felt easier in her mind.

'I hope that the Earl will come at once, don't you?' The normally ebullient Amy was subdued. 'Louise looked as though she was being led to execution.'

'Oh, don't say that!' Perdita shuddered. 'She will be safe enough until the date of the Assizes. I can't believe all this. What can Verreker hope to gain?'

'You think he is behind it?'

'Nothing is more certain,' Perdita told her. 'Perhaps he hopes that the Earl will buy him off if he agrees to drop the charges.'

'But, Dita, we know they are not true. We were there. We saw what happened. If we speak out in court?'

'We may not be believed. We are Louise's friends. We must be expected to support her.'

'But we would not lie on oath,' Amy said stoutly.

'It has been known. Oh, Amy, this is all so horrible! I cannot wait for Rushmore to arrive.'

Perdita tried to curb her impatience for the next few days, but there was no word from London, nor did the Earl appear in Bath.

'Where is he?' she cried in anguish. 'I won't believe that he has abandoned us.'

'He could be away from London,' Amy suggested. 'He'll get your letter when he returns. Meantime, shall we go to see Louise?'

'Oh, yes!' Perdita seized on the suggestion with relief. 'It will ease Aunt Trixie's mind if we are able to assure her that Louise is well. Possibly, she may come with us.'

That hope was quickly dashed. The attack of gout had flared alarmingly, and now it was impossible for Miss Langrishe to set her feet to the ground.

Her spirit was undaunted. 'Take what you can to make Louise comfortable,' she said. 'Chef shall provide some hampers of food. Perdita, you must ask the child if there is anything she needs...anything at all.' Her eyes grew sad. 'I feel that I have failed sadly in caring for her. Who could have imagined that it would come to this?'

'No one, Aunt, and you must not blame yourself.' Perdita frowned. 'How could you have guarded against such wickedness?' She sighed to herself in desperation. Where was Rushmore? Surely there had been time enough for him to return to Bath.

It was with heavy hearts that she and Amy set off for Ilchester. Miss Langrishe had not opposed the plan, though she had insisted that they took Ellen with them.

'Thank heavens that Father insisted that we kept our own carriage here in Bath,' Perdita told her aunt. 'I thought it an extravagance at the time, believing that we should have no use for it, but he said that the horses might as well be stabled here as in London.'

Miss Langrishe looked troubled. 'I won't forbid you to go to Ilchester, my dears, but I shall not rest until you are safely back again. You will have no gentlemen with you for protection.'

'We shall have our own driver and the groom. Besides, we shall have Ellen too. She would make a formidable foe should anyone attempt to offer us an insult.'

'And no one offers insult to Perdita, Aunt Trixie. She has a way of looking down her nose which is guaranteed to freeze the daffodils.' Amy's cheerful attempt at a joke succeeded in lightening the atmosphere, though Miss Langrishe was careful to point out that daffodils were not to be found in early autumn.

'She'll find something to freeze,' Amy assured her. 'Pray don't worry, Aunt. We shall not be gone for many hours. It is not as if we were planning a stay at any of the inns along our route. We shall stop only to bait the horses.'

'That's true…and if you carry provisions with you there will be no need for you to dine among strangers.' Miss Langrishe rang the bell to summon her chef. 'We must make up a basket for Louise. Heaven knows what the sheriff is giving her to eat.' She began to discuss a lengthy list.

'Dear Lord…Aunt is sending enough food to cover the fourteen years of transportation,' Amy whispered to her sister.

'That remark is in the worst possible taste.' Perdita frowned. 'It has given Aunt Trixie something to do. She longs to help Louise, but for the moment there is nothing we can suggest, other than to make her imprisonment more comfortable. Aunt feels that she has failed in her care of Louise.'

'She did try,' Amy pointed out reasonably. 'At one time I felt that she might strike the magistrate when he refused to leave Louise with us. For heaven's sake, did he expect that we should spirit her away?'

Perdita grew thoughtful. 'It might have been the answer. We could have taken her to London, to Aunt Prudence...'

'With the officers of the law hot upon our heels?'

'You are right. It would not have served. In fact, it would have made matters worse. Perhaps it's as well that the opportunity did not arise. It's just that I can't bear to think of Louise in that hateful place. She must be in despair, deprived of her friends and with such charges hanging over her.'

'We must take what we can.' Ever practical, Amy turned to the matter in hand. 'Must I fetch her things from the Academy? She will need a change of clothing. I'll think of some story for Miss Bedlington.'

'Will you do that, love? Perhaps if you mentioned that she wasn't well?'

Amy tried, but the scandal was common knowledge in Bath. Miss Bedlington saw it as a personal affront. The news that one of her pupils was held in a common gaol threatened to ruin her reputation

and deprive her of her livelihood. She made no secret of her disgust.

Amy lost her temper. 'May I remind you that in
this country a person is presumed to be innocent
until they are proved guilty,' she cried. 'Are you
judge and jury?'

'Hold your tongue, miss! Such impertinence! It
does not surprise me. You and your sister are a disgrace to the name of womanhood.'

'And you are its ornament? My sister is worth a
dozen such as you!'

'Get out, you little viper! You may take your own
possessions as well as those of your thieving friend.
If you return I'll have the law on you.'

'That won't be necessary, ma'am. If I never see
you again it will be too soon.' With this parting shot
Amy stalked away.

'That seems to be the end of my schooldays,' she
told Perdita. 'Must I tell Aunt Trixie?'

'You can't avoid it. Oh, Amy, did you have to
fly at Miss Bedlington? Aunt has enough to worry
about at present.'

Amy chuckled. 'Do I hear the pot calling the ket-
tle black? She insulted you, and she called Louise
a thief. I couldn't let it pass. You'd have done the
same yourself.'

'I suppose so. Well, we had best get it over with.
Let us hope that Aunt won't be too distressed.'

Miss Langrishe surprised them. She listened with relish to the story of Amy's confrontation with Miss Bedlington.

'Quite right!' she said at last. 'I never liked the woman. She's such a crawling, encroaching creature. Let her keep her precious respectability. She'll get no more recommendations from me.' Then she beamed at Amy. 'No harm done, I think,' she announced. 'The loss of a few weeks' schooling cannot harm you.'

'Aunt, you are a treasure!' Amy kissed the papery cheek. Then she looked at the list beside the old woman's hand, and she began to laugh. 'We are taking just the one coach to Ilchester,' she teased. 'I fear the horses will have a struggle to get us there.'

She was rewarded with an answering smile. 'Louise may have need of all these things, my dear. Far better to be on the generous side than to skimp our help.'

She was proved right. The girls made an early start on the following day and the journey passed without incident.

Perdita was unusually silent, and Amy guessed that she was dreading what they might find.

'Cheer up!' she comforted. 'We may be pleasantly surprised. Louise may be quite comfortable.'

Her optimism proved to be ill-founded. On arrival at the gaol they were directed to a dark and dismal dwelling built inside the prison walls.

'This can't be right!' Perdita cried in dismay. 'The sheriff is said to have six children. This house is much too small to house a family.'

Amy signalled to the groom, telling him to knock at the door and ask directions. When he returned he was accompanied by a stout individual who was clearly a stranger to the benefits of soap and water. The man opened the carriage door with a flourish.

'Welcome, ladies! You are the Misses Wentworth, I believe. Pray step down. Miss Bryant will be glad to see you.'

'You are the sheriff?' Perdita asked in disbelief.

'At your service, ma'am!' The man bowed, releasing noxious odours from his unwashed clothing. Combined with the powerful smell of gin, this was enough to send Perdita searching for her handkerchief. On the pretext of blowing her nose, she held it to her face.

Amy was made of sterner stuff. She jumped down with a smile, and offered the man her hand. The look she gave Perdita was filled with meaning. The sheriff must be treated with respect if he were to be persuaded to become their ally.

Perdita gave an imperceptible nod. Then she ordered the unloading of the coach. The number of large hampers brought a smile to the sheriff's face, and to the faces of the round-eyed children who poured out of the open doorway. Their numbers seemed to be endless.

Perdita's heart sank. The children seemed to be healthy enough, but there were so many of them. What must conditions be like indoors? She was soon to find out.

Pressed by the sheriff to step inside his home, Perdita felt a tug at her sleeve.

'Lord, Miss Perdita, I don't like this. Must you go inside? Miss Bryant could come out to you. I don't doubt that the place is full of lice, and the Lord knows what else besides.'

'Hush, Ellen! You need not come indoors, but Amy and I must not offend the sheriff. Wait here! We shall not come to harm.'

She spoke with a confidence she was far from feeling, but she stepped indoors to be greeted by a fat and blowsy woman with a new baby in her arms. Her clothing was stiff with grease and beer stains, but she smiled happily at her visitors, apparently oblivious of the dirty conditions in which she lived and the appalling noise. Dogs and cats roamed freely about her kitchen, and Perdita shuddered as she saw the state of her pot cloths. Possibly they had once been white. Now they were almost black.

'Miss Bryant is in her room,' the woman told them. 'Will you go up, ladies? It's small, but it is all we have to offer her.'

Perdita and Amy left the chaos behind and climbed the stairs. There were but two bedrooms, and they averted their eyes from the squalor visible through the open door of the chamber on their right. The other door was closed.

Perdita tapped gently, but there was no reply. Cautiously, she tried the doorknob and peered into the room.

Louise was sitting on a trestle bed, apparently in a stupor.

'Oh, my dear!' Perdita hurried towards her and gathered the girl into her arms. 'We had no idea! Can this possibly be worse than the gaol itself?''

Recognition dawned slowly in Louise's eyes. Then the tears came and she wept for several minutes against Perdita's shoulder.

'Forgive me!' she said at last. 'I meant to be brave, you know, but I cannot sleep for the noise and I am always hungry.'

'You cannot mean that they are starving you?' Amy was indignant.

'They give me what they can, but they are very poor and there are many mouths to feed. The sheriff's wife means well, but...but...I cannot eat what she prepares.'

'Why is that? Is she a poor cook?'

'I don't know. I haven't touched the food since I saw her licking her cooking utensils clean...'

Perdita closed her eyes in horror. Then she pulled herself together. 'There will be no need for you to do so. Aunt has sent supplies...enough to feed you and the sheriff's family for several weeks.'

Amy leaned out of the window and called to the groom to fetch a hamper to her. 'You must eat,' she insisted. 'You will need all your strength if we are to get through this.'

Louise gave her a pitiful look. 'I had hoped to see my guardian,' she whispered. 'Has he washed his hands of me?'

'Of course not!' Perdita was firm in her denial. 'We wrote to him at once, but he must be out of London. He has estates in Cheshire and in Derbyshire, you know.'

'But when will he be back?' Louise was fast losing her composure. 'The Taunton Assizes are not for some weeks. Must I stay here until then? I'd rather die—'

'No, you wouldn't!' Amy said firmly. 'Is the common gaol worse than this? Perhaps you could be moved?'

'Oh, never say so! You can have no idea. I can see the prisoners from my window…wretched creatures, most of them. They fight for food. It goes to those who can afford it. The others beg through the outer bars from passers-by.'

Amy and Perdita stared at her in silence.

'Then there are the women. I did not know such creatures existed. They sell themselves quite openly for favours and for money.' Louise's eyes grew sad. 'I cannot say that I blame them. How else can they survive?' She gazed at her friends in despair.

It was then that Perdita came to a decision. She would go to London herself. There, at least, she might learn something of Rushmore's whereabouts. She was convinced that her letter hadn't reached him.

If that plan failed she would seek the help of Thomas's parents, her uncle Sebastian and aunt Prudence. This would be a last resort. Thomas had inherited a fiery temper. Feeling as he did about Louise, Perdita would not put it past him to attempt to rescue her by main force. She knew how quickly gossip travelled in polite society. Now she prayed that the news had not yet reached him.

Once her decision was made she was impatient to put her plan into action, but she kept her thoughts to herself on the journey back to Bath.

Ellen looked at her averted face. 'Now, Miss Perdita, don't take on!' she begged. 'You have done all you can, giving that sheriff creature extra money and all that food.'

'And we promised him more if he could make Louise more comfortable,' Amy added.

'I know it, but what can he do? The place is a shambles.'

'It could be worse,' Amy told her quietly. 'Louise understands that they are not cruel people. They mean to be kind.'

'But she is suffering so. It is hard indeed when she is innocent.'

'Take heart, Perdita. For all we know, his lordship may have returned to Bath. He may be with
Aunt Trixie even now. He will know what to do.'

'Oh, yes!' Perdita cried with feeling. 'All else
aside, he must be told what has happened.'

That fond hope was to be disappointed. Only
Miss Langrishe awaited their return. She had not
seen the Earl.

'How is Louise?' she asked at once. 'Tell me how
you found her! Is she well in health?'

'I think so, but she is very low in spirits.'

'Well, that is to be expected, my dears. She has
her own room?'

'Yes, Aunt.' Perdita saw no point in explaining
that it was little larger than a cupboard. Nor did she
feel the need to mention the noise or the filthy conditions in the sheriff's home. 'Your gift of food was
welcomed,' she added. 'The sheriff and his wife are
very poor.'

'You left money with them? It is the best incen-
tive to take good care of a prisoner.'

Perdita hesitated, but Amy suffered no such inhibitions. 'Perdita gave them all we had,' she admitted.

Miss Langrishe reached into her reticule and
found a key. 'Unlock my desk, Perdita, and bring
me one of the leather bags you find there.'

Perdita was about to hand it to her, but Miss Langrishe waved the bag aside. 'Keep it!' she said.

'You will find enough in there to pay the gaoler when you go to Ilchester again.'

Perdita guessed that the bag was filled with golden guineas. 'It is too much,' she protested. 'Aunt, it will worry me to be in charge of so much money.'

'Then lock a part of it in your room. Won't you let me salve my conscience in this small way? At this present time I feel distraught…I did not tell you earlier, as I had no wish to distress you, but this has happened before.'

Both girls stared at her. 'You mean that another innocent person was accused?' Perdita exclaimed.

'It happened some years ago, to an elderly friend of mine. She too was accused of shoplifting here in Bath, and in the same way.'

'The theft of lace? Why should that be, I wonder?'

'Lace is expensive, Amy, and it is soft enough to be slipped quite easily into a lady's reticule.'

'Then this is just a copy of that crime?'

'In a different shop, but clearly the story has not been forgotten.'

'What happened to your friend?'

'She was found to be innocent, but the months in custody had a sad effect upon her health. It took her years to recover.' Miss Langrishe wiped away a tear.

Perdita took her hand. 'My dear Aunt, don't distress yourself. Louise is young. She will not suffer as an older person might. Let me write to the Earl again. My letter can't have reached him.'

'Will you do that, my dear?' It was with a heavy heart that Miss Langrishe sought her bed that night. She had grown sadly aged in the past few days.

'This isn't helping Aunt Trixie.' Amy commented. 'I wish we could do more to help her. Another letter to the Earl must take some time to reach him.'

'I don't intend to wait,' Perdita said decisively. 'Amy, I must go to London.'

Amy brightened. 'Yes, that is the answer. I'll go with you. Aunt must see the sense of it.'

'She is not to know in advance,' Perdita warned. 'She will either forbid it out of hand. Or insist that I take Ellen.'

'But if we are together?'

'I want you to stay here.' She stilled Amy's protest with a look. 'Have you not noticed? Aunt's gout is getting worse. Do stay with her, I beg of you. You can explain…'

'But what do you intend to do?'

'I'll try to find the Earl. He lives in Berkeley Square, so I understand.'

'But he may not be there. You can't roam the streets of London unattended.'

'I won't do so. If all else fails, I shall go to Uncle Sebastian. He and Aunt Prudence will help us.'

'But there is Thomas,' Amy objected. 'He can be a firebrand. He won't hesitate to go to Ilchester and confront the sheriff. He'll get himself arrested.'

'I know that, goose, but Thomas may not be there. There was some talk of his regiment being sent to Manchester.'

'I hope you are right, but what will you do if you can't find Rushmore and our aunt and uncle have left for Cheshire, as they do at the end of each Season?'

'Don't be such a pessimist! I'll come back to Bath, of course.' Perdita smiled. 'At least I won't be short of money.'

'No, but Aunt would have a fit it she knew that you were putting it to such use.'

'That can't be helped. It is in a good cause, and I'm sure that the Earl will repay her.' At the thought of taking action Perdita felt as if a great burden had been lifted from her shoulders. She looked at her sister's downcast face. 'I wish that you could come with me, love, but you must handle matters here. We don't know what may transpire in these next few days. Verreker may reappear and some further attempt be made at blackmail.'

'Oh, do you think so?' Amy's eyes began to sparkle. 'Let them try! They will have me to reckon with. When will you go, Perdita?'

'As soon as may be. Tomorrow we must walk to the offices of the mail coach. I'll buy a ticket and find out the times of departure. Now remember, no one must suspect.'

'Ellen will be the greatest danger,' Amy said slowly. 'She knows us both so well.'

'Then she must be diverted. I'll send her to Aunt when we go out. Doubtless she will have a sovereign remedy for gout.'

The plan worked as Perdita hoped it would, and by noon on the following day she returned to Laura Place with a ticket for the London Mail Coach hidden in her reticule.

Chapter Twelve

Perdita left the house before first light on the following day, easing open her aunt's front door with the utmost care.

She had taken the precaution of wearing her oldest cloak and bonnet, and as she hurried through the darkened streets she attracted no attention.

Now she blessed her aunt's decision to live in Laura Place. It was but a short distant to the courtyard of the inn where the Mail Coach awaited passengers. Perdita was the first to arrive, so she chose to take a corner seat facing the front of the coach. The air was chill and she shivered as she awaited her fellow-travellers.

Hopefully, none of them would recognise her. A journey by public conveyance was not the most favoured method of transport for Miss Langrishe's friends and acquaintances. Even so, she felt relieved when all the seats were taken by strangers.

It was still dark when the driver climbed aboard and gave his horses the office. They moved out slowly over the cobble-stones until they reached the outskirts of the city, where he urged them to greater speed.

Perdita was happy to discover that none of her companions felt disposed to talk at such an early hour. A young woman travelling alone must be sure to arouse unwelcome curiousity, and she had no wish to answer questions, however well meant. The driver already viewed her with suspicion. She had no luggage worthy of the name, and carried only a soft bag which held her night attire. She guessed correctly that he had no wish to be pursued by an irate father or brother, intent on removing the young lady from the coach.

Perdita shrugged. That would not happen. With luck it would be many hours before her absence was discovered, and far too late for her aunt to send anyone in pursuit.

She tried to suppress a pang of conscience. Would Miss Langrishe realise that she was acting for the best? The thought of adding to her aunt's worries was distressing, but the need to find the Earl of Rushmore must outweigh all other considerations.

She fell into a reverie, remembering that well-known smile and the twinkle in the dark eyes when he was amused. She sighed inwardly. His lordship would find little to amuse him in her news. He had promised to make enquiries about the loathsome Matthew Verreker. If only he had managed to discover some information which might be laid with the authorities, so that the creature might be prosecuted. With any luck the man could be transported to Australia or some such place, where he would be incapable of doing further harm.

Lost in thought, she was unaware that the growing light of day had revealed the faces of all the other occupants of the carriage. At last she realised that she was under scrutiny from a burly man who sat immediately opposite. He leaned forward to address the woman beside her.

'Do you care to travel forward, ma'am?' he asked. 'You may take my seat if you prefer to ride with your back to the horses.'

The woman favoured him with a long look. Then she transferred her gaze to Perdita. 'No, thank you, sir,' she said with an ironic smile. 'I am quite comfortable in this seat.'

The man nodded, but he continued to stare at Perdita. The pretty little chit was quite an armful, and she seemed to have no male protector with her. His curiosity aroused, he began to wonder about her. Was she seeking a position in London? There might be some opportunity for him there. On the other hand, her manner and her clothing suggested that she was a lady. Perhaps she was running away. He could still offer to be of service to her.

Perdita stirred uncomfortably. He was making her nervous. She was tempted to give him a downing stare. Instead she closed her eyes and leaned back in her seat, wishing that she had chosen a bonnet with a larger brim, which would have hidden more of her face.

Thank heavens the woman beside her had refused to give up her seat. How hateful it would have been to have the man in close proximity, doubtless with his legs and arms pressed against her own.

Her suspicions were confirmed at the first halt. She was the last to descend from the coach, and she found him waiting beside the steps.

He bowed. 'May I offer you some refreshment against the morning chill, miss?'

Before she could reply, the older woman stepped in front of her. 'This young lady is with me,' she said without preamble. 'She does not speak to strangers.'

The man backed away with a muttered apology, and as he walked off Perdita was amused to see that the backs of his ears were red with embarrassment.

The woman shared her enjoyment. 'There are some as never misses a chance to make a nuisance of themselves,' she announced.

'I have to thank you, ma'am. I must hope he will take you at your word. He was making me uncomfortable.'

'Ignore him, miss. He won't come near you again, else he'll feel the weight of my arm.' The woman chuckled as she hefted a well-filled basket as if it were a feather. 'I've seen the likes of him before, especially on this run. Sometimes I think they makes the journey just to pick up solitary maids. Shall you be wanting refreshment, my dear?'

'No, thank you, but—'

'I know. You'll be wanting to make yourself comfortable. Come along with me. I'll show you where to go.'

When they returned to board the coach, Perdita was glad to find that her tormentor had exchanged his seat inside the coach for one upon the roof.

'There now, that's better!' her rescuer announced. 'The cold wind will chill his ardour.' She laughed heartily.

Perdita thanked her once again. 'Do you make this journey often, ma'am?' she asked.

'As often as I can, miss. I visit my son in London town. 'Tis hard to live so far away when I have grandchildren waiting to see their Nan, but we are farming folk. 'Tis difficult to leave the work.'

'How old are the children and what are their names?' Perdita's question was enough to set her companion off upon what was clearly a favourite topic. In the next few hours she learned all there was to know about the little family in London.

'There now, I'm rattling on as usual,' the woman said at last. 'It's my besetting sin. Your ears must be ringing with my chatter.'

'It's a pleasure to hear of such a happy family,' Perdita said with conviction. 'I miss my parents so much. My father is a naval man, and they are away at sea.'

'So you are alone?'

'Oh, no, I have an aunt in Bath, and my sister is staying with her.' For a moment Perdita wondered if she were saying too much, but instinct told her that the farmer's wife was to be trusted. 'I also have relatives in London.'

'You are going to them?'

'Well, yes...but not at first, perhaps.' Perdita spoke with a confidence she was far from feeling, and after a brief glance at her face, her companion changed the subject, and lifted the heavy basket onto her knee.

'We had best eat now,' she said. 'Will you join me, miss?'

Perdita hesitated. 'Ma'am, I would not rob you of your vittles.'

This brought a chuckle from her companion. 'Bless you, there's enough to feed an army,' she announced. 'I make nothing of going short.'

When she opened her basket, Perdita realised that her friend had not exaggerated. Home-made crusty bread nestled alongside a fat cheese. A cold cooked chicken helped to fill the basket, as did part of a ham, and hard-boiled eggs were tucked into any available space. The woman handed Perdita a snowy napkin.

'Eat hearty!' she advised. 'There's nothing like good food for keeping up your strength.'

Perdita needed no further encouragement. The sight of the food made her realise that she was very hungry. Not a bite had passed her lips since dinner on the previous day. She removed her gloves, picked up the napkin and set about a piece of chicken with relish.

'I should have thought of this myself,' she admitted. 'I suppose I imagined that we'd be fed at the wayside inns where we stop to bait the horses.'

Her companion sniffed. 'There's no telling what you'd get. Sometimes the food is poor and pricey with it. Then, if the coach is running late, the driver don't give you time to eat.' She cut a generous slice of ham and handed it to Perdita on a slice of bread.

'You are very kind, ma'am. After all, you do not know me. My name is Perdita Wentworth. May I know yours?'

'I'm Bessie Griffin, miss. Aside from all else, my dear, it would not do for you to eat alone in a public dining-room. You've seen what can happen...' She jerked her head upwards to remind Perdita of the passenger outside.

Perdita looked away. 'You must think it strange for me to be travelling on my own,' she said at last. 'Believe me, the matter is urgent, else I should not have done so. I *must* find Rushmore.'

'Now, miss, don't cross your bridges before you come to them. For all you know, you may be in the gentleman's company before the day is out.'

'Oh, I *do* hope so,' Perdita said with feeling. 'He will make everything right again, I know it.'

Something in her tone brought the older woman's eyes back to her face and she smiled to herself. She knew the signs of a woman in love. She hoped with all her heart that the gentleman felt the same.

Their arrival in London was greeted with sighs of relief from all the occupants of the coach. The outside passengers were cold and windswept, whilst those inside were suffering from stiff limbs after their lengthy journey.

Perdita helped her companion down the steps. Then she stepped aside as the woman was greeted by a stocky young man who was the living image of his mother.

'No, miss, don't you wander off now!' Mrs Griffin extricated herself from her son's embrace. 'You'll be needing a hackney cab. Be quick and see to it, Ned.'

Ned was quick to obey his mother's wishes, but Mrs Griffin was not satisfied. 'Where to?' she asked Perdita.

The address brought a smile of satisfaction to the jarvey's lips. Only the quality lived in Berkeley Square, and it appeared that the young lady was to be his only passenger. His plans to charge her at least double the usual fare were soon destroyed.

'How much?' Mrs Griffin demanded.

The martial light in her eyes caused him to revise his estimate, but she brushed it aside with scorn.

'Highway robbery!' she announced. 'Ned, go and find another cab—'

'Nay, ma'am, don't take up a man so fast. Seeing that the young lady is alone, I'll make a special price for her.'

He tried to hold out for his price, but he was no match for Mrs Griffin and found himself agreeing to a fare which he considered an insult. Damn these country bumpkins. Sometimes their cunning could outwit his own.

Ned handed Perdita into the cab.

'Now don't you go paying this thief a penny more,' Mrs Griffin advised. 'I know his face. I'll have the law on him.'

Perdita was strongly tempted to giggle at the dejected appearance of her driver. How Amy would have enjoyed meeting Mrs Griffin. She leaned from the window of the cab, holding out her hand.

'May I call to see you, ma'am, when I return to Bath?'

'No call for that, Miss Wentworth. Still and all, I shall be glad to see you. You'll find us at Bluebell Farm.'

She waited until Perdita's cab had disappeared from sight. Then she took her son's arm and walked away.

Suddenly Perdita's confidence deserted her. She felt very much alone. Suppose his lordship should be away from home? It was with a sigh of relief that she saw the knocker still on the door. Rushmore must be in residence.

She paid off her dispirited driver, walked up the steps, and lifted the knocker. The door opened almost at once, and she was confronted by a stately individual in full livery.

'Yes, madam? May I help you?' the man asked politely.

Perdita summoned up her courage. 'I must see the Earl of Rushmore,' she announced. 'Is he at home?'

'His Lordship dines out this evening, ma'am. If you would care to leave a message…?'

'No…I must see him at once. Pray give me his direction. Is he at White's or Watier's?'

Gorton, the butler, knew better that to continue this discussion in the open street. 'Will you not step inside, ma'am? I should like to be of service to you.'

'Well, you can be!' Perdita told him bluntly. 'I'll find his lordship if you will tell me where he is to dine.'

Gorton led the young lady through into the salon, pausing to order ratafia from one of his underlings.

'With respect, miss, I should not advise it. The gentlemen's clubs are mostly to be found in St James's Street.'

'And so?' Perdita's chin went up.

Gorton looked hard at her. His ability to assess the position of his fellow human beings was legendary. He had no difficulty in coming to the conclusion that this was a Lady of Quality. Perdita was also a beauty. It was not his place to speculate upon her relationship with his master, although he had heard some talk of an orphaned ward. Perhaps this was the girl.

'Ma'am, the area is not used by members of the female sex,' he explained.

'I can't help that,' Perdita cried. 'Oh, don't you understand? I have come from Bath to see His Lordship, and this matter will not wait.' She rose to her feet. 'Will you call me a cab, if you please?'

It was clear to Gorton that her likely destination was St James's Street. If this was indeed the Earl of Rushmore's ward, he shuddered to think of his master's reaction if he allowed the young lady to destroy her reputation.

'That would mean an unnecessary delay,' he said carefully. 'No lady may gain admittance to the clubs. They may not even agree to take a message for you. Allow me to send out footmen, madam. That will be the quickest way.'

Perdita tried to hide her impatience, but a moment's reflection convinced her that he was right. She nodded, and he disappeared to give his orders.

When he returned he was bearing a tray. 'May I take your cloak, miss—?'

'I am Perdita Wentworth. Yes, thank you!' Perdita looked at the clock, and was shocked to find that it was almost midnight.

The difficulties of her present situation struck her for the first time. She had made no plans beyond finding Rushmore, but unless his lordship left at once for Bath she would have no place to lay her head that night unless she took a chance upon finding her aunt and uncle still in residence at their London home.

Now she bemoaned her own stupidity. She should have asked the jarvey to drive her past their house on the way to Berkeley Square. A glance at the knocker would have told her if they were at home.

Gorton looked at her troubled face and poured her a glass of ratafia. The young lady appeared to be exhausted. She sipped gratefully at the wine, but refused his offer of food.

'I am too tired to eat,' she told him simply. 'Will...will they be long, do you suppose?'

'It's hard to tell, miss, though I've warned them of the need for haste.' Gorton poked at the fire, stirring the logs to flame. 'Perhaps if you closed your eyes, Miss Wentworth, and tried to rest, the time would pass more quickly.'

He knew now who she was. The elder Miss Wentworth was a famous beauty, and extremely well connected. Most certainly she was not his master's ward, but she was a lady of some spirit. This was no time for speculation, but he could not help wondering at the reason for her errand. To present herself at Berkeley Square, alone, and at this late hour, meant trouble, he was sure of it.

Should he have sent for Rushmore? It might have been wiser to have denied his master, but Gorton knew determination when he saw it. This young lady was perfectly capable of sitting upon the doorstep until the Earl returned.

He looked down at her and saw that she was growing sleepy. The wine and the warmth of the fire had done their work. He waited until the sound of her regular breathing told him that she had drifted off. Then he slipped into the hall, prepared for a lengthy wait before the Earl returned.

It was minutes only before he heard the sound of running feet.

'Where is she?' Rushmore burst into the hall, all his famous composure vanished.

'Miss Wentworth is in the small salon, my lord. I believe she has fallen asleep.'

Rushmore brushed past him though he slowed his pace. He opened the door to the salon gently, and walked towards Perdita on silent feet.

She was sleeping like a child, long lashes hiding the lustrous eyes and resting softly upon her cheeks. As Rushmore looked at her, a wave of tenderness engulfed him. He took an unresisting hand and raised it to his lips.

She stirred then and looked up at him. Her smile made his heart turn over.

'Oh, Adam, I am so *very* glad to see you.' She held out her hands to him with a gesture that could not be mistaken.

'My darling!' Rushmore gathered her into his arms. 'Let me hold you to my heart! What is it, my dear one? The men assured me that not a moment was to be lost...'

Perdita rested her head against his shoulder. 'Didn't you get my letter? I had to come. I could not think what else to do,' she said. 'Oh, my dear, I don't know how to tell you.'

'No, I didn't receive any letter! Tell me what's wrong!'

Perdita responded to the urgency of his tone. Best to speak and be done with it. 'Louise has been arrested,' she said.

Perdita sensed his shock before he spoke. 'Tell me what happened,' he suggested quietly.

She kept the tale short. It was only when she spoke of the conditions under which Louise was living that her voice faltered. 'We cannot leave her there,' she said in broken tones. 'Oh, Adam, I am sure that Verreker is behind this wicked charge. Have you learned nothing of him?'

'I have!' Rushmore's face might have been carved in stone. 'He is known by other names. In Tunbridge Wells he attempted to elope with an heiress. There he was known as Martin Vincent. He left a trail in London too. This time his target was a wealthy widow. She knew him as Michael Vardy.'

'And it is the same man? How can you be sure?'

'The description is exact. And the Bow Street Runners are no fools. They tell me that in planning

an alias a man will almost always use the same in-
itials.'

'And is there evidence against him...enough to
prosecute?'

'Sadly, there is not. That is why he was able to
appear in Bath.'

'But what can we do? There must be something...?'

'I don't know, my dear one, but we shall beat
him, rest assured.' Rushmore rested his cheek upon
Perdita's hair. 'Your father has written to me, my
love. I am permitted to address you, but only after
he has learned of your wishes. I must confess that
my hopes were dashed by that condition.'

'Really, my lord?' Perdita gave him a demure
look. 'I wrote to my parents quite recently.'

Rushmore held her away from him, searching her
face for confirmation of his dearest wishes. 'Then
am I allowed to hope...?' he said in disbelief.

Perdita was no dissembler. 'Yes,' she told him
shyly. 'Oh, Adam, I love you with all my heart. I
did not know it until you went away. Then I thought
I'd lost you.' Her lips quivered.

'Never in this life!' His glowing expression banished the last trace of doubt. He tilted her face to
his and kissed her with a gentleness that stole her
heart away. She clung to him, not wanting the kiss
to end, but at last he put her from him with a rueful
smile.

'Have mercy on me!' he begged. 'I am not made of stone.'

Perdita did not stir. She felt so safe within the shelter of his arms.

'I must send you to your bed,' he said at last.

'Oh, I am to stay with you?' The prospect filled her with delight, but his lordship knew where his duty lay.

'I planned to send you to your aunt and uncle, Perdita, but Gorton tells me that they have already left the city, and I would not have you return to Bath tonight. It would be too exhausting. We shall make an early start tomorrow.'

Perdita nestled closer to his breast. 'I never want to leave you again, Adam. These past few weeks have been a torment.'

His lordship kissed her again, this time with rising passion. She was happy to respond to the urgency of his caress, but he checked himself once more. Her innocence was touching. Clearly she did not realise that he was on the verge of losing all self-control.

'You would tempt a saint,' he told her thickly. He rose and rang the bell. 'My housekeeper will take care of you, my darling. Sleep well. You are safe beneath this roof.'

Perdita clung tightly to his hand. 'I shall always feel safe with you,' she whispered. 'Oh, Adam, is it wrong to feel so happy when Louise is in such trouble? You *will* save her, won't you?'

'All will be well, I promise.' Rushmore dropped the lightest kisses upon her brow and delivered her into the care of the fresh-faced woman who was smiling at both of them.

Alerted by Gorton, Mrs Derby now shared his belief that the young lady in her master's arms would soon become the next Countess of Rushmore. She had known the Earl since boyhood and, like the rest of his staff, she had been troubled by the recent change in his demeanour.

Always courteous to those who served him, he had seemed preoccupied and almost unaware of his surroundings. Now she knew the reason for it. A glance at his face told her that he was his old self again, merry and cheerful, but with an added glow.

'He's radiant,' she told Gorton later. 'That's the word I'd use…but there's something else upon his mind.'

Gorton nodded, but there was no time for a discussion. His master had ordered the carriage and his fastest team to be ready at first light. There was packing to be done, and a groom to be sent ahead along the route to Bath. Of recent weeks Rushmore had kept fresh teams in readiness at certain coaching inns on the way and Gorton had wondered at it at the time. Keeping teams along the Great North Road was one thing, but Bath? It now seemed likely that the Earl had been expecting trouble.

* * *

Perdita had fallen into a dreamless sleep, though it seemed only minutes before she was awakened by two smiling maids. One bore her breakfast tray, and the other carried her clothing, freshly washed and ironed.

'Is his lordship waiting?' she asked anxiously.

'You are not to hurry, ma'am. My master hopes that you will make a good breakfast before you leave.'

Perdita sipped obediently at her chocolate, and buttered two fresh rolls which she spread with raspberry jam and ate with relish. The bowl of fruit looked tempting, but she was eager to dress and hurry to her love again.

He was waiting in the hall below. He came towards her and took her hands in his, kissing them each in turn.

'Ready?' he asked.

Perdita nodded shyly, aware that she was under benevolent scrutiny from a surprisingly large number of servants. Everyone in the Earl's household seemed to have found some task to perform in the hall that morning.

Rushmore too was aware of it, but he made no comment as he led Perdita to the waiting coach.

'Shall you require the services of a maid, my love?' he asked anxiously. 'One of the girls is ready if you wish it.'

Perdita looked up at him and her heart was in her eyes. 'No!' she whispered. 'I'd rather be alone with you.' Then she gave him a mischievous smile. 'I got here on my own, you know.'

Rushmore winced. 'So you did, my darling. The thought of that journey makes me shudder. I trust that you were not offered insult.'

She did not mention the man who had approached her. 'I was befriended by a farmer's wife,' she told him. 'She couldn't have been kinder.'

Rushmore settled her comfortably within the crook of his arm as the driver gave his team the office.

She was silent for so long that he grew worried.

'What is it?' he asked. 'Are you regretting your promise to me?'

'Oh, no, Adam!' She gave him a look of perfect trust. 'It's just that…well…I can't believe that I'm not dreaming. Am I truly to become your wife?'

Rushmore chuckled. 'I must hope so, otherwise you are in a most compromising position for a well-bred young lady.'

'Oh, you mean that I should not have stayed with you last night?'

'You did not stay with *me* my darling. You stayed in my home, guarded by a bevy of servants and an extremely moral housekeeper. I was referring to our present situation.'

Perdita snuggled closer to his breast. 'It can't be wrong to feel so happy,' she announced. 'When did you first know…I mean, when did you change your mind about me?'

'It took some time,' he told her in solemn tones. 'At times I was in fear of my life...those dagger looks were enough to fell me to the ground.'

'Well, I thought I hated you, you see. I thought you bored and quite puffed up with pride.'

'And the temptation to prick the bubble was too much for you? You were quite right, my love. I must have been insufferable.'

'You were!' She could not resist the opportunity to tease him. 'I despised you so! I thought it unworthy of a gentleman to come to see my parents and insist that I be punished.'

'I did not do so, dearest.'

'Oh, I know that now, but at the time I did not know about Louise.'

Perdita's face grew sad. 'We should have taken better care of her,' she whispered. 'I wish that we had never entered that wretched shop.'

'You could not have known what was planned. Try not to worry so, Perdita. Louise is in no immediate danger.'

'Oh, how can you say so? The conditions at the gaoler's house are enough to kill her.'

'No, they aren't, uncomfortable though they may be. Louise is young and healthy. I doubt if she will take much harm as long as there is no infection in the house. I feared abduction more. If the Duke had not required my presence here in London I should not have left Bath.'

'And now?'

'I have an extended furlough. I shall not leave you again.'

Perdita lifted her face to his. 'I am so glad,' she whispered.

He kissed her then, gently but insistently. It was a kiss which banished all her worries. With Adam she would have no fears for the future. She responded warmly, pledging her love to him beyond all doubt.

He held her close. 'Now you shall tell me, my darling. When did you know you loved me? I had given up almost all hope, you know... You seemed determined never to forgive me.'

'I have been so foolish.' Perdita blushed and hid her face against his coat. 'More than anything, my pride was injured. I soon knew that I was wrong, but I would not admit it. I am sadly stubborn, I fear.'

'A shocking character, indeed!' The Earl laughed and dropped a kiss upon her hair. 'I thank heavens for your stubborn nature. You don't give up, my dearest, do you? How many girls, I wonder, would have travelled unprotected on the Mail Coach?'

'Amy would!' Perdita assured him. 'In fact, she cannot wait to do so.'

'I believe you! But then, the ladies of the Wentworth family are quite out of the common way, are they not? I consider myself the luckiest man in the world to have captured the heart of one of them.'

Perdita lifted her face to his. 'You sound like Papa,' she teased. 'He always blesses the day he met my mother. He loves her dearly, as you must have noticed.'

'Who could not?' he answered gallantly. 'Your mother is a most remarkable woman. Her elder daughter is likely to follow in her footsteps.'

'Thank you!' she said gravely. 'You could not have paid me a more handsome compliment.'

'You have not welcomed any others from me. You surprised me from the first, you know. I think it was your total lack of vanity about your beauty—'

'But I told you, Adam. My appearance is an accident of nature, and not of my own making.'

'That's true, but many lovely women think it enough to absolve them from the need to use their minds.'

Perdita laughed. 'I've seen it for myself, but it must be very dull to sit about looking decorative, and without an idea in one's head.'

'You won't suffer that fate!'

'Perhaps not, but I wish I had some ideas as to how we can help Louise. Is there nothing we can do?'

'There is a great deal, Perdita. I believe that Verreker is still in Bath.'

'In hiding?'

'I think so. He must be behind this plot to injure her. It cannot be coincidence that she has been accused so quickly after she refused all idea of an elopement.'

'It was a wicked plan,' Perdita cried.

'But not original. Your aunt will remember the first occasion. That time no charges were laid against the perpetrators.'

'So Verreker must have felt that he too would be immune from prosecution if he were caught?'

'Possibly. He is a desperate man. He must have thought it worth his while to attempt blackmail.'

'But if he is in Bath it must be possible to find him, and what of the owners of the shop? They must be party to this plot?'

'There must be a strong connection, and we shall find it, never fear. I took some action after you retired last evening.'

'What did you do?'

'I sent for the experts, Perdita. The Bow Street Runners are already on their way to Bath. They will keep a close watch on the shopkeeper. Verreker will be anxious to know how matters are proceeding. He cannot fail to contact his friends before too long.'

'I still don't understand,' Perdita told him. 'What benefit can it be to him to lay these charges against Louise and have her taken into custody? It can only be a longing for revenge.'

'Not necessarily. He knows that she has powerful friends. Will they allow her to stand trial? He must believe that they will go to any lengths to avoid that slur upon her character.'

'But if she is found to be innocent, as she must surely be, he can gain nothing.'

'Mud sticks, my dear. Verreker will know it well enough. There are always those who claim that there is no smoke without fire. The damage to Louise's reputation will be immense if she appears in court.' Rushmore's face grew grim.

'And if you find him, Adam? What then?' Perdita looked up at the Earl and caught her breath. This was a man she did not know. At that moment he looked capable of murder.

She gave a little cry of anguish. 'You will take care, my darling? You must not kill him. He isn't worth it.'

'I shall not kill him, but before I have finished with him, he may wish that I had done so. Now, let us leave this unpleasant subject for the moment. We are coming to the inn where we shall change our team.'

'So soon?' she asked in wonder. 'The time has gone so quickly.'

Rushmore smiled down at her. 'We have covered many miles, my love. Come, you must be in need of some refreshment!' He helped her down as the landlord came bustling out to greet him. Bowing low, he led the Earl indoors.

Perdita's face showed her amusement as she was shown into a private parlour.

'Something amuses you, Perdita?' His lordship was puzzled.

'I was thinking of the contrast between this and my previous journey. It is all so…so comfortable.'

He caught her to him, then. 'That will always be my dearest wish, my dear. I promise to guard you from all harm. Now, try to eat. We have a long journey ahead of us.'

Perdita needed no further encouragement. As she looked at the table laden with viands she realised that she was very hungry. There were pies and pasties of every kind, flanking a massive joint of cold roast beef and a succulent ham.

Rushmore poured her a glass of wine.

'Is it not a little early?' she demurred.

'Drink it!' he said firmly. 'It will help you sleep. You have had a trying time, my love. Miss Langrishe is sure to be distressed if you arrive in Bath looking exhausted.' He waited until her glass was empty. Then he refilled it for her.

'I shall be tipsy,' she warned.

'Then I shall have you in my power,' he teased, twirling an imaginary moustache. 'Who knows, the evil Earl may have his way with you...?'

Perdita blushed, but she was laughing, much to his satisfaction. The look of strain had vanished from her face, and he was glad of it. She had borne enough in these past few days.

When they resumed their journey, he held her in his arms until she fell asleep. Then he looked down tenderly at the lovely flower-face. She would not suffer further if it lay in his power to prevent it.

This was not the time to tell her that he expected swift developments. Verreker needed money urgently. To obtain it he must act quickly. His most likely ploy would be to offer to drop the charges against Louise in return for a handsome settlement. It was fortunate that Perdita could not, at this moment, see the expression upon the Earl's face.

I'll see him in hell first! he vowed silently.

Chapter Thirteen

⁂

They arrived at Laura Place to find the family in a state of acute anxiety. Perdita had been dreading a confrontation with her aunt, but Miss Langrishe was too relieved to see her safely returned to Bath than to do more than to give her a reproachful look.

She took Perdita in her arms. 'Wilful child! Could you not have trusted me with your plans? Ellen or one of the grooms might have travelled with you—'

'Forgive me, ma'am. I had no wish to worry you, but it seemed to me that I must go to find the Earl without delay.'

'You were right!' Miss Langrishe turned to Rushmore. 'This is a pretty coil, is it not? What are we to do? I feel that I have failed Louise in every way.'

'Ma'am, that is not so, believe me!' His lordship looked grave. 'Louise may be living under wretched conditions, but at least she is safe. My fear was that she might be abducted. You took care to see that it did not happen.'

'We never left her alone,' Amy said quickly. 'But we did not expect this accusation. If you could but see her in the gaoler's house, you would not be so content.' She turned away to hide her tears.

'You think me content? Amy, you do me less than justice! I shall not rest until the charge is dropped.'

'But, Adam, what can we do? Perdita will have told you that she and Amy tried to see the owner of the shop, but he was nowhere to be found.'

'He cannot stay away for ever. The Runners are here in Bath. They will find him, and Verreker too.'

But in the event it was Perdita who saw Verreker first. As she and Amy crossed the Pulteney Bridge on the following morning, he strolled towards them, doffing his hat politely. When he made as if to pass them, Perdita stepped in front of him.

'You?' she cried in disbelief. 'I wonder that you dare to show your face in Bath.'

'And why should I not do so, Miss Wentworth? This is still a free country, I believe.'

'It should not be so for you. You should be behind bars—'

'Like your friend Miss Bryant? A sad business, that! I was taken in by her. It had not occurred to me that such a girl would take to thieving.'

Amy stepped towards him with an arm upraised, but Perdita held her back. 'No!'' she said firmly.

'This criminal will get his just deserts when the Earl of Rushmore catches up with him.'

'Ah, yes, the noble Earl! Such a warlike gentleman! Will you pass on a message from me, Miss Wentworth? If the Earl should offer me violence in any way, I'll have him charged with common assault.'

'You cur!' Perdita could contain herself no longer. 'Any man worthy of his salt would have found employment instead of preying on defenceless women.'

'Are you accusing me? That would leave you open to a charge of slander, my dear. You should take care to curb your tongue. After all, you have no shred of proof. I was deeply shocked to hear that your friend had been taken in charge.'

'Liar!' Amy hissed. 'You are behind this plot!'

'Miss Amy, I will make allowances for your youth, and your affection for your friend, but really I cannot allow you to make such statements without contradiction. What possible connection could I have with this haberdasher's store? I am not in the habit of buying lace and ribbons either for myself or my friends. You are quite mistaken, but may I give you ladies a word of advice?'

He waited, and smiled when he received no answer from either of the girls.

'You may not welcome it,' he continued. 'But there is a simple answer to the problem. In these cases I understand that a charge is often dropped if suitable recompense is offered.'

Perdita gave him a look of cool disdain. 'I thought it must come to this,' she said. 'We are now at the hub of it, are we not? Let me assure you, Mr Verreker, we shall not buy you off. You will not receive one penny for this attempt at blackmail.'

'Then, ma'am, though I can only refute these hysterical and unfounded accusations, I fear that your friend must stand her trial. Such a pity! It will quite destroy her reputation in Polite Society.' Verreker gave them an ironic smile. 'That, of course, must be the happiest outcome. If she is found guilty I doubt that she will be hanged, but I wonder how she will enjoy life as a convicted felon in Australia…' He brushed past them, and strolled unhurriedly across the bridge.

'I could kill him!' Amy was trembling with rage. 'I'd like to stab him through the heart, though I doubt if I could find it. Oh, Perdita, what are we to do?'

'Adam will know,' Perdita told her quietly. 'Don't worry! Verreker will not best him!'

'You seem very sure of that, but love has made you blind. You heard what Verreker said. He knows how to use the law. I'd hoped that Rushmore could force him into a confession with the use of a horsewhip, if necessary.'

'Adam won't do that, though he was tempted. To lay himself open to a charge of assault could serve no useful purpose.'

'What then?'

'He feels that we must not frighten away our quarry. Up to now Verreker has had the luck of the devil on his side. It cannot last. Sooner or later he will make a mistake and then we shall have him.'

'But what of Louise? We have no time to lose. It is but weeks to the Assizes. She must be out of her mind with fear at the thought of standing in the dock like a common felon.'

'Adam has gone to see the magistrate,' Perdita comforted. 'He may have better news for us.'

Amy shot a sharp look at her sister. 'Something has happened between you two, I think. I saw it at once when you returned last night. In spite of all, you both have a certain look…'

Perdita smiled. 'How quick you are!'

'Lord, it would be obvious to a babe in arms! Have you accepted him?'

'Yes. He knows now that I love him. Oh, Amy, I have no right to feel so happy in the midst of all our troubles.'

'I don't see why not,' Amy said stoutly. 'Thank heavens that we have something to celebrate at this awful time.'

'We cannot celebrate just yet, but you are happy for me?'

'Of course!' Shaken though she was by the encounter with Matthew Verreker, Amy managed a
teasing grin. 'What a pair you are! You will deal
together famously, though I expect that battle will
be joined at frequent intervals. Never mind! It will
remind his lordship of his fight against Napoleon.'

'It won't be in the least like that,' Perdita said
with dignity. 'We shall be a sober married couple.'

Amy laughed aloud. 'I'll believe that when I see
it. Oh, Dita, are you sure? You hated him so much
at first.'

'I was a fool! It was not love that blinded me,
but my own stupid pride. I am such a stiff-necked
creature. I refused to see what was under my nose.
Adam must be a saint. He loves me in spite of all
my faults.'

Amy laughed again. 'He does not strike me as a
saintly creature, which is probably as well. You
could not live without a challenge, sister dear.'

'But you do like him, don't you? You forgave
him long before I did myself.'

'I discovered that there was nothing to forgive.
We misjudged him, but I believe that he loved you
from the first moment he laid eyes on you.'

Perdita's eyes were shining. 'He told me that
himself. Oh, Amy, I'm the luckiest person in the
world. I can't believe that I'm to be his wife.'

'Have you told Aunt Trixie?'

'No, of course not. I wanted you to be the first to know, but we planned to keep our love secret until Louise is freed.'

'Then you must not go about looking starry-eyed,' Amy scolded. Then she smiled. 'Your news will come as no surprise to Aunt Trixie. She foretold this very outcome whilst you were in London.'

Perdita had the grace to blush. 'I haven't been very clever,' she admitted. 'I did not know that I had advertised my feelings.'

'Only to those who know and love you, Dita.'

'Thank heavens for that. Come, Amy, let us hurry back to Laura Place. Adam must have returned by now. He may have news for us.'

This was so, but the news was not encouraging. As Adam had expected, his rank availed him nothing in pleading Louise's cause. The magistrate had made it clear, if not in so many words, that in England no one was above the law.

'Then she must stand trial?' Miss Langrishe had aged visibly in the last few weeks. Her gout was worse, and now she could not move without pain. 'It seems so wicked that she must be humiliated in this way to answer a trumped-up charge.'

'It may not come to that,' Adam said quietly. 'Verreker is being watched. My men have found him here in Bath.'

'We spoke to him this morning,' Perdita said softly. 'He was crossing the Pulteney Bridge.'

Miss Langrishe gasped. 'And what had he to say to you? I wonder that he dared to show his face in public.'

'He is quite untroubled, Aunt. He denies all knowledge of any plot, claiming that he does not know the owners of the shop. He did suggest, however, that it might be as well for Louise's friends to pay what he termed ''compensation''.'

Miss Langrishe grimaced. 'I have been wondering... Adam, do you think perhaps it might be as well—?'

'Out of the question, ma'am!' he told her firmly. 'Pray do not give up hope that we shall come about. There is still time.'

'I hope you may be right, but if anything should go wrong? The child would not survive a voyage to Australia, penned in the hold of some prison ship with those who are treated as cattle.'

'Oh, Adam, you would pay before you let that happen to her, would you not?' Amy pleaded.

Adam took Perdita's hand. 'Am I to believe that there is only one among you who has faith in me?' he said.

Amy and Miss Langrishe were quick to reassure him, but they still had questions.

'I want to believe you, Adam,' the older woman said. 'But, if this case should come to trial, how is Louise to prove her innocence?'

Adam frowned. 'I'll admit that it won't be easy,' he said quietly. 'She may not give evidence on her own behalf, nor may her friends give evidence for her.'

'How unfair!' Perdita was incensed 'What of her counsel, then?'

'He, too, may not address the jury on her behalf.'

'And this is English justice?' Perdita was pale with anger.

'He is allowed to examine and cross-examine witnesses.'

'I see.' Perdita lost her temper then. 'I wonder that you can be so sanguine, my lord. It seems to me that Louise is to be condemned unheard.'

'Not so, my dear!' Rushmore took Perdita's hand in his. 'There have been developments.' He reached into the pocket of his coat. 'This letter was delivered to me this morning.'

'What is it?' Miss Langrishe eyed the missive as if it were some loathsome reptile. 'Not more bad news, I hope?'

'Not at all.' Adam unfolded the paper. 'The letter is anonymous, of course, but it contains some interesting information. Apparently the three plotters are disappointed that no effort has been made to buy them off. Each would like to propose a compromise, but they are afraid of the other two.'

'But what does this mean?' Perdita cried. 'It cannot help Louise.'

'It is the first glimmer of hope,' Adam assured her. 'I have never believed in honour among thieves.

When these men are taken, each will attempt to save his own skin by revealing details of the plot.'

'But you will need evidence against them,' Perdita cried in despair. 'As yet we have nothing.'

'Don't give up hope, my love!' Oblivious of his companions, the Earl dropped a kiss upon her brow. 'This news is encouraging, believe me!'

Miss Langrishe recalled him to a sense of decorum. 'My dear Adam, you forget yourself!' she accused. 'That is, unless you have offered for Perdita.'

Adam did not hesitate. 'You knew of my intentions, ma'am. Perdita's father gave me permission to address her. Now I am happy to tell you that she has agreed to become my wife.'

'Oh, my dears! What joyful news! Perdita, come and kiss me! I wish you both happy, indeed I do, but bless me, there can be no doubting it. You are well matched and must have years of loving companionship ahead of you.' Suddenly, Miss Langrishe looked more her old self. The colour returned to her cheeks and her worn expression vanished.

Perdita was blushing furiously. 'Aunt Trixie, you don't seem surprised,' she whispered.

For the first time in weeks Miss Langrishe laughed. 'Your secret must have been obvious to a blind man,' she teased. 'The symptoms were all there, my dear, though it took you some time to recognise them for yourself.'

Perdita clung tightly to his lordship's hand. 'I didn't think it possible to feel so much in love. It is quite wonderful...' When she looked at Adam her heart was in her eyes. 'But, Aunt, we have agreed that this is not the time to celebrate our betrothal. We shall wait until Louise is cleared of this monstrous charge.'

'I hope that may be soon.' Amy began to pace about the room. 'How can she clear her name if she is not to be allowed to speak in her own defence?'

'I did not say that,' Adam assured her. 'If the worst should happen and she is brought to trial, she will be allowed to assure the court of her innocence. Her lawyers, I can tell you, will be the finest in the land, and there will be many witnesses to her good character.'

'It may not be enough.' Amy was close to tears. 'She must be terrified.'

'I intend to reassure her, my dear. Tomorrow I shall go to Ilchester—'

'How can you offer her any hope?' Amy would not be comforted. 'What can you say to reassure her?'

Adam looked at the anxious faces of his companions. 'I don't wish to raise unfounded hopes, but today I had a long talk with the magistrate and I told him the full story. He is a reasonable man and he accepts that Verreker, after failing in his first attempt to gain Louise's fortune, is probably behind this latest attempt. He is ready to proceed against the man with the full rigour of the law, but he must have proof.'

'And in that we are sadly lacking.' Amy was disconsolate. 'We need a miracle, and they are hard to come by.'

'Stranger things have happened. Now, Amy, what do you say? Will you go with me to see Louise?'

Perdita looked startled. 'Am I not to go to Ilchester too?'

'My love, I need you here. I believe that events will now move fast. My men have orders to report to you if they have any news.' He bowed to Miss Langrishe. 'Forgive me, ma'am! I would have asked that you be told, but I thought you not in the best of health.'

'Your news has cheered me, Adam. Perdita and I will see your men together should the need arise. There may be something we can do.'

'No!' he said firmly. 'I beg that you will take no action, however tempted you may be. I know my little hot-head here!' He slipped a loving arm about Perdita's waist. 'She is fully capable of entering the fray alone. It would be a mistake. The quarry shall not escape us, but he will flee if he suspects that we have any evidence against him.'

Miss Langrishe struggled to her feet. 'Come, Amy! Let us leave these love-birds to their billing and cooing. If you are to visit Louise we must find some more comforts for her. You will tell me what she will need most.'

Amy looked more cheerful as she followed the older woman from the room. She longed to see

Louise again, and although the Earl had not been specific as to his future plans he had succeeded in lifting her spirits.

As the door closed behind them, Adam took Perdita in his arms. He slid a finger beneath her chin and looked deep into her eyes. 'It is a lifetime since I kissed you, my lovely bird of paradise.'

Perdita twinkled at him. 'I thought that term was reserved only for females of a certain profession,' she teased.

He smiled. 'You are well informed, my love. How do you come by these slang terms?'

'Amy is forever quizzing our cousins,' she admitted. 'Are you shocked?'

'Never, my darling, but in this instance my compliment comes from the heart. Your aunt described you as a love-bird, but to me you are something far more splendid. Have you any idea how much I love you? It is not your beauty alone, my dear one, though that is a joy to behold. I love your spirit, your courage, and your loyalty to your friends.'

He kissed her then, and Perdita returned his kiss with a passion which shook them both. All her inhibitions vanished as his warm mouth sought her own. She threw her arms about his neck and held him to her, murmuring inarticulate words of love.

'Ah, what a jewel you are!' he said softly. 'You are all I want in life.' He kissed her eyelids and then the corner of her mouth, straying from there to press his lips against the soft flesh of her neck. 'When shall we be married, Perdita? You will not keep me waiting? Already I dread to lose you to another.'

'That can never be,' she told him. 'I am yours and always will be.' She began to chuckle. 'You do not mention my faults, my lord, but they are legion. How are you to deal with a wife who has a hasty temper and is stubborn into the bargain?'

'I shall think of a way,' he promised with a wicked look. 'Ah, my love, where should we have been without your stubbornness? It carries you through against all manner of difficulties. You speak of faults, but I have plenty of my own.'

'Indeed you have!' She gave him a demure look. 'One, in particular, I find very hard to bear.'

'And what is that? Tell me, and I shall try to correct it.'

Perdita heard the note of anxiety in his voice. 'Why, sir, I doubt if you will manage it. You have an unnerving habit of always being right. It has infuriated me on more than one occasion.' She laughed happily, secure in the certainty of his love.

'Minx!' He drew her to him and kissed her soundly. 'You had me worried, dearest. More remarks like that and my hair will turn quite grey—'

'Nonsense!' Perdita reached up to stroke his cheek. 'Kiss me again!' she whispered. 'I could stay in your arms for ever.'

'Temptress!' He held her away from him and shook his head. 'This is more than flesh and blood can stand. Let us join your aunt before I forget myself completely. What do you say to a drive about the town this afternoon? Miss Langrishe might enjoy it.'

Swift colour rose to Perdita's cheeks. Innocent though she was, she could not mistake his meaning. She jumped to her feet. 'That is an excellent idea,' she said hurriedly. 'I will go and speak to Aunt Trixie at once.'

Adam pressed a kiss into the palm of her hand and closed her fingers over it. 'Keep this, my love! It is a promise for the future.' He released her then and turned away, conscious that he had come close to giving his caresses an urgency which was far beyond the bounds of decorum. Yet he knew that he had not frightened her. Perdita would never behave in a missish way. She had given her love to him without reserve, in the open and honest way so natural to her.

He knew now that his passion was returned a hundredfold. He gave a rueful smile. That knowledge made it difficult to control his feelings, but he would do so. His lovely bride would be well worth waiting for.

He rang the bell and ordered his carriage for later that afternoon, hoping as he did so that Miss Langrishe would feel well enough to drive abroad.

She did not disappoint him. Though still in some pain she assured him that she was well enough to make the expedition.

'I feel so much better, Adam,' she told him. 'There is nothing like good news to give one's spirits a lift.'

'Then, ma'am, let us hope that we shall have more of it.' He rapped on the roof of the carriage and the horses made their way slowly through the crowded streets.

Miss Langrishe waved to her acquaintances. Clearly, she was delighted to be released from the confines of her home.

'Bath has changed so much since I first came to live here,' she observed. 'Adam, may we drive along the Royal Crescent? The houses there are very fine, and the view across the town is wonderful. How I should have liked to live there, but the climb to the heights is steep, and the Crescent was too far to be conveniently placed for the life I lead.'

Perdita could not agree with her, though she looked with pleasure at the graceful sweep of the Crescent. 'This must be the most beautiful city in England,' she cried warmly. 'I wonder that everyone does not come to live here.'

'Great heavens, Dita, don't say that!' Amy was laughing. 'The place would become impossible. Let us keep Bath a secret for as long as possible.'

Adam smiled at their enthusiasm. 'Do you care to drive out for a little way?' he asked Miss Langrishe. 'The view from the heights above the city is quite spectacular.'

He was right, and for a time his companions gazed with delight upon the scene below, with the city set like a golden jewel in a bowl of the Somerset hills.

'You have made a fortunate choice, ma'am,' Adam remarked. 'The place has so much to commend it.'

'And you must not regret the Crescent, Aunt.' Amy would have none of it. 'I, for one, am glad to be near the shops and the Pump Room and the Theatre.'

'Not the historic sights, Miss Amy?' Adam was disposed to tease her.

Amy chuckled. She was not in the least put out. 'They are well enough in their way,' she admitted 'But they are not so exciting.'

He laughed and let it go, but Amy quizzed her sister later.

'Does Adam think me a featherhead?' she asked as they prepared for bed.

'Of course not! What gave you that idea?'

'I don't know. I suppose it's because he laughs at me. Still, I like him in spite of it. Do you mind that you are not to go with us to see Louise?'

'No, I can understand his thinking. I trust his judgment, Amy. If he thinks it best for me to stay here, I will do so.'

Amy gave an unelegant whistle. 'There's a turn-up for the book! I thought I'd never live to see the day.'

Perdita frowned at her. 'Up to now he has been right. Now, what are you taking to Louise?'

Amy listed the clothing, the blankets, the food and the little luxuries which Miss Langrishe had insisted on providing.

On the following morning they were quickly stowed away inside the coach, and Perdita waved Adam and her sister off with no expectation that the day ahead of her would prove other than uneventful.

She was mistaken. As she was engaged in writing to her parents she was summoned to the salon. There she found her aunt in conversation with a burly man who introduced himself as a Bow Street Runner.

'Have you news for us?' she cried eagerly.

'Yes, ma'am. The subject is here in Bath.'

'We know that. We spoke to him yesterday. Have you discovered anything more about him?'

'He is known to us, Miss Wentworth, though under another name. We tracked him first in Lunnon town, where he's wanted for forgery, as well as theft and fraud.'

'Great heavens, is that not enough? Why is he not taken?'

'Proof, ma'am. We are building a case against him, but we must have proof. If he is charged and we have insufficient evidence, he will escape the law as he has done before.'

'Could you not search his rooms?'

'Aye, if we could but discover where he's staying. He's gone to ground, miss.'

'But he walks about the town quite freely—'

'And then he disappears. Oh, he has rooms at the Saracen's Head, but he ain't never there.'

'Perhaps he should be watched more closely,' Perdita's tone was icy.

'Quite, ma'am, but he's a slippery customer. We are doing our best.'

'Of course you are,' Miss Langrishe soothed. 'Be sure to let us know if you have further news…'

When the man had left she looked at Perdita's averted face.

'Don't lose heart, my love. I know that you had hoped…'

'I'm beginning to feel that any hope may be misplaced,' Perdita told her despairingly. 'The weeks are going on and the Assizes will soon be held. Oh, Aunt, this man is old in the ways of wickedness. Shall we ever be able to defeat him?'

'I thought that you had faith in Rushmore,' Miss Langrishe told her lightly. 'Will you give up on him because we have had no success as yet?'

'No, of course not!' Perdita's voice was shaking. 'It is just that…oh, Aunt, I can see no ray of hope on the horizon.'

'Take heart, my dear. Do you finish your letter to your parents. It will help you to feel closer to them.'

The advice was easier offered than taken. Perdita found herself unable to concentrate. It was as she was gazing endlessly into space that she was summoned for the second time.

'Miss Wentworth, there is a person here to see you.'

'I can see no one. Send him away.' Perdita could think of no one among her acquaintance who would be welcome at that time.

'The person is most insistent, ma'am. She says that it is most important that she speaks to you.'

'A woman?' Perdita was mystified. 'I can't think what...? However, you had best send her in.'

She did not recognise her visitor at first, but something about the thin figure seemed familiar.

'Good morning!' she said politely. 'Have we met, ma'am? I'm sorry, but I can't recall—'

'Yes, Miss Wentworth, we have met.' The woman stood just inside the doorway, clearly ill at ease in such opulent surroundings. 'You were kind enough to take my part at the haberdasher's shop when the owner threatened to dismiss me.'

'Oh, yes, I remember.' Perdita frowned at the recollection. 'A brute, if ever I saw one! I must hope that he didn't make good his threat when we had left.'

'No, ma'am, not immediately, but something happened the following week...' She was swaying
where she stood and Perdita hurried to her.

'You are ill!' she cried. 'Will you not sit down?'
She grasped the woman's arm and was startled to
find that it was almost fleshless. Perdita rang the bell
to summon Bates.

'Bring me some wine if you please,' she ordered
swiftly. 'This lady is not well... She is in need of
a restorative.'

But when the wine arrived her companion refused
it.

'I need a clear head for all I have to tell you,
madam. I did not know until last evening that your
friend had been accused of stealing lace. It is untrue,
of course. I saw it being slipped into her reticule.'

Perdita gasped. 'By whom?' she demanded.

'By the owner's son...the man who followed you
out of the shop to ask if Miss Bryant had it about
her person. He knew I'd seen him, but he passed it
off as a practical joke, instigated by his friend.'

'And this friend? Did you know him, Mrs...?'

'My name is Margaret Tarrant, ma'am. I did not
know him then. It was not until the following week
that I heard a curious conversation. I was in the
storeroom above the shop when one of the panels
slid aside. I had not noticed it before. I could see
into the room beyond quite clearly, and I was surprised to see that it was comfortably furnished...not
like a storeroom in the least.'

'A hidden room?' Perdita was growing excited.

'Yes, Miss Wentworth. The two men within were quarrelling. There seemed to be some argument as to the speed with which they should proceed against Miss Louise. The stranger was all for haste, but the owner's son would not hear of it. He was all for caution.'

'Can you describe this man?'

'He was tall and fair…quite handsome in his way and dressed like a gentleman, though his language was not that of any gentleman I ever heard. His name seemed to be Virkir, or something like that.'

'Could it have been Verreker?' Perdita felt a sudden surge of hope.

'Yes, ma'am, that was it. I didn't mean to eavesdrop and I hoped they hadn't seen me. I was at the back of the store behind some boxes, but my cough gave me away. I was dismissed that same afternoon.'

'Oh, my dear, I am so sorry, but if only you had come to me before! So much unhappiness might have been avoided.'

'I have been ill, Miss Wentworth. I knew nothing of your friend's arrest until last evening when my friend gave me the news. I could think of nothing but my son, you see. I could not work, and I feared the child would starve.'

'That will not happen,' Perdita told her firmly. 'You must let me help you. You have done us a service far beyond anything that I might have hoped for. Now, ma'am, you shall come to meet my aunt. She takes some light refreshment at this time of day and will be glad of your company whilst you tell her what has happened.' Perdita had guessed that her companion was faint with both hunger and distress.

'I did not come to beg,' Miss Tarrant told her quietly.

'I know that, ma'am. You came to help us if you could.' Perdita gave her a smile of encouragement. 'Will you not trust me and set your pride aside for once? It is a difficult thing to do as I know to my own cost, but we owe you so much. It would make me happy if you would accept my help. Will you deny me that pleasure?'

A faint smile was her reward. 'You make it difficult to refuse you, Miss Wentworth…'

Perdita's heart was singing as she led her companion into the salon and Miss Langrishe saw the change in her at once.

'What has happened?' she asked quickly. 'And who is this lady, Perdita? We have not met before, I think.'

'Oh, Aunt, you will be happy to know her. Mrs Tarrant has brought such news.' Perdita made the introductions quickly. 'She can prove that Louise is innocent.'

This was enough to bring Miss Langrishe upright in her chair. 'Pray sit down, ma'am, and tell me what you know.'

Perdita was on fire with plans, but she waited long enough to explain that Mrs Tarrant had come to Laura Place in haste, and without breaking her fast.

'My dear, you must be starving...' Miss Langrishe rang her bell and ordered substantial additions to her mid-morning tray. 'Now, Perdita, please be patient! Let me hear what Mrs Tarrant has to say...then we shall see what is to be done.'

Perdita was only half-attending as the story was repeated. Her head was filled with plans. First of all she must summon the Bow Street Runner back again. He had left her his direction. If Mrs Tarrant could be persuaded to wait until he returned, the man might act upon her information. She broke into the conversation to suggest this to her aunt, and received that lady's agreement.

Perdita gave her visitor an anxious look. 'What of your son, ma'am? Shall you be able to leave him for so long?'

'He is with my friend this morning. Pray do not worry, Miss Wentworth. Davy will take no harm for an hour or two.'

'Then, Aunt?' Perdita looked a question.

'Yes, send for the Runner, my dear. There is no time to lose.'

Chapter Fourteen

When the man returned he questioned their visitor for so long that Perdita grew alarmed.

'This lady is not well,' she protested. 'You are tiring her beyond endurance.'

Mrs Tarrant waved aside the protest. 'I feel much better, ma'am. Pray do not concern yourself. I'd like to help in any way I can.'

Perdita eyed her closely. The small amount of food she had eaten seemed to have revived her. Now she was able to answer the Runner's questions clearly and without prevarication.

The man's smile saluted her courage. 'Thank you, madam. You are a vital witness. May I ask if you are willing to give evidence on oath?'

Mrs Tarrant nodded. 'Yes, I shall tell the truth.'

'Then, ladies, I shall leave you for the moment. Matters must be set in train. We have already searched out quarry's rooms at the Saracen's Head without success.'

'Did you not need a warrant?' Perdita looked surprised.

The man closed one eye in an elaborate wink. 'Chambermaids can be obliging, miss, and if a certain door is left ajar it don't take above a few minutes for experienced men to look about them. Course, that won't apply to searching the shop premises. For that we'll need the magistrate's permission.'

'His lordship will see to that,' Perdita told him. 'Can you return this evening? The Earl will be back by then.'

'Yes, ma'am. Thanks to this lady we have some news for him at last.' He bowed himself out of the room.

Mrs Tarrant too was ready to leave.

'How shall we ever be able to thank you, ma'am?' Miss Langrishe wiped away a tear. 'I had almost given up hope of seeing any happy outcome to these wicked charges. Mrs Tarrant, I know that your life is hard. Will you not let us help you?' She reached into her reticule.

'Not money, ma'am, I beg of you.' Mrs Tarrant flushed.

'Why ever not? You have a son, I believe. You could make his life more comfortable.'

Their visitor shook her head again. Then Perdita intervened.

'Mrs Tarrant is right, Aunt Trixie. To offer money might be construed as bribery, but there can be no objection to sending Davy a few small luxuries.' She turned to the embarrassed woman again. 'Do say you will accept them,' she coaxed. 'Your son will enjoy them, will he not?'

Mrs Tarrant caught her hand. 'You are too good,' she said in a broken voice. 'My child has cried from hunger, and it broke my heart to be able to give him nothing.'

'Then come with me!' Perdita led her to the kitchens, and there she filled a basket to overflowing with cold fowl, a joint of beef, a piece of ham and a large fruit pie.

Mrs Tarrant raised a hand in smiling protest. 'No more, Miss Wentworth, if you please. This is enough food to feed us for a week, and I am grateful to you.'

'Don't speak of gratitude, ma'am. We shall be always in your debt. Now give me your direction. The Earl will wish to see you. You may be sure of it.'

Miss Langrishe was lost in thought when Perdita returned.

'I have been wondering if we should expedite matters,' she announced. 'Shall I invite the magistrate to dine with us this evening? It would not seem unusual. Frederick dines here often in the ordinary way.'

'With respect, Aunt Trixie, I believe that it would not be wise just now. He is involved in Louise's case. It might be seen as an attempt to influence him.

'I suppose so.' Miss Langrishe sighed. 'Oh dear, how I wish that Adam might have chosen another day to go to Ilchester. He will know what to do.'

'He will, and at least we have splendid news for him. I can't wait for his return. If only the hours would pass more quickly...'

As the day wore on, she ran to the window a dozen times to catch a first glimpse of his coach. When it arrived at last she flew down the stairs, and, regardless of the curious glances of passers-by, she seized his hand and almost dragged him into the hall.

His eyes began to twinkle. 'What a welcome!' he teased. 'Am I to believe that you have missed me?'

'Come into the salon,' she urged. 'And you, too, Amy. So much has happened whilst you've been away.'

'You do not ask about Louise.' Amy spoke in a low voice. 'Oh, Dita, she is so crushed in spirit. She has lost all hope.'

'But she must not do so! That is what I want to tell you!' Perdita hurried them through to greet her aunt. 'We have such a story for you. Aunt, will you tell it, or shall I?'

'You had best do so, my dear. You have been bursting with excitement since this morning and I fear you may explode.'

Perdita laughed. Then she rushed to give them an account of the day's events, speaking so quickly that a childhood stutter returned to trouble her.

Adam cast aside his cloak and slipped an arm about her waist, drawing her to sit beside him on the sofa.

'Slow down, my darling!' he advised. 'This is all good news indeed. Can there be more?'

'Oh, yes! The Runner is coming back tonight, but he must get a w-w-warrant from the magistrate.' Perdita looked at the faces of her companions and in their expressions she saw growing hope.

'Oh, Adam, they must release Louise,' she cried. 'Don't you agree?'

'We may have to wait for a time,' he said cautiously. 'We have only Mrs Tarrant's word that the lace was placed in Louise's reticule. It may be thought that she has made the accusation in revenge for being dismissed.'

'You would not say so if you had met her,' Perdita cried hotly. 'And what of Verreker? He told me that he had never visited the shop. Amy will bear witness to that. Why is he living in a secret room?'

'There is no law against it, dearest. You say that his room at the Saracen's Head holds nothing suspicious.'

'So the Bow Street Runner said.'

'Then the room above the shop is our best hope. When I have seen the man I will visit the magistrate.

If the case against Verreker is promising we may get the warrant to search the premises.'

'Oh, Adam, I felt so sure...' Perdita could not hide her disappointment.

'Patience, my love! You are right in all respects, but we are dealing with a slippery customer. He will take advantage of a single loophole in the law and we must not lose him now.'

Perdita could only agree.

However, Perdita did not rest until Adam returned late that night with the promised warrant.

'Satisfied?' He showed her the document. 'Now we must hope that the Runners find evidence.'

'When will they search?'

'Tomorrow. Verreker is in the habit of visiting the Pump Room in a morning, doubtless searching for another gullible victim. They will seize the opportunity to surprise the owners of the shop.'

'He spoke of jewellery, too.' Perdita reminded him with an anxious look. 'He said it was too dangerous to sell it at present.'

'That is our best hope, my love. The Runners have a description of the pieces. They need only find a single stolen item if they are to charge him. I would stake a handsome bet that his ill-gotten gains are in that secret room.'

'I hope you may be right.' Perdita rested her head against his shoulder. 'I thought it would be so easy to get Louise released. Now, it seems, we are still beset with difficulties.'

Adam kissed her very gently. 'They will be overcome,' he assured her. 'I promise that by noon tomorrow you will be easier in your mind.'

Perdita raised her face to him. 'I believe you,' she said softly. 'Oh, my love, you are my rock. How should I ever live without you?'

'You need never do so, my dearest.' His mouth came down on hers and she was swept away on a dizzing tide of passion as his warm lips claimed her own. She was breathless when he released her but he continued to rain kisses on her eyes, her cheeks, the corners of her mouth and the tip of her nose.

'Go away, you temptress!' he exclaimed at last. 'You would seduce a saint, and I am no saint...'

'Why, sir, you shock me!'

Adam saw the laughter in her eyes and tried to grab her as she danced away from him, but Perdita was too quick. Still laughing, she fled for the safety of her room, though it went much against the grain to leave him.

An unknown longing seized her. Their love was incomplete, she knew that well enough, but it was hard to wait for true fulfilment. Now she prayed that the months would fly until her parents returned. Only then would she be able to wed her love.

Amy was waiting for her. 'Did Adam get the warrant?' she asked eagerly.

'Yes. The men will search tomorrow. I pray that they may be successful.'

'So do I. Louise is at the end of her tether. You would not care to see her looking so...so resigned. She seemed like a stranger to me.'

'That will change,' Perdita comforted her. 'Let us see what tomorrow brings...'

It was better news than they had hoped. Verreker had been taken as he left the Pump Room, charged with the theft of a diamond necklace, sundry brooches, and two valuable bracelets.

It was enough to persuade the magistrate to reconsider his decision to prosecute Louise.

He gave orders that the prisoner be returned to Bath, under arrest, where he could re-examine the case against her.

'There is no direct connection with the alleged theft of the lace,' he explained to Adam. 'But I have heard enough to have my doubts about the owners of the shop. Will you present yourselves at a hearing in three days' time?'

'And Miss Bryant?'

'Will be released into your custody, my lord. Remember, you are surety for her!'

Adam nodded his thanks. He had said nothing to Perdita, but he too had been worried about Louise's state of mind. The girl was a shadow of her former self. She was silent, biddable, but seemingly with no will of her own. She could not be persuaded to discuss the case, even to proclaim her innocence.

'She looks as if she has gazed into the pit!' Amy was in despair. 'Will the magistrate take her silence as proof of guilt?' She tried to curb her growing anger. 'Louise should not have been sent to Ilchester. Why could he not have left her in Adam's care before this? The experience has scared her. I doubt that she will ever be the same...'

'He can do so now because we have new evidence,' Adam told her.

'And Louise will recover her spirits,' Miss Langrishe added. 'The young are resilient. Just give her time. Then she will think of this as a bad dream.'

'But only if we are successful.' Amy resumed her pacing of the room. Then she stopped in front of Adam and faced him squarely. 'What if aught should go wrong?' she demanded. 'Will you spirit her away? You cannot let her be transported.'

'She will not be transported,' he told her firmly. 'Don't cross your bridges before you come to them, my dear. Let us wait for the hearing.'

To everyone at Laura Place it seemed an age before that day arrived, but three days later those connected with her case met at the Magistrate's Court.

'This is not a trial,' he explained at once. 'But new evidence has come to hand, and I intend to make sure that there is no miscarriage of justice in this case before committing the prisoner to the

Assizes.' He looked about his court until eye rested upon the owner of the shop who was sitting beside his son.

'Well, Joshua Keay, have you anything to add to your previous evidence against the prisoner?'

'I stand by every word of it,' Keay insisted. 'What I should like to know is why this person is present here today?' He pointed to where Verreker sat, flanked by a couple of Bow Street Runners. 'This case is no concern of his.'

'You seem very sure of that,' the magistrate told him smoothly. 'Perhaps he is well known to you?'

'I never set eyes on him before this day.' Keay glared at his quietly spoken questioner.

'Strange! The items which he is alleged to have stolen were found upon your premises, hidden beneath a floorboard in a private room.'

'That is naught to do with me, I've been away, sir. Bath is overcrowded, as you may know. Sometimes visitors beg us for accommodation as a favour. We have no way of knowing their past history.'

'And your son was equally unaware of the presence of this person upon your premises?'

'Speak up, Jem!' Keay glanced in irritation at his son.

'No, sir...I mean, yes, I did not know of it...I was with my father...' The young man went red and white by turns.

'So your staff are at liberty to let accommodation without your knowledge? You are very trusting, sir.'

The sneering tone was not lost on Keay. He shot a malignant look at the magistrate, but that gentleman was unaware of it. He was signalling to the usher.

The Keays stiffened as Mrs Tarrant was led into the room, and Perdita glanced at Matthew Verreker. He had been lolling back, apparently at ease and untroubled by the presence of the guards. Now his hands betrayed him. He clenched them until the knuckles went white.

Once Mrs Tarrant's identity had been established, the magistrate began to question her.

'I must ask you, madam, do you know anyone in this room?'

'Yes, sir. I know the Earl of Rushmore and the ladies. Mr Keay was until recently my employer. I know his son, of course, and the young man's friend, who is sitting over there.' She pointed to Matthew Verreker.

'It's a lie!' Jem Keay was on his feet. 'I do not know this man. He is no friend of mine.'

His father managed an ingratiating smile. 'Pay no attention to her, sir!' He addressed the magistrate direct. 'This woman was dismissed for theft and insolence. This is her way of taking her revenge—'

'Silence!' the magistrate thundered. 'I'll have no further interruptions!' He turned back to Mrs Tarrant. 'Now, ma'am, since it was your evidence which led to the recovery of certain stolen items, will you tell us how you came by this information?'

Mrs Tarrant was pale but composed as she began to speak. 'I had gone up to the storeroom at the shop, sir. I could hear voices, which surprised me as there seemed to be no one in the room apart from myself. Then a panel slid aside and I could see into the room beyond. Mr Jem Keay and his friend were quarrelling about a sale of jewellery—'

'All lies!' Jem Keay's voice rose to a shriek. 'What has this to do with the charges against the Bryant woman?'

'We shall come to that in time, young man.' The magistrate's expression was stern. 'You deny again that you know this man?' He pointed to Verreker.

'I do!' came the sullen reply.

'Then how could Mrs Tarrant have known about the items hidden in the room unless she had overheard your conversation? Your unknown lodger would not, I imagine, have been talking to himself.'

'She's a thief! She could have put them there herself.'

'But she did not know of this room. I believe the entrance is so well concealed that the Runners had some difficulty in discovering it.'

'She's sly! Who is to know what she finds when she is poking about in secret?'

'What, indeed? Now we know that Matthew Verreker has been living upon your premises. You claim that this was without your knowledge?'

'I do.' Jem was at pains not to look in Verreker's direction. 'Mrs Tarrant must have let the room to him.'

'This sly creature had the authority to do so in your absence?' Everyone in the room was aware of the magistrate's disbelief. 'Indeed, you do surprise me!'

He began to shuffle his papers. 'Now we shall come to the charges against Miss Bryant. You have given us fresh evidence, Mrs Tarrant. Will you please repeat it to this court?'

'The young lady fell into a trap,' she said. 'She had left her reticule open upon the counter whilst she was purchasing some ribbons. I saw Jem Keay slip the lace inside. Later, he followed her into the street and asked if she would look for it. There were a number of witnesses... Then he asked for her direction.'

'Why do you listen to her?' Jem Keay shouted wildly. 'Will you take her word? Can't you see that she is trying to destroy us?'

Joshua Keay placed a restraining hand on his son's shoulder. Then he rounded upon the magistrate.

'It is one person's word against another,' he snarled. 'Have you proof which will stand up in a court of law?'

'Why, yes, I believe we have!' He looked at the Earl of Rushmore. 'My lord, will you tell us what happened next?'

'We received a letter,' Adam said. 'The writer offered to drop the charges against Miss Bryant in return for a settlement.'

'You did not pay?'

'No, sir. I regarded it as a cheap attempt at blackmail.'

'And you have this letter still?'

'I have it here.' Adam produced the letter from his pocket.

The magistrate smoothed it out with every appearance of satisfaction. 'And here we have some accounts made out to certain customers of the shop owned by Mr Keay.' He bent to examine the papers on the desk before him.

'Jem Keay, you will approach the bench,' he said as he held up a slip of paper. 'This is signed by you. Will you confirm it as your writing?'

'I don't know!' Jem's eyes darted about the room and settled upon his father as he begged for reassurance.

'You do not recognise your own hand? I must disbelieve you. Now, young man, cast your eyes upon this note! The likenesses in the characters are impossible to ignore, are they not?'

Jem cracked then. He swung round screaming as he looked at Matthew Verreker. 'You devil! You made me write it, didn't you, to keep your own hands clean?'

Then his father was beside him. 'Be quiet, you fool!' he hissed. 'Will you condemn yourself out of your own mouth?'

'I won't swing for him!' Jem was beyond control. 'He is the one who planned the whole. We were to share...he promised...'

One of the Runners was already out of his seat, ready to restrain the hysterical figure, but no one was prepared for what happened next.

Verreker moved with the speed of a striking snake. In a single movement he caught the remaining Runner in a choking grip, seizing the man's pistol with his other hand.

'Stand back!' he ordered in a pleasant tone. 'I doubt if any of you will care to have this man's blood upon our hands, and I shall not hesitate to kill him if I must.'

Slowly he backed towards the door at the rear of the court, dragging his captive with him.

'He goes with me,' he continued lightly. 'Try to follow and you will find a corpse.'

'Give it up, man!' Adam began to move towards Verreker and his captive. 'You can't escape, and this will make things worse for you.'

Verreker's harsh laugh echoed around the room. 'Stay where you are, my lord, and spare us your heroics. Worse, you say? I think not. You, above anyone, have ruined all my plans. It would be a pleasure to kill you, and I am strongly tempted, but you shall not persuade me into wasting a shot.'

He paled as Adam continued to advance on him.

'Stand back!' he screamed. 'If you take another step, I'll put a shot into this fellow's brain.'

Adam smiled and shook his head, but he did not stop.

Verreker's face was a mask of indecision. As he had threatened, he could fire at the Runner, but Adam was likely to prove the greater danger. With a grunt of satisfaction he levelled the pistol and fired.

The shot took Adam in the shoulder, halting him in mid-stride. With a cry of horror Perdita flew to him, gazing in anguish at the spreading stain upon his sleeve. She looked up at Verreker.

'I'll kill you for this,' she promised.

'You may try, Miss Wentworth, though I doubt if you'll succeed.' Verreker was smiling as he looked at her. 'It is a flesh wound only, I believe. Such a pity! I was aiming for the heart!'

'You dog!' Perdita ground her teeth. 'You won't escape the law.'

'Always the warrior, my dear? What an accomplice you would have made, unlike these weaklings whom I took into my confidence.' Verreker cast a withering look upon Keay and his son. 'I should have known that they would crack at the first sign of pressure.'

'You can't get away,' Perdita insisted. 'Give up now, and your case may be reviewed more leniently.'

'I am for the hangman's noose. You may depend on it. Do you suppose that your noble lord here has any other plans for me? Now, Miss Wentworth, let us have no more heroics. Pray do not follow the example of your friend, I beg of you. Your face is quite extraordinary. It would be a pity to reduce so much beauty to a mass of pulp and a few slivers of bone.'

Perdita ignored him. She was looking at the flow of blood which poured steadily from Adam's wound.

'It isn't as bad as it looks,' he whispered quietly. 'Stand away from me, my love! That pistol holds but two shots and he has wasted one of them. If I could but persuade him to fire again...' His eyes told her that he was in mortal fear for her safety, but she rose and rounded on Verreker.

'I'll strike a bargain with you,' she announced. 'I can't allow his lordship to bleed to death. Give me your cravat to staunch the flow and I will help you.' She was well aware that she must hold Verreker's attention, and if, possible, give Adam the opportunity to reach him. Her heart misgave her. Just how badly was Adam injured? He knew well enough that she might lose him, but the firm pressure of his hand stilled all her fears.

Verreker nodded in quick appreciation of her words. 'I have to hand it to you, madam. You are worth fifty of that milk-and-water miss I planned to wed. Here!' He snatched at the snowy linen about his throat and threw it to her.

It fell short and Perdita moved towards him, but he backed away, still holding his gun against the Runner's temple.

'No tricks!' he warned as he edged towards the door. 'I shall not hesitate to shoot, and my next shot will be fatal. Now, ma'am, how do you propose to help me?'

Perdita was trembling and her mouth was dust-dry, but her main emotion was one of fury. Verreker must not be allowed to get away, but she could not think of a plan to stop him. He was now too far away from her to give her the chance to stumble against him, but even if she had been able to do so she would have put the Runner's life at risk, to say nothing of her own.

She stared at him helplessly, hating the smirk of triumph on his lips. How many other lives would he go on to ruin, she wondered? Beside her Amy's face was the picture of outrage, and Louise had fainted. It was then that the door behind him opened, and Thomas burst into the room. For the moment he did not understand what was happening in the court.

'Where is she?' he shouted. 'What have you done with Louise?'

Startled by the intruder, Verreker dropped his guard for just an instant, but it was enough for Adam. Even with his left arm hanging useless, he moved with astonishing speed, knocking the pistol aside, and using a strong right hook to connect with Verreker's jaw. The man fell like a sack of coals.

Then pandemonium reigned as the Runners hurried to secure him and his two accomplices. Perdita saw nothing of it. She was on her knees beside Louise, trying, with Amy's help, to restore her friend to consciousness.

Thomas thrust them both aside and gathered Louise to him. She opened her eyes and gave him a loving look.

'Oh, Thomas, I have been so frightened,' she whispered.

'That is all over, my dearest. You will never be frightened again.' He picked her up and looked at Adam. 'Where is your carriage, my lord?' he asked stiffly.

'It is waiting. Do you go ahead to Laura Place with the ladies.' Adam was swaying on his feet. 'Perhaps you might request the services of a surgeon for me?'

'You are injured, sir?' Thomas softened his tone.

'Merely a scratch, I believe, but the ball should be removed...'

'I see. Well, sir, Louise must be my first concern, but I shall wish to speak to you later.'

'I'm sure you will!' Rushmore grimaced as he looked at Thomas's retreating back. The boy had a right to be furious with him. Louise might so easily have been killed. As a guardian he had fallen far short of his own high standards.

Then a soft hand slipped into his own. 'Don't blame yourself!' Perdita said. 'You saved her in the end.'

Adam took her in his arms. 'You should go back with the others, my love. This has been a terrible ordeal for you. I wonder that you did not faint when Verreker threatened you. I confess that I was terrified for you.'

Perdita lifted her face to his and her eyes were twinkling.

'Why, sir, I did not dare,' she told him. 'I recalled that you have no time for missish vapourings...'

'You are a wonder!' he said fervently. 'I don't know what I have done to deserve you. Come, my love, let us see the magistrate. I believe that the charges against Louise will be dismissed.'

He was right. Jem Keay was already babbling out his evidence faster than the Runner could record it, in an effort to save his own skin.

'And Verreker?' Perdita was anxious to know the fate of her adversary.

'He will either hang or be transported, Miss Wentworth. Either way he will no longer be a danger to society.'

'I am glad of it.' Perdita held out her hand. 'My aunt is hoping that you will dine with her at Laura Place, sir. Will that be possible, do you suppose?'

'It will be my pleasure, ma'am. This case will go to the Assizes. It is now out of my jurisdiction.'

'Come, Perdita!'' Adam took her arm. 'Your aunt will be awaiting you. Shall we walk back to Laura Place?'

The sun was shining when they reached the street, and as they strolled along in the balmy air the world seemed a better place. Perdita felt that a dreadful weight had been lifted from her shoulders.

'I can't believe that it is really over,' she said softly. 'Now we have nothing more to worry us...'

'Speak for yourself, my darling!' Adam gave a wry smile. 'I suspect that I am in for a most unpleasant interview with young Thomas.'

His suspicions were well founded. They saw Thomas sitting outside Louise's room, his head in his hands, and slipped away to wait for him.

'Well done, miss!' The physician patted her hand as he finished his task. 'You have been brave. I would guess you to be a soldier's daughter.'

Louise gave him a misty smile, but she was looking beyond him towards the door.

'I'll send the young man in,' the physician said. 'But you must rest, my dear. I have prescribed a sedative, but you must not let him tire you.'

'He won't do that.' Louise sighed with content as she rested her head against the pillow. 'He is always so gentle with me.'

She spoke no more than the truth. Thomas approached her as if she might shatter to fragments before his eyes. She lifted a hand to wipe a stray tear from his cheek.

'I am stronger than you think,' she whispered. 'You must not worry so.'

He bent his head and kissed her hands, but speech was beyond him. He sat motionless for several minutes until she drifted into sleep. Then he went to find the Earl.

He walked in upon a family gathering. Miss Langrishe was seated with the girls, whilst Adam explained that the charges against Louise had been dropped.

Thomas stalked over to him. 'Can you spare me a moment in private, sir?' he said.

'I can spare you all the time you need to give me a dressing-down, Thomas, but it need not be in private. I am well aware of my shortcomings. Whatever opinion you have of me, it cannot be worse than my own.'

'I am glad you think so, sir. Let me tell you that your role as a guardian leaves much to be desired. Louise has been neglected and today she was almost killed. Good God, sir! Imprisonment…humiliation… what else will you let her suffer?'

'Stop!' Perdita was on her feet at once. 'How dare you, Thomas? We have been dealing with a man who would stop at nothing to gain his ends. Adam saved our lives today. You might remember that!'

'Perdita is right, my boy!' Miss Langrishe said gently. 'No one could have known the depths to which this man would sink. We were all outwitted...but Adam did his best to ensure Louise's safety.'

'Without too much success, I fear!' Thomas was still smouldering with rage.

'Don't be such a gooby, coz!' Amy said inelegantly. 'Must we have a family feud? Adam is to wed Perdita, and you, no doubt, will offer for Louise. May we not be friends again?'

'Well, sir, may I offer for Louise?' Thomas gave the Earl a belligerent stare.

Adam's smile lit up the room. 'With my blessing, Thomas. Indeed, I hoped that you would do so.' He held out his hand.

Thomas was nonplussed. He had expected opposition...an argument...an outright refusal. Now his dearest wish was to be granted. A surge of happiness overwhelmed him.

'Well, that's all right then!' He took the proffered hand and beamed upon the assembled company. 'I must tell Louise. How long shall I wait? I must not wake her, I suppose.'

A chorus of protest answered him until abashed, he returned to sit by Louise's bed until his love should wake.

Perdita stole a look at her aunt's face. Miss Langrishe looked exhausted. The events of the morning had taken their toll, and now reaction was setting in.

Amy caught her sister's eye and nodded. 'Aunt, will you not rest for an hour or two?' she coaxed. 'Perhaps, when we dine tonight, we may allow ourselves a celebration. After all, we have much to celebrate today, and you will wish to enjoy it to the full.'

'You are right, my dear.' Miss Langrishe allowed herself to be helped from the room.

Adam turned to Perdita. 'And what of you, my darling? Do you also wish to rest?'

'Great heavens, no!' Perdita beamed at him. 'This has been an adventure! Just think! If I had gone to Gibraltar I should have missed it!'

'Fraud and lies and attempted murder, Perdita? In our future life together I shall be hard put to provide you with enough excitement, but I shall try.' He was laughing down at her.

She gave him a wicked look. 'I'm sure you will succeed, my lord, though I can't think how.'

'I shall have to prove it to you before too long. How soon may we be married?'

Perdita nestled happily against his chest. 'As soon as my parents return to England. It is late autumn now, and they return in early spring. Of course, by then I may have changed my mind...'

'About what?'

She heard the anxiety in his tone and chuckled to herself.

'Why, sir, about becoming a Countess. You cannot be surprised. After all, it was you who told me that I had no hope of doing so. An ape-leader was the term you used, I think.'

'Why, you little minx, am I never to live that evening down?'

'I hope you will remember it for all your life, my love.' Perdita's eyes were shining. 'It was the night we met. I, for one, will never forget it.'

'Nor I!' He kissed her then, and they were lost at once in a world which promised nothing but happiness for the future.

*   *   *   *   *